THE FACE OF INNOCENCE

BOOKS BY ELISABETH OGILVIE

The Face of Innocence
Bellwood
Waters on a Starry Night
The Seasons Hereafter
There May Be Heaven
Call Home the Heart
The Witch Door
High Tide at Noon
Storm Tide
The Ebbing Tide
Rowan Head
My World Is an Island
The Dawning of the Day
No Evil Angel

BOOKS FOR YOUNG PEOPLE

The Pigeon Pair
Masquerade at Sea House
Ceiling of Amber
Turn Around Twice
Becky's Island
The Young Islanders
How Wide the Heart
Blueberry Summer
Whistle for a Wind
The Fabulous Year

THE FACE OF
INNOCENCE

Elisabeth Ogilvie

McGRAW-HILL BOOK COMPANY

New York   St. Louis   Toronto   San Francisco

Düsseldorf   Mexico   Panama

THE FACE OF
INNOCENCE

CHAPTER 1

ON A SEPTEMBER afternoon a woman named Susan Linden sat at her dressing table applying lipstick while her daughter read Emily Dickinson's poetry aloud in the taut and breathless voice she considered suitable for the material. At the close of "For Susan Is a Stranger Yet" she fell into a dramatic silence.

"Very nice, dear," said Susan, as soon as she finished with the lipstick. "Can you tell me what it means?"

"Well, I *think* it means that a lot of people would be surprised to know just what a mystery this Susan really is. Of course that doesn't apply to you. We know all about you." She giggled. "Do you have a haunted house, with a ghost in it?"

"I *am* a haunted house," said Susan. "Haunted by PTA fund drives, cooked food sales, your brother's teeth— did you ever see the ghost of a tooth?—and getting you into college three years from now."

"Well, it doesn't seem to be wearing you down any,"

said Amy. "You're the best-looking mother in town, but please don't tell anybody else's mother I said so, or the kids'll hate me, hate me, hate me."

"I shan't let anyone know that you're guilty of any such heresy as admiring a parent," promised Susan. "Now go freshen up if you want me to go out with you."

Amy leaped off the bed and was out of the room in a swirl of tartan pleats and long legs, leaving Susan's spread rumpled and Emily Dickinson standing casually on her head. Susan turned back to the mirror and studied herself with a critical and objective gaze. If I saw this woman coming toward me anywhere I could tell exactly what she was, she thought. I would know by instinct about the Scouts and the Hospital Auxiliary, the PTA, the sort of husband she has, the town she lives in, and the friends she has.

It was not a depressing theory but a satisfying one, for nobody but Susan knew what this picture of herself represented in terms of pure, passionate, dedicated will power. The woman in the mirror, wearing misty tweeds and a fine sweater, the discreet earrings and circle brooch, the casual short hairdo proper for daytime walks down Main Street on a September afternoon—this woman with the wide forehead and the calm, gentle brown eyes was even more her own creation than her children were— because they were half their father's.

Susan did not think in so many words, *I am thus and so*. She had stopped thinking it long ago, when she realized that she had at last become what she had set out to be.

She picked up her handbag and went out of the room, and met Amy at the head of the stairs. Dark auburn hair like her mother's shone like polished mahogany where she had brushed it tightly back over her skull; her pony-tail bounced out proudly behind. Susan realized the sleek coiffure was in her honor. For the hours spent among her peers Amy preferred long curtains of hair falling straight past her eyes. Amy had her father's bones, for which Susan was thankful. She thought her own bones were nondescript in terms of distinction, though she was proud of her ankles.

Amy wore a forest-green blazer with silver buttons over her yellow sweater, and her mother said, "You look very nice, dear." She was careful, as always, not to dote. Amy was so much what she had dreamed of being at fourteen, even surpassing the dream, that at times Susan feared it couldn't be so, and she must one day wake up to brutal reality.

"You do too, Mother," Amy said. They smiled in mutual pleasure and went downstairs side by side. At the foot they stopped and listened. There were loud thumps and uncouth outcries from the kitchen.

"The entire Wolf Patrol, I presume," said Amy wearily. "Do we have to make contact with it and ruin my mood?"

"You go on out, and I'll make sure that tonight's dessert is safe." Amy gave her an otherworldly smile and drifted toward the door. Susan detected an aura of Emily Dickinson and wouldn't have been surprised if Amy had turned like a swaying flower to declaim, " 'Parting is all we know of heaven, and all we need of hell.' "

She did not, and Susan went into the kitchen. Amy was a necessary delight, but Barry was a fearful joy. At twelve he was as intense about baseball, scouting, his father, his friends and his enemies, and all animals, as Amy was about everything good and evil in her world. He was handsome in a thoroughly masculine way, with his father's splendid gray eyes.

"Hi, Mother!" He greeted her with the hail-fellow-well-met air he'd had from bassinet days. "Hello, Mrs. Linden!" the rest of the Wolf Patrol chorused, politely stowing their food in their cheeks when they spoke.

"What are you eating?" asked Susan. "No, don't tell me. Peanut butter and marshmallow sandwiches. I know it must be delicious, but don't talk when your mouth's full of it. I can't stand it." They laughed wildly at that; for some reason she had a reputation with Barry's friends as a great wit. "Don't touch anything else, it's all spoken for. And clean up, of course. What are you doing this afternoon, anyway?"

"I told you, we're going over to Mr. Sanborn's to work on our carpentry badge." His scowl was ridiculously like his father's.

"I'm sorry, Barry, but I'd need the FBI to keep track of the affairs of everybody in this family. About six agents, but I don't know where we'd keep them."

The Wolf Patrol rolled in their seats and held their sides. Barry looked modest. He could afford to be nonchalant about this paragon of humor, since he owned it. She said goodbye and left them.

Theirs was an old house in the old part of a town that had once been the center for outlying farms, before Exurbia took over and the well-to-do commuters began building split-levels and swimming pools on what had once been superb pasture for dairy herds. Susan did not envy them. Her house was the kind that she had always wanted from earliest childhood. She loved the age of her house, and its eccentric nooks and corners, and the old-fashioned things like the shaggy barberry hedge, the evergreens and the maples, and the large back yard that was unashamedly a back yard. True, it had an outdoor fireplace, but it also had apples, and a grape arbor where the children gorged themselves. One corner was left completely wild and shrubby, enjoyed equally by birds and boys. Beyond the driveway there was that treasure too rare in modern times, a vacant lot which Richard had bought when an old house burned down.

She and Amy went out through the gate in the barberry hedge and down the wide sidewalk under the shade trees. These pavements were perfect for roller skates, tricycles, and baby carriages, and in the warm, richly colored, aromatic September afternoon there was plenty of this wheeled traffic.

"Now, Amy," said Susan, when they reached Main Street and had to wait for a light to change, "tell me about this exhibit. Yes, I know you gave me the leaflet, but if you can tell me when I've had a chance to read it I'll give you a dollar."

"I could lie, I suppose," said Amy, "because I could use a dollar, considering the allowance my old-fashioned parents keep me on. But I won't." She slid her hand under her mother's elbow and started her across the street. "Well, when Miss Absalom marched us to the museum yesterday to see an example of fantasy in art, we thought we were going to see some of that stuff you just can't act reverent about without feeling like an awful fool."

"And is it?"

"No! Mother, it's just out of this world! An exhibition

of dreams, the folder calls it, and if anybody could paint their most gorgeous dreams, they'd be like this. Only Miss Absalom says this girl was probably schizophrenic. She died awfully young, after she painted all those marvelous fantasies she'd had. I suppose she just kept withdrawing from the world until she practically willed herself out of existence."

Susan glanced down at her. Amy could always astonish her at the most unlikely moments.

Just as they reached the opposite curb the lights changed and a car shot past them on a noisy gust. Amy whipped around and yelped ecstatically. "That's Tracy Jones! He's got a *Jaguar!*"

"Not for long, if he doesn't improve his driving habits," said Susan.

"He's so conceited," said Amy, gazing wistfully after the car. "He drives it to school, and all the senior girls are so crazy to ride with him they're disgusting. Making perfect fools of themselves. Of course the only reason his parents let him have a car like that is they're *nouveaux riches* and don't know any better."

Susan thought a television executive like Tracy Jones, Sr., hardly qualified as *nouveau riche,* but the phrase obviously tasted so delicious to Amy she wouldn't question it. "Tell me more about the exhibit."

"No, you've got to be taken by surprise, to get the impact the way I did. I'll tell you one thing, the people from Beacon Heights are simply thronging to this show. They're just mad about it, and they're very *avant-garde* up there, you know." Another lovely phrase, to be pronounced meticulously and with relish.

"You mean the *nouveau riche* gang?" asked Susan.

"That's Tracy Jones's family. The rest aren't that way. They're terribly cultured, really, Mother, and they *know*. They make a real thing out of buying pictures, Miss Absalom told us. And then of course there are the Glen people, the ones who *really* have money. I mean *money*-money. They build up collections the way Barry collects baseball cards."

The Glen people would love that, thought Susan. It should cut them down to size, them with all their *money*-money.

The small elegant Federalist mansion, which had once been the home of the Somerset family and was now the museum, sat tranquilly among its chestnut trees at the head of a gracious green slope. Susan was pleased to notice that Amy pounced greedily on two beautiful chestnuts while she continued her short introductory course on modern art. "I suppose that's why this man brought the pictures here. He knew they'd be appreciated. And, Mother, it's up to us to do everything we can to encourage things like this in Somerset."

"Would you like to buy a season ticket for the Community Concerts right now and do your bit, darling?" asked Susan. "Who couldn't be bothered to go to any of them last year, with her own mother on the committee?"

"Oh, all right!" Amy snapped, then glanced sidewise at her mother and grinned. They went inside. Marshall Jury, the director, stood in the entrance hall talking to his young female assistant. He exclaimed in pleasure and came across the black-and-white floor to meet them.

"Susan! This really makes my day," he said. "It's quiet right now, but there have been people streaming through here who never set foot in the museum from one year's end to the next, when we feature local talent. So help me, I haven't recognized four-fifths of them. I was beginning to think I'd been transported, museum and all." He was a stout and bearded man whose heart lay a few million years back in the geological history of the broad valley in which Somerset lay.

"Oh, yes, I've been hearing about the *avant-garde,*" said Susan. "I didn't know we had one until my daughter told me." Amy had already gone in.

"We've got something, but I don't know what you'd call it."

"Seriously though, those paintings are lovely in an other-worldly way," said his assistant.

"Oh, yes, yes," agreed Jury. "The use of color is quite inspired, and the lines and shapes—and Henry Lyons assures me the work has merit, in fact he recommended the show. But oh, Lord!" He waved a large hand at her. "The interpretations I've been listening to, the symbolism that's been discovered—not by Henry, to give him credit—a mad hash of Freud and *The Golden Bough,* chanted by people who could pass by a chunk of Devonian limestone without turning a hair. The marvel of the natural world means absolutely nothing to them."

"Well, it means something to me, Marshall," Susan assured him. "Far more than these pictures are going to mean. But Amy's excited about something besides the latest teen-age singer, and that's what counts." She smiled and went off across the black-and-white diamonds toward the main gallery.

"Isn't she a lovely person?" asked the young assistant.

"Yes, she is," said Marshall Jury. "She respects rocks."

Susan walked into the long drawing room where the Somerset family had entertained Lafayette. Pale walls and
lighted cornices gave a cool, shadowless illumination in
which colors glowed with a deep radiance that tran-
scended mere canvas and pigment squeezed from tubes. In
fact her first impression was of waves of color all about the
room, tender and translucent or deeply vibrant, in shapes
of gemlike clarity. She felt relief; no need to pretend. She
could unashamedly admire.

There were a few people at the far end of the gallery; a
tall woman with a well-behaved wirehair terrier on a leash
was Mrs. Henry Lyons of the Glen, whose husband had assured Marshall that the pictures were authentic art.

Alone at one side, Amy stood in touching reverence before a picture. "Just look at this one, Mother," she whispered. "Stand here and try not to think, just *feel.*"

Susan obeyed. She concentrated so hard that the outer
edges of her vision blurred. Only the picture was alive,
pulsing like live coals at the center of wavery grayness.
The masses fell into shape, distance became evident, a
sunny distance viewed from beside a corner or pillar of
rough stone; one felt the roughness against one's cheek
and sweaty palms, the gritty warmth of it, as the hot and
aching eyes stared across the glaring miles toward the
blinding flash of sun off metal breastplates.

The Marching Men.

"Can you read that card from here?" a young voice
asked incredulously, and she knew she had said the words
aloud.

With a physical act of will she pulled her gaze from the
scene and looked into Amy's questioning face. "That's

what it is, isn't it?" she said with a laugh which sounded like a gasp to her. "Marching men?"

"That's what it's *called*, but how did you know? Can you actually see them? Can you sort them out of all those lines? If you recognized them right off, I'm going to tell Miss Absalom you're a genius!"

Susan kept looking into Amy's light-speckled brown eyes, thinking, This is my daughter. Nothing can hurt me. It's all a dream, except for Amy, and Marshall talking out there in the hall. ... The wirehair barked once at Marshall's booming laughter. Amy, frowning, said, "Most people, if they're sensitive enough, sort of *feel* the mystery in the pictures because the titles tell you what *she* saw, but you saw it without reading the title!"

She was dragging at Susan's arm. Susan felt as if she would pitch forward if she didn't pull back as hard as she could. The colors blossomed out at her from every side in a fantastic and evil burgeoning. "Amy, wait," she protested. "I'm dizzy, I don't know why. I'll have to come back another day." In spite of herself she saw and recognized the next one. *The Judgment*. She would not look again. She was free of Amy and trying not to run out into the hall where the black-and-white diamonds winked and quivered as if through heat waves. She heard Amy's frightened feet behind her. The assistant was rising from her desk saying, "Mrs. Linden, are you all right?" Marshall was standing in his office door.

"Dizzy, that's all." She smiled blindly at them and went out, breathing the sharp, leaf-scented air in gulps.

"Mother!" Amy's voice shook with fright. "What's the matter?"

"Nothing serious, dear. I may be coming down with some bug or other that hits all at once like this."

"I'll call Father—"

"No, you will not," said Susan sharply. She patted the girl's shoulder. "I feel better already, out in the air. Let's go across the park, and if I feel rocky when we reach Main Street we'll take a taxi."

How indescribably precious the iron deer on the lawn, the sweet-sad whiff of petunias and the frosty scent of dahlias, the blue quality of the shadows; how bitterly, painfully beautiful because of the nightmare behind the museum doors. Just let me get home, she prayed. Into my room, into my bed, pretend I'm sick before Richard has a chance to see my face.

CHAPTER 2

Now THE ROOM that was hers and Richard's, where her children had been conceived, became another place entirely. A gallery; but not the one from which she had so recently fled. All that associated the two were the pictures. The same paintings had hung in that long-ago place, as far away from the Somerset museum as from one world to the next.

It had been a different world and she'd been a different person, and eighteen years lay between *there* and *here*. She was carried now, shivering and frightened, back into the very skin of Leslie Danton. The years were shed like dead leaves, like dead leaves they went up in smoke; out of the smoke her mother, Olivia, spoke to her.

"Turn around," she said.

Silently the girl revolved in the dark green velveteen dress with its lacy white collar and cuffs. Her eyes were fixed on unseen distances, her face blank as a store window mannequin's.

"Very good," Olivia said. *"Very* good. She's got that look—what is it again, Naomi?"

"Une jeune fille bien élevée," said Naomi in her impeccable French. She was a tall, aloof woman who looked rather like Edith Sitwell.

Olivia nodded curtly; Naomi's effortless control of languages always stung her. "Just what we want. They have to believe she's sheltered and innocent. Well, she *is,* but she should look the part. Leslie, pretend I'm Mrs. Montgomery."

She stood off, a pretty blond woman, flower-delicate in pink suit and a cap made of violets. "So this is Leslie!" she crooned. "How do you do, my dear?"

"Very well, thank you," Leslie replied with less animation than a talking doll.

"Where's your curtsey?" her mother snapped, and Leslie came angrily alive.

"Curtsey! Oh, Mother, I'm eighteen, and this is the twentieth century! I refuse to do that stupid bobbing one more time!" Her gaze avoided her mother's suddenly quiet face, going toward David, who sat on a corner of the desk behind Olivia. He winked at Leslie and that filled her with a fresh, gay courage.

"In fact," she said expansively, "I don't know why I even have to go over there tonight. I'm not supposed to say anything except that I don't know how I paint the pictures, then *you* start telling what the pictures mean, so why do you need me at all?"

Her heart began to beat hard as she saw the deep flush kill Olivia's pastel fairness. The woman stood perfectly still. They were all waiting, David's blond head bent as he stared intently at his swinging foot; Naomi poised against the blazing paintings like a Plantagenet effigy in modern dress; Pauline, big and gypsy-dark, her long cigarette holder halfway to her mouth. For once her dangling earrings were still.

Leslie swallowed. This was taking all she had; she wished David would look up and wink again. But if she didn't go on, the fine brave start would be lost. Well begun is half done, she encouraged herself.

"You're always telling me," she said, "that the pictures are everything. We should all realize that our only importance is in taking care of the pictures and interpreting them. Otherwise we aren't anything at all. I'm only Princess Nen-a-tifa when I'm painting or when you're showing me off, but otherwise I'm just a stupid little girl, no more than the brush for a dead hand out of the past. So I mustn't give myself airs."

The red deepened frighteningly in Olivia's face. Her eyes were almost shut as she listened to her own words coming back at her.

"I want to go home," Leslie said. "If I'm really nobody, why can't I go home? Maybe I'll start painting again," she said craftily. "Look how long it's been since I've done anything. Remember what Mr. Martin said, that I could lose whatever it is. Maybe I've lost it already."

"You've been forbidden ever to mention that man's name again," Olivia said, her lips hardly moving. She glanced at Naomi. "Has she been secretly in touch with him?"

"I don't know when she'd have the chance, Olivia."

"Les isn't a sneaky kid," said Pauline loudly. Olivia didn't turn to David, who seemed to be staring even harder at his foot, as if deciphering a code message on the toe of his shoe.

"You could have asked me, Mother," Leslie said. "Anyway, I don't need to have anybody tell me I want to go home. I've been wanting to go home for three years. Why can't we just take the pictures and *go?* People can come there to see them. If we're meant to meet somebody very rich that's one of us, they'll find the pictures wherever they are, even back in Belmont Falls."

"Leslie," said her mother in the voice that always reminded her daughter of tinkling ice cubes. "You are to go straight back to the hotel, take one of your pills, and stay in bed till it's time for tea with Mrs. Montgomery. Pauline, see that she does it."

Pauline sighed loudly, which meant she felt put upon. She never got a chance to stay in the gallery when the people began coming in. Leslie kept her eyes on her mother. "I don't want a pill, I don't want a nap, I don't want tea with Mrs. Montgomery. We've been three years on the road with those pictures and nobody's bought the collection, nobody's offered to finance any searches for the truth, or take us all to Egypt to look for my grave. And you wouldn't let me go to that university where they wanted to study me. Now we've given everything a fair trial, and *I want to go home.*"

"How long has this been coming on?" asked Olivia.

"For quite a while," said Leslie, feeling slightly drunk. "But I've never had the courage to say it until today. And I wouldn't be saying it in front of everybody like this if you'd given me a chance to say it in private."

"So you realize how abominable your behavior is," said

Olivia. "That's something, I suppose. Now go back to the hotel with Pauline like a good girl, and we'll overlook the whole thing and start out fresh."

"Come on, kid," said Pauline. "We'll stop for a soda on the way. My treat."

"Thank you very much, but no, Pauline." She was proud of her calmness. What a difference it made, just having David there. She wanted to fight this through alone without calling on him, but his presence gave her the strength she needed. *Of course you can do it, sweetheart,* he'd said. *You're eighteen now, you can get married without permission.*

Only he'd wanted to elope and tell Olivia afterwards. It was her idea of what was fair, to give her mother a chance to consent. She seemed so fond of David, always saying it was like having a son of her own to have him around, that Leslie hadn't really expected any trouble. But Olivia just wouldn't give her a chance to talk to her alone, and so this scene in the closed gallery had exploded unexpectedly. The curtsey had been the match set to the box of fireworks.

"Mother," she said in appeal, "I *am* going home. Please understand! David and I are going to get married there, and then he's going to find a job, and I can get something to do too, and—"

"*Married?*" Olivia was no longer red, but so white that her lipstick looked purple. Her eyes swelled and grew shiny. "*You?* To this nobody I brought in off the street, out of pity? This—this—" She swung around and looked at him. He stood up quickly, his fingers twitching a little at his sides. He was blushing to the ears, but he looked straight back at her, and Leslie was enormously proud.

"He's not a nobody, Mother," she said. "Remember what Pauline saw in the crystal, and then Naomi read it in one of the pictures? The Fair Lover from the North? You all decided David must be the one, the way you found him. As if he was led to you. Remember? And the way he and I"—it was delightful pain to come out with the sweet words—"felt about each other from the start, it was like something that really began centuries ago."

"Fiddlesticks!" Olivia snapped. "It's utter unscrupulous nonsense! Twiddling things around to suit yourselves! We don't know anything about him, he could have lied about his family and all his troubles in college, just to get our sympathy!"

Leslie's mouth dried. Olivia had been practically kittenish about the Fair Lover idea, but now—

"Mrs. Danton," David said, and she turned contemptuously toward him.

"I told you the truth that night in the Automat," he said, "and I'm telling the truth now when I say I love Leslie and I want to marry her."

Her eyes swept him from head to foot. "Oh, you do! And I suppose you expect that when you marry her you'll also marry the pictures."

"The pictures have nothing to do with it. I love Leslie for herself."

"But I'm sure," she crooned, "that you aren't *ignoring* the pictures. I'm sure you've taken them into consideration, where you'll keep them, how you'll show them, and so forth."

"Well, after all, they're Leslie's work!" he shouted. "They're hers!"

"Oh, no, they aren't. Leslie gave me a power of attorney on the day she was eighteen. I wasn't taking any chances on anything like this happening. I knew she'd fall for the first man who paid attention to her, and he'd have the pictures and be gone before she knew it!"

David moved back against the table as if he felt unsteady, his eyes seeking Leslie's. She looked back, remembering all the times when she had signed her name without seeing what she was signing.

"That time on my birthday," she said feebly, "I thought it was something to do with insurance. You let me think so."

"It *was* insurance. Against your being made a fool of. Now go back to the hotel and lie down. You don't want to look like a zombie tonight."

"But the pictures don't matter!" she cried. "Do they, David? Keep them, I don't care! We're going to get married!" She ran to him and he held her clumsily, not as he had when they were alone, but she knew he was upset and embarrassed, and she forgave him. "Let's go on the bus tonight, David," she pleaded. "We can be in Belmont Falls in five hours."

He took her by the shoulders. "Now wait a minute, Leslie," he said, smiling anxiously at her. "Let's not rush. You didn't want your mother mad at you, remember? Let's give her time to get used to the idea. After all, we'll have all the rest of our lives."

"David, I can't stand it here another moment! I hate this gallery—I hate that hotel—oh, please, let's go!"

He didn't move, looking past her at Olivia, moistening

his lips. She pulled at him, tried to shake him, pulled again. He was like rock. Pauline burst out with some emotional profanity, and Olivia said icily, "Pauline, that's why I don't like to have you around the gallery." She began giving the other woman a lecture in deportment, as if she were allowing little Leslie to have a harmless tantrum in one corner. Nobody was to notice her; even David was looking stonily away from her.

She tried once more, frantically, to move him. Then she let go of him and ran out of the gallery and across the anteroom toward the outer doors. She grabbed up her coat on the way, and then, decision and act coming together with no conscious planning, she seized her mother's handbag.

Nobody saw her do it; she had moved so quickly they hadn't a chance yet to follow. Anyway, they wouldn't think she was going far; no farther than back to the hotel like an obedient robot. But outside she kept on running for a block before she stopped.

Apparently nobody thought anything of a young girl running along a busy Boston pavement in a bright March noon. She could be running for the subway, a dental appointment, a class. Nobody stopped her, nobody caught up with her, least of all David. She still hoped for him to follow.

When she got around a corner she stopped, breathing hard through her mouth. Her throat felt scalded, and she was sweating. With the natural instinct of the fugitive she slipped into a group waiting for the lights to change, and crossed the street with them. Then onto the Common and running along the path, sending the pigeons up in clouds. She felt light enough now to run forever, knowing no one could catch up with her except David, and *he*—she stopped by an elm, peeked around it back at the noon-time strollers. No fair head showed among the other bare ones—yes, there was one, but it belonged to someone who didn't look a bit like him.

At the hotel she gave the elderly desk clerk a little smile and nod, and hurried toward the elevators and the equally elderly operator, who also got a smile; they had been very nice to her, these old people. The hotel itself was old, and not very expensive, but it was respectable. Olivia would never stay in any place that wasn't respectable.

The elevator creaked and jerked upward. Leslie, her whole body straining ahead, wished she'd taken the stairs.

She let herself into the room she shared with her mother, locked the door behind her, and went across the room shedding clothes. The velveteen dress she put on a hanger. It was a pretty dress. Under other circumstances she'd have loved it. She put on a sweater and skirt, and changed her shoes for crepe-soled ghillies. She got her dressing case from the closet and was putting her pajamas and toilet articles into it when someone tapped at the door.

"Les, honey." It was Pauline, trying to be hushed, but her clanging tones were always penetrating. "I know you're in there." She sounded out of breath. "Listen, kid, I know how you feel, but . . . Are you all right?"

Leslie didn't answer, staring bright-eyed at the locked door, and Pauline said, "Look, you haven't gone and taken a whole bottle of those things, have you?"

"Don't worry," Leslie said, sounding drowsy. "I just took one." Moving as delicately as a cat stalking a bird, she put more things in the case.

"Oh, boy." Pauline blew a loud gust of relief. "The way you took off scared me silly. Listen, forget that David. He's a weak sister, a mama's boy. That's why Olivia can twist him around her little finger. And look, maybe this old Lady Montgomery's the One, and we can all come to roost somewhere for a while."

"Let's hope so," said Leslie with a good imitation of a yawn.

"You go to sleep now, honey. So long. I'll be in my room right down the hall."

"All right. So long." Leslie dragged it out as if she were falling asleep. She waited a few moments, then opened her mother's bag. Olivia's billfold was comfortably thick. Leslie transferred fifteen ten-dollar bills to the neat little handbag Olivia had given her for Christmas and which had never yet held any money but a handful of change.

Everything in Olivia's bag carried her faint scent of carnations, and it caused waves of sickness in Leslie. She didn't linger over it, though as an afterthought she opened the bag again and took out some ones and some silver.

She put on her coat again, tied a bright scarf around her head, took her things, and went out into the hall. It was the drowsy hour after lunch when the residents took their naps. Nobody was in sight, though she could hear the elevators creaking and groaning around a far corner.

She ran down the stairs as she and David had always done, arriving in a narrow corridor at the back of the lobby, and slipped out a side door into the alley. She went on down the alley past the back of the hotel and came out on another street. She saw a Yellow Cab coming with no passengers, and ran across the sidewalk, signaling. When it pulled in to the curb she felt as if she'd accomplished a miracle with a wave of her hand. Now *that* could really make one feel like a princess.

"The Greyhound Bus Depot," she told the driver. He accepted it. He didn't gaze coldly into her face and say, "You're running away." He behaved as if she had a perfect right to be where she was. She almost laughed out loud.

Though she had ached for home for so long, and now to be so close was agony, she knew that Belmont Falls was the first place they would look for her. She saw the Maine names on the busses through a hot dazzle of tears, and passed them by.

She went to New York.

CHAPTER 3

WHEN THEY REACHED the house she gave Amy a few instructions about dinner, and went up to her room. "Shall I bring you up a nice hot cup of tea?" Amy called after her.

"Yes, do that, dear, and I'll take some aspirin." She went across the room and looked into her mirror, searching for the woman who had been here earlier. That happy woman. *Complacent,* her lips formed mockingly. Pride goeth before a fall and a haughty spirit before destruction. Destruction. The word was like a hammer blow; it rocked her down onto the edge of her bed, and a despairing hand gripped the nearest thing, a book. She picked it up, and a line leaped out at her like a message shouted in her ear. *But Susan is a stranger yet.* It was almost as if the poem read so lightheartedly by Amy had been an incantation, summoning up the evil that had befallen her in the last hour.

She heard Amy on the stairs and got up quickly, took a

robe, and went into the bathroom. "Just leave it on my desk, dear," Susan called to the girl as she appeared at the head of the stairwell.

"All right." Amy was no longer frightened. She loved to whisk around in the kitchen by herself.

In the bathroom Susan scrubbed her face as if to scrub away what had happened, then went back to her room, hung up her clothes, piled pillows behind her on the bed, and sipped her tea.

She felt safe here in the stillness and the blurring velvety dusk, so different from the light in the museum in which she had felt like a butterfly impaled alive on a pin. She tried to think how many people were there, what they looked like, if she had actually run from the gallery, and if anyone had noticed besides the wirehair.

The last time she had seen those pictures was in a Boston gallery. She had run then, too. She had never looked back, never gone back. In eighteen years, at first with a terror that had turned her forever into the passionate friend of the hunted fox, rabbit, and deer, she had built herself into a new person in a new world. To see the pictures now, in Somerset, by the side of her child, was not to be endured; she clapped her hands against her ears as if the throbbing in them were a pounding siege against the fragile citadel that was Susan Linden.

After a while the courage that had sustained her eighteen years ago came back, though she did not think of it as anything at all except a lessening of the squeezing pressure. Coherent thoughts emerged, a dim plan for the next step. In those days one never saw more than one step ahead, and prayed it would be in the right direction.

Who had brought the pictures to Somerset? Her

mother? The possibility set her heart to beating violently, shaking her body, turning that body back to the slender, springy frame so often shaken in those days. But she had the feeling that it wasn't her mother. She couldn't imagine Olivia's showing the pictures without being close by to watch for the certain secretive glance around that signified the Elect.

She used to move in on the ones who looked promising. She was charming, sunny, tactful, flattering. *Do you like it? Do you see what is meant there? I knew you did, I could tell.* And if that struck a spark, she would go on. *It was all around you when you came in. I haven't been able to take my eyes off you. I said, "This is one who knows."*

Afterwards, over coffee made on the hot plate in her hotel room, Olivia would be shining-eyed, telling the circle. *You should have seen the furs. And there was a diamond and emerald clip—I know gems, and hers were genuine. She's coming back tonight. She's fascinated, she can't keep away from the pictures. Oh, she's one of us, all right. She'll want to give a tea for you, dear, and believe me, we'll meet Money* . . .

Olivia's soft voice was insistent in the dusk-blurred room, and shutting your eyes didn't shut out the relentless smile and the shining eyes. . . . No, it wasn't Olivia who'd brought the pictures to Somerset. She is not even alive any more, thought Susan. I would know if she were. I think I must have known when she died, wherever it was. It was like being let go. But how could I have believed the pictures died with her, moldering away in a damp cellar somewhere or burned up in an attic fire?

All right, she said sharply to herself. *All right.* Not Olivia. Who else? Pauline? No. Hadn't it already been wearing thin with Pauline before Susan ran away? ... The complaints in the harsh, clanging accent: "Hitler's dead, so who does she think she is? Telling me what to wear, not to talk, not to mention my crystal ball ever! We're class, she says. At least you and she are. This isn't carnival stuff, this is for real, and I can tag along and maybe pick up a few cents when you hit the money, if I lick her boots for her in the meantime! Let me tell you, kiddo, I've had more money come into my place than she'll ever count. Why, I've had clients swore me to secrecy, big in the government, big in the theater, because it would be murder if it got out!"

This was over a soda in a crowded drugstore in Philadelphia on a winter's night. Olivia had wangled an invitation to a cocktail party, promising that she'd come back with news to make their eyes pop. Susan—Leslie then —had been told to stay in her room because she'd been discovered in bashful adolescent conversation with a bellhop. Pauline, made up to the eyes and looking more like a gypsy than ever, dangling earrings and all, had dragged her down to the drugstore. "You're a nice little kid. Sure, I'm willing to figure you a lost princess buried somewhere in the Valley of the Kings, because those pictures of yours bug me, I can't figure 'em out. But what I want to know is, does your *mother* believe it? Because she doesn't treat you as if she did. *She* wants all the glory."

"She's smart," Leslie said feebly. "She's a business-woman. But of course she believes it, Pauline. She's *honest*." Her head spun in the steam and the lights and the noise, and the flash of Pauline's earrings hurt her eyes. She thought, What if it *is* all just a big hoax to trick gullible people out of their money, the way crooked mediums

[2 6]

do? It was terrible to think your mother was a crook too, not somebody fighting a lonely and desperate battle to bring a message from the past to the right ears. But if I'm *not* a reincarnation, she thought, am I just an ordinary seventeen-year-old girl? If she was, *wonderful* was the word for it, except that she didn't dare think it; it was a frightening disloyalty, it called her mother a confidence woman, a trickster. And did ordinary seventeen-year-old girls paint such pictures without knowing how or why? And then sit there afterwards yawning, drained of life, listening to the interpretations the circle gave to a new painting? The latest installment in the tragic life of the young daughter of a pharaoh, centuries ago.

If I am not the Princess Nen-a-tifa, Leslie's terrified mind ran on now, doubling back on itself like a pursued rabbit, then I am insane. And Olivia knows it . . . or doesn't know it . . . whichever is worse . . .

She was back in her room. Not the hotel room where she was supposed to stay until Olivia told her how to dress for the afternoon at the gallery—"And don't talk to *any-one!* You're above that sort of thing, you're *royalty!*"

No, it was her room in Somerset, with the streetlight now shining through the maple tree outside the window. Barry was calling, "So long!" across the yard. A dog barked down the street. A car door slammed. Richard home? She shrank back against her pillows and waited, but he didn't come.

No, it wasn't Pauline who had the pictures. After Leslie ran away, the Lost Princess really lost, Pauline had probably gone back to her cozy existence with her crystal ball and her steady clients.

[2 7]

What about Naomi, the intellectual daughter of a long line of educators? She supplied many of the interpretations for the pictures out of the vast library in her head, even though Olivia did not always give her the credit for it. The girl Leslie used to wonder what had drawn her into the tail of the comet. Susan the woman knew now that she was looking for something, but what? Did she really believe, or was she trying to? How many times had she walked out with dignity, denying the tears in her eyes, but had come back? And *why?* Because she had nothing else to go to? Leslie had been too shy to ask her questions.

Good Lord! Susan thought now in honest and invigorating astonishment. What was she doing with us? She could have been teaching somewhere. She could have been married, instead of trailing around in Olivia's train. Unless she really believed with all her heart that I was the princess. That was the only explanation. She was quietly but passionately sincere, otherwise she would never have stayed on under the velvet-tongued humiliations heaped on her when Olivia thought someone enjoyed talking with Naomi more than with her. No, if the pictures had fallen into Naomi's hands they would never be shown as mere romantic fantasies. The truth must be told as Naomi knew it. So, if it was neither Olivia, Pauline, nor Naomi, who was it?

Through the layering walls of the past eighteen years she heard her doorknob turn. Her voice sounded queer to her as she called out, "What is it?" and she wondered if this was how people felt as they began to withdraw from reality. Barry's answer sounded as if it came from a great distance. "You asleep, Mother? You got a headache?"

"No, I'm not asleep and yes, I have a headache," she called back. "Is Father home yet?"

"Nope." He went on to his room. I should put on the light, she thought. Dress. Wash my face in cold water. But inertia held her there. She felt weightless and without strength against the pillows, as if her hands would not obey her if she commanded them to move.

Who else? She knew then she had purposely saved David for the last, and she had to make a great effort to consider him objectively. She could see him clearly as he'd been on that last day before she fled the gallery. A slight boy with fair hair brushed back, looking from her to her mother with worried blue eyes, sometimes moistening his lips, starting to say something and then stopping. She could remember how he'd resisted her appeals, and how his arms had felt when she pulled at them.

He'd joined them late, only a few months before her flight. He had been living alone in the YMCA in Philadelphia, and Olivia, with her unerring instinct for charming the young, had gathered him up in a lunchroom one day. Sensitive, poetic, eager, he had approached the pictures as a shrine toward which he had been on a lifetime pilgrimage. And he had seen Leslie as—what?

For a long time she'd hated him for his betrayal of her. Now she saw him as an immature boy who'd been appalled, maybe terrified, to find himself the object of Olivia's fury. And she owed him her freedom, because his cowardice had given her the desperation to run.

No, it couldn't be David who had the pictures. After that final scene he'd probably fled gladly to the safety of the family business in Detroit, and now entertained his children with amusing and much-embroidered accounts of his adventures while attempting to make his fortune in the East.

The door opened gently. Light came in from the hall

like a blow. She flung an arm up across her face. Richard said softly, "I'm sorry. Did I wake you?"

"I'm glad you did," she said. "I was dreaming. Come in, darling, I'll put on the light."

As it filled the room she saw Richard standing near the bed, tall, a little stooped, his tweed jacket hanging loosely on his bony frame, his strong, big-nosed face wearing the gentle smile that had first attracted her to him. "Welcome home, Richard," she said, and held out her arms.

"And what a welcome," he said in mild amusement as he embraced her. He could not guess the panic that made her hold him with all her strength. She felt words springing up wildly in her throat; she wanted to cry into his neck now, cradled like this against his chest, *Richard, I had the most terrible experience today!*

But she could not. If she could not think of it all without loathing, how could he hear it without loathing? Their whole life would be tainted.

They broke apart and he sat on the side of the bed looking at her. "Amy says you're sick. You look a little drawn, but you don't feel hot."

"I don't know what struck me, but I feel better now, I think. I shan't eat much supper, though."

"Good idea. And stay in bed until tomorrow morning. You've been on the go too much, you haven't had a chance to rest and invite your soul. How long is it since you've spent an afternoon or an evening reading?"

"Too long," she said.

"Then tonight you read. What would you like?"

"I love you, Richard," she said.

"Well, don't look so sad about it."

"I *am* sad."

He stood up. "Drop off a few committees and you'll feel better. Let's spend more time together. Remember the evenings at home when the children were small?"

"Did we know how blissfully happy we really were then?"

He leaned down and took her face in his hands. "Whatever has struck you, I don't like it. You sound as if you were full of premonitions, forebodings. You know, 'By the pricking of my thumbs something wicked this way comes.'" He laughed. "Have you kept it from me all these years that you're really a witch?"

She pulled her head back from his hands. "Who can tell?" Her smile felt like a grimace.

With Richard smoking his pipe and reading his paper in their room, and the children coming and going, she imagined the museum retreating farther and farther away from her. She felt strength rushing back into her, physically and mentally. She even looked forward to tomorrow, viewing with gratitude the commonplace things that had seemed sometimes bothersome until today. Amy brought in her English homework for a little help. Barry lay on the rug and studied the ads in the evening paper. "Pups, half-shepherd, half-collie, free to good homes," he read ear piercingly. "Hey, why can't we have one?"

Amy appealed to her mother. "How can he be so *disloyal* to—" She still couldn't say the name of the old dog who had died two months ago, saddening the summer for them all.

"He's not disloyal, Amy, he's lonely," said Richard. "But the whole thing is up to your mother. She'll have most of the care of a puppy."

"Do I have to decide tonight?" said Susan. She felt deliciously relaxed. A wonderfully sensible solution to the puzzle of the exhibit had occurred to her. Someone had taken the pictures after Olivia died, and had sold them for a lump sum, perhaps to a secondhand dealer or to someone with a good imagination and a sense of showmanship. The story of the schizophrenic girl dying young would catch the fancy of many people. . . . Yes, that was not only possible but probable. The chain between her and the pictures existed only in her mind. Marshall had mentioned Henry Lyons in some connection. That proved there could be no link with the past.

The more she thought about it the more certain she was that it was only a wild coincidence that had brought the pictures to Somerset. There was nothing for her to fear; her past was still as deeply buried as she had buried it. To all intents and purposes the child who had painted those pictures was dead.

"You mean," Barry was saying, "there's a *chance?*" She looked down into his luminous gray eyes and said, "Yes, darling, there's a chance, but I'm not promising anything tonight."

"Well, if we *are* going to get another dog," said Amy, "why can't we have a poodle? A big one. Michele, Simone, Gigi," she went on dreamily. "Or Pierre, Zhack, Ro-bair —"

Barry said, "Oh, for Pete's sake! What's the matter with these half-shepherd, half-collie pups, free to a good home? Boy, I'll bet they're some dogs!"

Susan wondered if Amy were imagining Gigi or Ro-bair riding with her in Tracy Jones's Jaguar. . . . Flirting comfortably with her new sense of security, she decided she might even go back and take a good look at the pictures, face them down once and for all, and then forget them.

In the morning there was rain, but she didn't mind. She had slept well and had awakened with that glorious sense of relief one feels upon waking from a nightmare to the safety of one's own bed. She assured Richard that she felt fine, and promised to think seriously about shedding some of her outside activities, if she could decide which. "If you don't decide, I shall," he said, and she answered meekly, "All right, Mr. Rochester, or am I dealing with Heathcliff?"

Barry begged her to spend the day considering the puppy, and left the newspaper propped up on her work counter in the kitchen to remind her.

"If he gets that dog free, why can't we buy a poodle?" Amy asked. "I'll feed it out of my allowance." She left.

As soon as Susan thought Marshall Jury had arrived at the museum she called up and asked to speak to him. After an exchange of courtesies so courtly on his part that she felt like a French marquise, she asked, "Marshall, who is responsible for the show in the main gallery? I mean, where does the work come from, how did you happen to have it, and so forth? What does Henry Lyons have to do with it?"

"Well, as you know, I have a free hand here because nobody else wants the job, but I depend on advice from a few experts when it comes to anything in the way of pictures and sculpture—especially the modern stuff. And I can always find somebody good at the special exhibits— the Revolution in the Somerset Valley, the old ship-building days, and so forth—What is it, Maisie?" Maisie's voice was heard, distant and indistinct.

"Oh, tell him to do anything he likes," Marshall said testily. "I'm having an important conversation with Mrs. Linden."

Susan said, "You can call me later if you want—"

"I want to talk to you now," said Marshall. "You were asking about this Leslie Danton show. Well, I had a letter from this chap asking me if he could bring the show here. He's been taking it to museums around the country, apparently trying to reach the hinterlands with the gospel of impressionism or abstraction, whatever it is. Lettie Absalom's been telling me for a year that I'm a reactionary old fogy and won't show anything unorthodox if I can help it, so I thought I'd let the old bird see I was impartial. Then it transpired that Henry Lyons had seen the stuff in some little place in New York called The Vine and Fig Tree, of all things, and was enthusiastic about it, and had put the idea in the man's head."

"And is the man staying in Somerset while the show's on?"

Marshall chuckled. "Are you after him too? I'm ashamed of you, Susan. I didn't know you'd follow the herd."

"*After* him?" she asked in surprise. "What do you mean?"

"Oh, he's very much sought after, both by the crowd on the Heights and the aristocrats of the Glen."

"Where they have the *money*-money," said Susan.

"I beg your pardon?"

"In Amy's set, *money*-money is the kind you inherit along with stables of hunters and ancestors who entertained Lafayette, as compared to just plain money that you earn."

"I'm glad to know the fine difference. Well, Randall Emery knew what he was doing, wanting to show his collection here. He's found a hotbed of kindred souls."

"A pretty phrase," said Susan. "Well, thank you for all the information, Marshall. I was curious, that's all. What's his name again?"

"Randall Emery. He's back and forth between here and New York, staying at the Somerset House when he's here. If he accepts all his invitations he'll never again have to pay for a meal or a bed."

"That's quite a life," said Susan. "Well, thank you again."

"I was happy to be of assistance," said Marshall, at his most chivalrous.

She left the telephone with her assurance intact. The name Randall Emery meant absolutely nothing to her. He was the clever entrepreneur she'd imagined and he would know nothing about her, so she was right to believe that the chain was broken and she was safe. Her spirits rose as the day worsened. Perhaps it was a good thing the pictures had come to Somerset, forcing her to face what she had refused to look at for so long. Now she could honestly forget it, instead of knowing always that she was hiding from herself.

CHAPTER 4

ANN ELLENBURG HAD been Susan's first friend in Somerset when she'd come there as Richard's wife sixteen years ago. They were still close friends and so were their husbands, though their children had developed a sort of protective antipathy toward one another since they'd outgrown being wheeled together in the park or paddling nude in the Ellenburgs' wading pool. Ann called Susan up on the afternoon of the rainy day and said, "Guess what."

"I can't," said Susan.

"I've snared—yes, *snared*—Randall Emery right from under Mrs. Tracy Jones's snub nose."

"You mean Mrs. Tracy Jones, the mother of the Jaguar?"

"Oh, do you hear about that too? My daughter is disgusted with me. She says if I've made Mrs. Jones mad I've ruined all her chances. I told her that at fifteen she wasn't riding in anybody's Jaguar unless I'm along too, but she feels that she's headed for premature old maidhood. . . . Aren't you thrilled about my getting him?"

"Not particularly," said Susan. "What's so special about him? Why is everybody mad about the man?"

"Well, for one reason he's charming, and for another reason those pictures are going to make history in the art world and be in *Life* and *Time,* and, oh yes, on television, what with everybody on Beacon Heights trying to be In ... I mean, darling, that a Leslie Danton painting will shortly be a very impressive status symbol. And who is the man who controls them? Randall Emery."

"I still don't get it," said Susan.

"I think you glory in being a non–status seeker. You and your back yard and overgrown barberry hedge and your husband owning a hardware store. You're an affront to something or other. And so am I, let's face it. My husband doesn't commute either. He's the lawyer all the farmers get to make their wills, and when somebody wants a divorce he says, 'Now you don't really want to leave old George, do you?' " She sighed heavily. "So with all that, we've just got to have Randall Emery, don't you see?"

Susan began to laugh. "I'll say so, just to shut you up. When are you having him, and how? Boiled or barbecued?"

"At a quietly elegant little buffet supper on Sunday. Discreet music on the stereo, and a small but suitable group."

"If Richard and Joe are samples, we'd better brief them beforehand."

Ann giggled. "I've put it to Joe that we're simple, hospitable townspeople, being nice to the stranger in our midst. But I do expect to have a few who are going around swooning about Leslie Danton's pictures, because they think it's the thing to do—I'm sure they can't make head or tail out of them. Well, you know." She named a few. "Can't you just imagine Veronica Porteous being reverent?"

Laughing quite irreverently, they said goodbye.

Leslie Danton. It was queer, the name meant nothing to her, no throb in an old wound, no flick of pain in a new one. Leslie Danton died and Susan Hedges was born in that indescribable hotel room where she had cowered against the headboard all night long, staring at the doorknob with the chair propped under it, more afraid of being found by the police than by the lost souls who restlessly or drunkenly roamed the halls all night. A red neon sign across the street had lit the room at intervals like rhythmic reflections of hell, and there was a period before daylight when, in her fever, hunger, and fear, she had felt her mind swinging dizzily on those reflections and thought she had not outrun madness after all.

The dirty gray dawn crawling into the room and the crash of glass in the street below as the trash men made their collections were beautiful because they meant she had survived the night. She was faint with hunger and lack of sleep, but she was sane.

She could remember even now her breakfast in the grimy one-armed lunch on the corner, the good smell and taste of it, never minding the thick mug and the tough, cooling toast, or the queer-looking people at the counter with her. It had been good, it had been manna on her tongue and in her quivering stomach, because it was eaten and drunk in freedom. In the mirror behind the counter she saw herself behind the specials chalked in different colors, and studied the phenomenon with fascination as she sipped from the mug; dark red shoulder-length hair pushed back behind her ears, the uneven bangs she'd cut with nail scissors in an attempt to disguise the childish curve of her forehead, the wide eyes seeming bigger than usual because of the gray-violet shadows around them. But with her tweed coat collar turned up and the gay scarf blossoming out of it she looked like any girl her age, she told herself. And *looking* made it so.

Susan Hedges knew nothing of Leslie Danton. Susan Hedges was looking for a job. The reason she was away from home so young was that she had no parents, and the aunt she lived with wanted to marry again, and the man didn't care for having a young niece on his hands too. . . . She was delighted at the way the story sprang alive while she sipped the scalding coffee. She could even see the aunt: thin, shrill, worried, wanting to do her best for the child, but not wanting to lose this one last chance. *He* had a good job too, some sort of supervisor in an aircraft factory. He was rough-talking but solid, he liked beer and bowling. But Susan made him nervous, with her big eyes and her timid way of talking, and the way she jumped if he so much as cleared his throat. He wanted Aunt Selma to himself, and that was natural.

The counterman, a thickset Greek with a scarred face, asked her if she wanted more coffee. His manner was worried and paternal. "You just moved in around here?"

"Not really. I've only been here one night," she said nervously. "I'm looking for a job."

"You're too young to be away from home."

"I'm older than I look." Would he report her to the police? Now was the time to tell her story, and it tumbled out too fast. "I want to be on my own," she finished up.

"I'm sensible, I won't get into trouble—" Her mouth wanted to shake, and she wiped it hard with her napkin.

"I think you better go home again," he said. "A big city like this is no place for you. Even if you don't want to live with your aunt, live where you can call her up now and then. A girl needs a family in touch."

She looked down at her coffee mug, ready to cry with tiredness, and he said gruffly, "Well, at least get out of that flea-bag next door. Look, if I give you the address of a decent boardinghouse, will you go there?"

She nodded dumbly. He scribbled an address on the back of a slip. "Ma Agnopolous is tougher than nails. She'll look out for you better than your own mother. I'll call her up and tell her about you, and then get you a taxi. Okay?"

"Okay." She gave him a wobbly grin.

She stayed with Ma Agnopolous in the crowded, noisy, old brownstone for over a year. An older boarder got her a job in the stockroom of a department store, the younger ones took her under their wing as a kid sister and showed her New York, all the places you could go for nothing, all the cheap things that were fun. At nineteen she met Richard in the cafeteria of the Museum of Natural History, where she and Theo Agnopolous had gone to see a black dance group from Sierra Leone.

She thought back to the counterman now, eighteen years later on the Sunday evening when she and Richard were dressing to go to the Ellenburgs'.

"What are you smiling at?" Richard asked her.

"A nice man in my past. Will you fasten my dress?"

His fingers were warm, stroking her back. "When a woman starts dreaming about her life before she met her husband, isn't that a bad sign?"

"No, because his kindness to me led directly to *you*. . . . You know about him, the counterman who bullied me into going to the Agnopolous house. If I hadn't been staying there, I'd never have been in the museum with Theo to see that dance troupe on the same day you went to see that exhibit of crystals."

"A Hellenic Cupid, so to speak," said Richard solemnly. "What made you think of him tonight?"

"I don't know. Suddenly he came into my mind. I've never really appreciated what he must have felt to be so concerned about a young girl. He was very kind to me."

"I'm grateful to him, too." Richard's lips brushed her nape. "Am I kind to you?" he whispered. She turned quickly into his embrace and held him hard. "Oh, Richard," she whispered. "Sometimes I'm so happy I don't know how it can last." He stopped her mouth with his own. "Stop that now," he said sternly. "Don't start that superstitious twaddle. We're not stealing our happiness from anyone else. It's all *ours*."

They walked to the Ellenburgs' through the mild early dark. Lights and faint music floated out through the long windows.

"Don't let's hurry," she said.

They stood listening, looking up through the trees to the first stars. Suddenly everything took on an unbearable poignance for Susan. She didn't want to go in. Yielding honestly to impulse she would have turned and run for the car, dragging Richard with her.

"What's the matter?" he said as her hand tightened on his arm.

"Nothing. It's just so sad all at once. It's as if the house is filled with the ghosts of all the boys and girls who danced there."

"My grandparents, for four of them," said Richard. "But they're very happy ghosts, I'm sure. You're in a strange mood lately, my girl. You'd better snap out of it."

"It must be my age," she said starkly, in imitation of a woman they knew, and they both laughed and went on up the walk. The bad moment was gone.

Ann hurried toward them. "Susan, dear! And Richard, how do you manage to look so distinguished? I wish Joe was bony like you. Come on into the library and meet the guest of honor, and then you're on your own." She linked arms with both of them. "You'll be able to stand it, Richard. Joe likes him already."

They went into the library. Joe, stocky and short with thinning sandy hair, was holding an exquisitely executed sloop model, whittled and rigged by his stubby fingers. "This is a Friendship," he was saying. "You see the clipper bow."

"Wasn't there a spoon-bowed Friendship sloop?" the other man asked. His back was toward the door. He was taller than Joe, and in the lamplight Susan could see only that his hair was either fair or gray.

"Yes," Joe answered, "but—hello, Susan! Hi, Dick!"

The stranger glanced over his shoulder, wearing the all-purpose smile for such occasions. It was David.

It seemed as if everyone was frozen in action for minutes. But really everything was going smoothly. David put the framed photograph he was holding down on the desk and turned toward them, smiling, his voice deeper than it had been eighteen years ago.

"Mrs. Linden," he was saying.

"How do you do, Mr. Emery?"

He moved on to Richard, and Susan said quickly to Ann, "Is there anything I can do to help, Ann? Last minute touches and so forth?"

Ann was looking bemused. "Why, no . . . oh, yes, there is, come along!" It meant there was something she wanted to confide. Susan followed her out of the library and down the hall to the kitchen. She was astonished at her own detachment, after that moment when her mind and vision swam out of focus. It was as if she had expected this to happen; she'd known it from the moment when she'd stopped on the brick walk and held Richard's arm, and wanted to turn and run. *Presentiments and forebodings,* Richard had said. *Are you sure you're not a witch?*

Had he recognized her? Was there anything at all in the movement of his eyes, the pressure of his fingers? She wasn't sure. The light wasn't good there just inside the library door, with only the lamp on Joe's desk. But there had been that moment when he saw them, and then had turned to place the photograph carefully on the desk, and straighten it with both hands as if to line it up just so with the blotter. It could have been a gesture made to win time for himself.

"Isn't he *nice?*" Ann was demanding. "Joe's crazy about him. I'll bet he'll even go and see the pictures now." The old-fashioned bell jangled, and Ann turned and ran. Susan stood where she was, her head bent, thoughtfully studying her hand where it rested on the countertop. This, she told herself firmly, is a hand that has fed children, combed a dog, caressed a husband's cheek, signed checks for the grocer, held the gavel at PTA meetings; stirred oatmeal, frosted birthday cakes, admonished, beckoned. It is the hand of Susan Linden, housewife. It is not the hand of Leslie Danton. Leslie Danton is dead.

There was a great deal of animated conversation at the front of the house. Everyone seemed to be having a good time. She kept on looking at her hand. She wanted to go home while she was still convinced that it was her hand and not Leslie Danton's. Leslie was the ghost in the house, not all the pretty girls who had danced there years ago.

"Leslie," David said behind her, and she turned, betraying herself. He was standing in the kitchen doorway. He came quickly, taking her hands in his. She stood quietly, her fingers passive, and looked into his face.

It was older, stronger, the young mouth thinned and hardened under a small fair mustache. The clear skin she remembered was still clear, but much paler and pulled very tight between cheekbone and jaw. His eyes were as blue as she remembered, but different; they looked deeper-set, as if illness or strain had worn the flesh away from the sockets. He was handsome in a fine-drawn way; she would have expected him to grow solid and ruddy.

He was smiling slightly. "What are you thinking, Leslie?"

"I am not Leslie," she said.

"You are, and I thought you were dead." His smile was an obvious effort. She saw sweat on his forehead, and felt the nervous contraction of his fingers around hers. "My God, I identified you, Leslie! I saw you buried beside your father in a cemetery in Belmont Falls, and it was

snowing, and I was so cold into my bones that I—
Leslie!"

Though his voice was just above a whisper, it had the
effect of a shout. It nearly rocked her on her feet, but she
had to hold on. "Please let me go, Mr. Emery!"

"I'm David," he said savagely. *"David."* He held her
hands so hard her rings were causing her agony. "I can't
believe this, but you're real! Were you the woman who
got sick in the gallery the other day and had to get out
quick? Pris Lyons was kidding me about it—she said
the pictures were overpowering. It must have been you.
For God's sake, what did you think when you saw them?"

"My hands," she said. "Please."

He didn't let go, and she wondered now if it were the
overhead light that gave him such a ghastly color. He
went on. "Who was that girl? Her face was so cut up we
went by her size and her hair. She had all new clothes and
no identification. Naomi said that's just how you'd travel,
and nobody else claimed her."

"I don't know what this is all about," Susan said, "and I
don't want to know. Will you please let go of my hands?"
Looking dazedly into her eyes, he released her. "I'm Susan
Linden, Mr. Emery. Nobody here ever knew Leslie. She's
really dead, one way or another. Therefore she has no further interest in the pictures. That's the truth, Mr.
Emery."

"You're talking as if I were an enemy, when I'm so
happy to find you alive that I can hardly contain myself. I
may not look it, because I'm still in shock. When I saw
you dead, or rather that poor girl with no face and no
name, I wanted to kill myself, but I was a coward—as always."

"It's a good thing you were, because you see before you a happy woman. You can forget the other one."

"It won't be that easy to quiet my conscience. For eighteen years I've been haunted not only by that cemetery in the snow, but by the way you looked at me before you turned and ran. Like someone half-insane with desperation. Your mother tried—physically—to keep me from following you. She kept saying you'd only gone to the hotel. Well"—he gave her a rueful grin that brought back the old David for an instant—"I couldn't knock her down, though I felt like it. When I reached the street there was no sign of you. Then when we saw you'd gone from the hotel I was frantic, but Olivia wouldn't let me call the police. She said you'd be back when you were hungry, you couldn't carry on alone, there was nobody in Belmont Falls for you to go to."

They could hear Ann's merry heels hurrying along the hall, a laughing remark tossed back. Susan said in a bright social voice, "I hope you enjoy Somerset, Mr. Emery. It's a rather interesting town in spite of its small size. Tonight you'll meet most of the noncommuters. We all live our lives right here in town."

His eyes took on a blue blaze in his taut face as she ran on. Over his shoulder she saw Ann in the doorway, glowing with humorous expectancy, and Richard behind her.

"At the risk of sounding smug, Mr. Emery," she said, "I love the life I live here. In fact, I never really lived until I came to Somerset. Hello, Ann and Richard. Don't you think I should write promotion material for the Chamber of Commerce?"

Ann applauded. "Or go into the cloak-and-dagger business for the government. You have Mr. Emery simply spellbound."

"He was taking the line of least resistance by retreating into a coma," said Susan. She laughed, and went past him to Richard. "And if you should want a nice bicycle, a power mower, or assorted nails, Mr. Emery, my husband is the man who can supply them."

David said, "He looks like the sort of man who could supply everything."

"Believe me, he is," said Susan. David's eyes held hers for a moment, then he smiled and inclined his head slightly. Ann laid her hand on his arm. "Come and meet more of our friends, Mr. Emery. And then we'll eat. Joe hates dragging out the cocktail hour, and so do I."

Susan and Richard followed them down the hall. "What's the matter?" Richard asked in amusement. "It's not like you to give this big pitch. All you needed were a few flags to wave and a brass band. Did he rile you up by calling us a nest of Philistines?"

"Poor Mr. Emery," she said. "No, he didn't say anything of the sort. He wasn't even patronizing. I guess I thought that I'd better explain the difference between our crowd and the Beacon Heights set." She looked seriously at Richard. "When you come to think of it, there *is* a sort of distinction in being the backbone of the town, don't you think?"

"I don't know about the distinction, but there's a certain satisfaction in being the only hardware business in town, especially when the emigrants from New York come in to browse on Saturday. They're all big impulse buyers. Let's go eat."

It was a successful evening in the terms of performance. She laughed and talked with her friends, appeared to enjoy herself immensely, and by skillful diversionary tactics she kept from being cornered by David until just before the party broke up. She found herself briefly alone near the phonograph, and suddenly became aware of a gentle passage from *Swan Lake* which, as soon as she gave it attention, took possession of her, making her conscious of her weariness and a sadness that must have been there all the time. Instinctively she shut her eyes and saw longingly a winter-bound emptiness, an empty silver lake rimmed by dark evergreens, with here and there a birch gleaming among the firs. She could feel the silence; the thin pure thread of the melody made the silence, and spread it like a veil of snow over the bright and inhabited room. The voices grew distant. She could smell the clean wintery air. Nothing moved along the edge of the dark woods or across the dull silver lake.

"Leslie."

Someone was there. Someone calling her through the cold silence. She opened her eyes and saw David.

Her sight was blurred for a moment and he seemed very young. Behind him the room was a kaleidoscope of color and movement. David said, "Aren't we ever going to have a chance to talk?"

"I don't know," she said. Her vision cleared, and her eyes ranged, anxiously seeking Richard. She made an effort. "It's not that I hate you, or anything like that. It's just that I can't mix two worlds. I've put all that behind me and as far as I'm concerned it never happened. I was born when I was seventeen years old. Susan Hedges. Now Susan Linden. Can't you understand, David?"

"I do understand," he said in a low voice. "But there are the pictures. You can't deny those. We have to discuss them."

She shook her head. "I must go. It was nice meeting you, Mr. Emery."

"I shall look forward to our next meeting, Mrs. Linden," he said formally as she turned away. "I hope it will be soon."

"What was he like, Mother?" Amy bedeviled her at breakfast. "Brilliant? Cosmopolitan? Does he know loads of famous artists?"

"I don't know," said Susan. "I talked very little with him."

"That wasn't his fault," said Richard from behind the paper. "He started on a beeline for her more than once, but each time someone trapped him or she disappeared. He caught her once in the kitchen, and once in the corner by the phonograph."

"Really, Mother?" Amy's eyes danced. "You mean he was smitten? When are we going to have him over?"

"When are we going to get our dog?" asked Barry.

"I'll call up today," said Susan.

"Can I do the table decorations?" cried Amy. "I've got the best idea for something—oh, you know, *stark,* with rocks and some of our driftwood, and—"

"Hey, are you some kind of a nut?" Barry asked. "Table decorations for a pup? Hey, Mother, why don't you call now? Gee, with pups in the house they're probably up."

"She wasn't talking about dogs, brat; she's talking about Randall Emery," Amy said haughtily.

"She's talking about a nervous breakdown, if you ask

me," said Susan. She put her hands over her ears. "I am going to ask about the pup, but we aren't thinking about entertaining Mr. Emery. Anyway, he's booked up for the rest of the time the pictures will be here."

"Oh, darn it!" cried Amy in despair. "When am I going to meet him? I bet Linda Ellenburg met him. I bet she was right there, all bright-eyed and bushy-tailed. I bet—"

"As a matter of fact, Linda was away for the weekend at her grandmother's." She looked drearily at her coffee cup and Richard said in the crackling voice he didn't use often, "All right, you two. Clear out, brush your teeth, powder your nose or whatever it is you have to do, get your lunchboxes, and *go*."

They looked outraged, but they never argued with that voice. Susan gazed after them with relief and regret, and Barry looked back at her with silent pleadings from the doorway. "I'll call," she told him. He bounded out after that.

"You're going for a checkup," Richard said to Susan. "And that's that."

"I don't need a checkup," said Susan. "I need a change, though." The words came from a mysterious wellspring of inspiration. "Look, I think I'll drive out to the shore! That would rest me as much as anything. Unless you came too, and that would be even better," she added, feeling guilty. She knew he wouldn't leave the store for an extemporaneous holiday, and she needed to be alone.

"You do anything you feel like," said Richard. "It'll be fine down there. September on the ocean is so spectacular it's a sin we have to miss it. All the good days come in the middle of the week, damn it. . . . If anybody calls the store and says they can't reach you, I'll tell 'em you eloped with the milkman." They both laughed at the picture of her hurrying out to old Sig Olsen's truck, and then Richard's smile deepened around his eyes. "Or with Randall Emery. That should give them pause. Everybody saw him trying to corner you last night, and I can say, reluctantly, and with obvious pain, that I found the two of you holding a rendezvous in the kitchen."

"Why pick *him?* Why not a real blast, like the husband of my best friend?" It was foolishness but she felt the sun was too bright on her face; that he read something in her eyes.

She hurried through the early morning chores, made a thermos of coffee, put a can of sardines, some crackers, and a peach into a basket, and changed into slacks. Then she remembered to call about the pups. The woman said they'd started running the ad early, and the pups were too young to go yet. But she'd vouch for their character and brains; the father was a friend of the family, so to speak. Certainly Susan could bring her little boy over to see them and choose one. "We buy all our paint and tools and things like that at Linden's Hardware. Mr. Linden is so *nice!*"

"I think so too," said Susan. Shared laughter, thanks, and goodbyes. She seized her lunch and ran out the side door to the garage. The telephone rang but she kept on running, and let the engine drown the sound if it kept on. There was a moment of sick suspense when she backed her car between the corner maple and the barberry hedge, but the street was empty. It was just after the older children had gone to school, the little ones hadn't come out yet, the postman and the dry cleaner's truck and the TV repairmen hadn't started out on their rounds.

The street belonged to the birds, and to a cat who sat
tall and composed in a pool of sunshine. Susan was too far
away to see its eyes, but she knew it was observing her, as
cats observe. It looked like a stylized cat, an alabaster sculpture found in an Egyptian tomb. ... As the fancy took
her mind, a warm, dry, ancient scent blew across her face
and into her nostrils, the memory of incense burned long
ago, and spices buried with a young girl.

The cat in this painting was the sculpture of a pet. Naomi's voice, dry and scholarly. *He shared her food, so he
died from the poison too. The murderer was doubly
damned because both the princess and the cat were sacred
objects.*

Oh God, Susan thought numbly now. She tried not to
drive too fast, tried to gulp in the morning's damp, cool
fragrance. She had never actually breathed the air of that
tomb. *Never!* It was only the abnormally vivid imagination of a disturbed child. If she had painted a cat without
knowing why, then, she knew why now; because she'd always wanted one, but Olivia feared cats (with suitably occult reasons for it, of course). And that cat back there on
the sidewalk was the Johnsons' cat, Nellie, who had never
given her a squeamish moment or a shiver along the spine
in the ten years they had had her.

Heron Cliff was a part of the coast that still belonged to
the families of the founders of Somerset. It rose beyond
the busy harbor where the Somerset River entered the sea,
and was occupied by five sprawling, shingled cottages
whose broad porches faced the Atlantic and whose back
windows looked into the woods across a lane. The beach
below the cliff was reached by several tortuous paths
winding down among juniper and bay. It was sheltered at

either end by rugged slopes and falls of ancient volcanic rock over which children had climbed for the last hundred years, making them forts or castles or the Himalayas, and playing in the tide pools.

Richard's great-grandfather had built a cottage there, and so had Henry Lyons'. Though the Lyons family had gone on to great wealth, Henry still cherished his cottage as an enclave of peace and quiet against the demands made on him and Priscilla out in the world, so to speak. Another direct descendant of a Somerset incorporator owned a third cottage, and the two others belonged to young offshoots with large families like litters of puppies.

Behind the cottages the woods had been left strictly alone, by common consent. This pocket wilderness descended gently over its hidden granite terraces to the black road along which Susan drove this morning. A cluster of mailboxes on her left marked the dirt road heading into the woods and climbing the slope. It was steep and rutty, and one suddenly emerged from the woods as if directly into the sky; leveling off, one faced for a moment a broad, wild field running to the cliff's edge, and then ocean as far as the eye could travel. Another sharp left turn led into the shadowy lane that ran between the cottages and the woods.

The cottages were set wide apart along fields of bay, blueberry patches now turning scarlet, alder clumps, wild rose thickets, wind-stunted spruces, spreading juniper. The Linden place was the last one in, with woods on the far side as well as behind it.

The Lyons place was the third one, almost entirely fenced in with chain link, but not to show exclusiveness; it was to keep in their wirehair terriers. Henry and Pris

[5 3]

didn't have to demonstrate exclusiveness; they were born into it, they couldn't escape it. At Heron Cliff no one paid much attention to them, and Susan thought this was one reason why they fled there whenever they could.

She saw that they were here this morning, though all the other places were closed up. The Land Rover was in the drive, and two wirehairs were playing a rough-and-tumble game on the back lawn. She was glad Barry wasn't with her, or he'd want to swap the predictable dignity of the collie-shepherd for the exuberance of a wirehair. She drove slowly, watching them; their fun in this clear, beautiful morning was a reminder that David and his pictures were only an infinitesimal part of existence, and that she should be able to cope with something so small. Yes, she *should* be, if only the mere thought didn't send shooting cramps across her midriff and make sweat break out on her neck.

Suddenly Priscilla Lyons appeared around the corner of the garage with a basket of late flowers, waved, and came to the gate. Susan stopped and got out of the car. Henry came strolling behind Pris, smoking his pipe. They looked curiously alike, as if they were cousins; both tall, fairish, with the long features Amy always called aristocratic, and pleasant smiles. Perhaps they were cousins, Susan thought; keeping all the money in the family, like the Rothschilds.

"Hello, Susan," Pris said. "Couldn't you stand it in town today, either?"

"No, and I tried to get Richard to play hookey, but he wouldn't."

"You see," said Henry gravely, "I convinced myself I had to check on the electric pump, and that had priority over New York."

"Especially when there's nothing wrong with the pump," said Pris, "and he can saunter on the beach and contemplate the ocean and invite his soul." She gave him a swift sidewise smile. "Anyway, I'm glad he came with me. He's been altogether too tense these days, and I don't intend to lose my husband to a coronary before he's fifty."

"I think the hardware business is more tranquilizing," said Susan.

"You're right." Henry pointed his pipe at her. "Whenever I go into that store I can browse for an hour and come out a new man." They all laughed. The dogs came rushing at the sound and had to be talked to. Yes, it was a good world, Susan thought. The sun on her head, the gulls circling, chickadees across the lane, the happy dogs, the pleasant people. She'd manage, of course she would, if she could only *think* hard enough . . .

"I saw you and that lovely little girl of yours at the Leslie Danton show the other day," Pris said, "but only for a moment, and then you had that dizzy spell."

"That was the darnedest thing," Susan heard herself, gay and glib. "I'd just gotten into the gallery when it hit me, and I had to get out fast. I never get dizzy, so this scared me a little. But I guess it was just a mild virus attack. I intend to go back and really see the show."

"It's worth seeing," said Pris. "As the youngsters say, it's out of this world. The painter was, literally so. But what visions, what dreams, what colors!" She turned to Henry as if to appeal for his corroboration, but he was wrestling a stick away from a growling terrier. "Henry saw the pictures first, and I thought, Oh, it's simply another Young Wonder, they're popping out everywhere like these singing groups with the weird names, but he assured me that Leslie Danton didn't paint pictures of soup cans and cartoons." There was a warm flush across her cheekbones; she took on a young, soft look which, with her distinctive features, gave her a kind of genuine beauty. "Henry gets so excited about these things. It's one of his nicest traits."

"I wonder how the work came into Mr. Emery's hands," Susan said cautiously to the side of Henry's head as he played with the dogs. "Is he a relative? Or does he manage the show for her estate, or what?"

One of the dogs leaped into his arms and he straightened up, hugging it. *"Now* I've got you! . . . I'm not sure, Susan. I've talked with him a few times, we've had him to dinner once, and he's pretty knowledgeable about art in general, but all he's ever said about Leslie Danton is that she's dead. As you said, he's probably managing the pictures for her heirs and of course he'll want as high a price as possible for the collection."

"Is it for sale?" Did she sound too sharp, too startled?

Pris said, "Oh, in these circles, everyone's very coy. No one ever comes right out and says, It's for sale, and I want so much. It's almost Oriental, the amount of indirection and mystery required, and all the getting together for drinks. Even Henry's being subtle. For instance, his wife doesn't even know if he wants to buy the collection or not, supposing Randall Emery will sell."

"But does his wife think she can *live* with it?" Henry teased her back. If she showed flashes of beauty for him, his glance at her revealed a masculine tenderness which, when Richard showed it, made Susan weak.

"I can mention several of your treasures that have called for a great deal of will power on my part," said Pris. "But these pictures—they really have a strange fascination, and not just for me. One friend of ours turned dizzy like you, Susan, and not with a virus. She said the vibrations were just too powerful to be endured." She said it straight-faced, and Henry said, sucking on his pipe, "Anabel gets her most powerful vibrations from a bottle of Scotch. She was already revved up when she went into the gallery that day."

They laughed again, and Susan turned to the car. "I'm like Cinderella, I have just so long."

"Stick around, I'd love to see a car turn into a pumpkin," said Henry.

"It's what my house turns into that's fascinating, if I'm not there when my son gets home," said Susan. "He may bring the entire sixth grade with him."

Priscilla's smile had a sad humor. For the first time Susan wondered if the Lyons' childlessness were really from choice; if they'd gladly give up Europe or South America for an Amy or a Barry of their own.

CHAPTER 5

THERE WAS A good stretch of field between the Lyons'
place and the next one, then more open land between
that and the Linden cottage, so her sense of solitude was
not disturbed by any human reminder as she drove in.
She knew deer moved without fear in the woods near by.
A cloud of young goldfinches took off, chirping in questions, from the dandelions on the back lawn. A chipmunk
rushed into the neat pile of birch fireplace logs beside the
doorstep. As always, there were gulls circling on the wind
currents far overhead.

She felt almost cheerful as she went around to the front
of the house. If David wanted to sell the pictures he
could, as far as she was concerned. The artist really was
dead, to all intents and purposes; he had the collection, he
could do as he pleased as long as he went away and the
subject was closed. If Henry Lyons bought it and hung it
in the special air-conditioned wing of the big house in the

[ELISABETH OGILVIE]

Glen it would go out of existence for her. Out of sight, out of mind.

Except that it wouldn't be quite that simple. "You have this many steps to go before you come into your kingdom," Olivia used to tell her. "So many lives to live before you can be free."

"Who's going to murder me in this one?" she had asked, and Olivia's eyes had flashed. "Don't be impertinent, Miss! And don't you go into one of those Hedges sulks! I had enough of that with your father."

So many lives. . . . Fate, or fluke, or freak coincidence had ordained that she live at least one of them over again now before she could discard it for good; the existence of young Leslie Danton.

She crossed the lawn, scattering more goldfinches, toward the gate in the low stone wall along the cliff's edge. At Belmont Falls there was a stone that had her name on it, or rather Leslie's. The impact of seeing David had dulled the other fact, but it came to her now in shuddery aftermath, as if in some way it really had been she who had died and been buried on a bitter day with the snow coming down past the black spruces. The dead girl became immediate and personal to her. Where was she going, what was she running from? Where had they found her, and why was it David who had identified her, not Olivia?

Anyway, in her sudden death she had become a friend who had released Susan Hedges into the world. I shan't forget you, Susan promised.

She almost fell over a horseshoe stake. They were both in place, and the shoes left where they'd landed in the final ardent game between Barry and his father on the last

[5 9]

weekend they'd been out here. I must put them in before
I go home, she thought, as she opened the gate and went
down the long flight of wooden steps to the beach.

She took off her shoes and socks and wiggled her toes
luxuriously in the warm sand. For a few moments she simply *was,* taking in the heat of the sun and the brilliant colors, walking to see what treasures had been imprisoned in
the rim of dried rockweed black on the pale sand; salvag-
ing a brightly painted lobster-pot buoy cast up on the
rocks. But she knew that all the time she was simply putting off the inevitable.

Finally she lay down in the sun with her extra sweater
folded under her head, and shut her eyes. She didn't know
what it would gain her to think; she knew only that not to
think about it would make her sick. It was as if she had
completely lost the strength of will which had kept her
free of it all these years so that she had even stopped
dreaming of it after a while. But she knew she had to free
herself again, this time forever, or she couldn't survive.
Leslie *had* to go ... and that meant David too, and he
must understand and agree, if he had really been concerned about her for so long.

His conscience hurts, she thought wryly, for making
love to me, promising we'd brave the world together, and
then betraying me the minute he had to face Olivia. And
the excuses, even now: *I was frantic. Olivia held on to me.
I couldn't knock her down. Olivia wouldn't let me call
the police.*

Maybe she was being too hard on him; Olivia had been
strong medicine for a boy adrift, a college drop-out in his
senior year, lonely, yet not wanting to go home because
his family was against him and his girl had married some-

one else. Olivia's sympathy could be very potent. It could always rope Leslie back with a lariat of tenderness whenever she got too jumpy and wild-eyed. . . . Olivia would have been compassionate to David, after insulting him, when Leslie ran out of the gallery.

"You couldn't know what you were getting into, dear. Why do you think I tried to keep you apart? She's only a child, much more of a child than most girls her age. Otherworldly, of course. She can't cope with the simplest difficulties of this life. Those bursts of temper, that rage—it used to make slaves tremble, and she's terrified when I don't break down under it. I was the strong governess who could always control her when no one else could. That was why, when she was incarnated, she was born to me; no one else would have known what to do with her. They might possibly have—put her away." This would have been almost whispered; Leslie had heard it thus more than once, the velvet threat and then the tenderness, the promise to care for her always, to keep the world at bay.

"That frightened, determined little soul trying to break through!" Olivia would have gone on. "Just think, it might have been locked up forever. But the Masters arranged things as they always do, and so Leslie will never go far from me. She can't. It's not in her karma. But you've been deceived, David, dear. She can never love as other girls do."

And her smile would have forgiven and comforted him.

Susan sat up and opened the thermos. The coffee was hot and burnt her lip, but the pain helped restore her. She began deliberately to remember Olivia in the days before the first picture. They lived in the small, elm-bowered

town of Belmont Falls, and Olivia worked in a law office.
She was busy, but kind and loving, calling Leslie Puss and
Kitten and My Precious Baby; sometimes My Precious
Fatherless Baby, if only her Daddy could have lived. . . .
But in the early days Leslie didn't miss what she hadn't
known, especially with a pretty, twinkly-eyed mother who
looked enchanting when she tucked her child in at night
and went out on a wave of chiffon and perfume to whatever man waited in the living room.

Then for a little while there'd been a jolly stepfather
named Bill Danton. But he died in the Pacific, during the
war. Now Olivia and a friend spent a few evenings a week
trying to "get" Leslie's own father and Bill Danton on a
Ouija board. As Leslie learned how to read she sometimes
spelled out the titles of books that Olivia left around: *The
Mystic Afterlife; My Seven Incarnations; The Return of
Atlantis; Secrets of the Pyramids.* But, aside from the il-
lustrations, especially those in the books about Ancient
Egypt, there was nothing much to interest her in them.
She preferred books about animals, over whose sorrows
she cried herself sick. She couldn't have a dog because
they lived in an apartment, and Olivia had that phobia
about cats, anyway. She used to walk home from school
past houses into which she dreamed herself—the kind
of house in which Susan Linden now lived.

Olivia remained pretty, social, and a demonstrative
mother. Even when Leslie began to shoot up, she was dis-
played fondly as My Tall Child, and given dancing lessons
to help out. Leslie had not liked them but one would
have tied one's legs into figure eights to please Olivia, all
the while wondering wistfully if the day would ever come
when men waited in the living room to whisk *her* out into

the wonderful night world of parties and theaters. It was the doubt, squatting in her soul like the toad in the princess' bed, that drove her in upon herself when she edged clumsily into the teens. She rode her bicycle alone out into the lovely surrounding countryside where her ancestors had settled. She read vastly in the long evening hours, and thought up frantic excuses for not going to parties and school affairs.

Then one night Olivia asked her in a voice gone suddenly cold, "Doesn't *anyone* ever ask you for a date?"

"No," she said almost inaudibly. Olivia, still watching her with expressionless gaze, picked up her bag and wrap. Then she went out.

That night Leslie painted the first picture.

One of Olivia's friends had given Leslie a small oil-painting kit for Christmas, but until now she hadn't felt any inclination to touch it. Left alone in the evenings, she fled to her books as to a drug. Tonight, roaming the apartment, feeling as if some menace were stalking her outside the windows and would come in through the door with Olivia, she finally got out the paints. At first she was nervous and discouraged. But mixing colors on the palette interested her, and after the first timid stroke on the canvasboard she hurried on. Blue was the color she tried first; a strong blazing blue. *Sky, lots of sky,* she thought, *absolutely clean and pure and hot.* It was a gray January, with a raw cold that bit to the bone, but suddenly she was lost, she was far from the apartment, the apprehensive fear, the miserable winter. When at last she returned it was as if she had been to a far country, and the evidence of her journey lay before her, a pyramid of tawny stone rising from limitless yellow-white sands into a sky of scorching

blueness. She looked at it and marveled. It warmed her all
through. She could smell and feel the heat and the silence.
She knew a longing that suddenly made her cry.

Years later, on the beach, Susan's coffee had turned
cold, and she couldn't remember pouring it out. You
mustn't forget like that, she told herself. You mustn't go
back into it so thoroughly. It was the way you went into
that picture. Into all of them. As if into a trance. They
said it was a trance.

Who said it first? There was a dizzying succession of
people who saw the pictures. Some kept their faces immo-
bile, giving her quick alert glances from the sides of their
eyes as if to catch her in some deception. She told them
the truth. "I don't know why I painted it. I don't know
what I was thinking. I didn't think anything that I can remember."

Some were excited, and Olivia expanded in their atmosphere like a night-blooming cereus, tenderly smiling at
the girl, calling her sweet names while the excited ones
gazed at her as if she were something rare and unworldly.
They fell back in awed respect when Olivia held up her
hand and said, "No, I can't let you question her any more.
She must rest now. We must cherish this gift. She must
live like a novice in a convent, otherwise the messages
don't come through."

Oh, God! Susan thought in disgust. My mother! She even
convinced *me.* That was why I was so ready to smell the
air of the tomb, to remember how it looked, to say that
the description of the interment services was familiar to
me. I was a faithful mirror to her, to all of them who

came and went through those years. But those things I de-
scribed to them, the Fair Lover from the North, my
death, the burial rites—didn't I believe them? Couldn't
I have sworn I'd experienced everything I painted? *Didn't
I swear it?*

With a gasp she put her hands to her face and covered
her eyes, trying to fight her way out of a sea of darkness.
And another voice came, cool as rain.

Tell me about it, Leslie. Mr. Martin. His face came
with the words, an ugly, jowly face with a shaggy mustache, grizzled hair, small eyes deep-set under ferocious
brows; a face that regarded her neither with skepticism,
wariness, nor greedy excitement, but with tranquil kindness toward a sixteen-year-old girl. Without raising his
voice he had got rid of Olivia, which was enough to make
Leslie view him as some sort of deity.

"Tell me what *you* think of your paintings, Leslie, not
what your friends say they mean."

They were sitting on a bench in Central Park on an
April day, and he had brought things to feed the pigeons.
She had never fed pigeons before, or sat on a park bench
with a man in April. She hoped people around would
think he was her father, or a beloved uncle. It gave her a
wonderful sense of being ordinary. She answered him with
thoughtless honesty.

"They're not my friends, they're my mother's friends.
They hope I'll make money for them, like a race horse. I
—I don't know about the pictures and what they mean. I
don't like much to think about it."

"Why?"

She wanted to tell the truth, because no one had ever

desired it of her, or given her time to tell it, since the night when Olivia asked, *Doesn't anyone ever ask you on a date?* She tried very hard to put it into words. "It seems to me that I've got two choices and they both scare me. I don't want to be insane, and I don't want to—to be in touch with other worlds. But it's got to be one or the other, hasn't it? What else could it be?" The understanding in his face almost made her cry, but he had known how not to go too far. He was a good man, what everyone dreams of for a father. Wise and kind. She wished now she could have told him so, but perhaps he saw it in her eyes then.

Later that day she had listened at a door for the first time of her life. It was a small hotel with narrow corridors, and their rooms were at the far end of one, so nobody ever passed by. She stood in the dim light, pressed against the wall between her room and her mother's, listening to the voices coming over the transom. If she saw Pauline or Naomi coming she would move quickly away from her listening position. She wanted to shut her eyes so she could concentrate entirely on Mr. Martin's voice, but she didn't dare take a chance on being caught.

"I can't tell you anything definite about the pictures," he said. "They are remarkable, certainly, but it would take a great deal of study to discover their source."

"We have discovered the source, Mr. Martin," said Olivia, playfully firm.

"You *may* have discovered it," he corrected her. "It's not for me to say, one way or the other. I haven't been in contact with the child long enough; I know nothing about her, what her life has been, what her private world consists of. I do know that there are strange wellsprings in the human brain, and much has grown from them, as green ferns flourish around living water."

"A man in your position and with your great knowledge, Mr. Martin," Olivia said, "should have no doubts. The thing is as beyond question as the miracle of television. Only in this case the voice and the picture come not from *now*, but from thousands of years ago." This was Part One of Olivia's speech to the waverers who wanted to be convinced but didn't quite dare to give in. Her musical voice was hushed, yet strong with emotion; this tone always made Leslie's stomach roll.

"Only one thing is certain, for me," said Mr. Martin. "If this child is really an instrument through which the past ages can be heard, I would be the happiest man alive. Do you realize what a precious gift this would be to the world, if it could be proved beyond doubt? And it may be proved some day. She is young, and has her whole life before her. If the gift exists, it won't go away unless it is so abused that it ceases to exist."

"*Mr. Martin.*" Icy and regal now. "*I* am her mother. I protect and care for my child."

"Do you?" he asked gently. "Do you care for her enough to stop exploiting her and take her home to grow up as a normal girl, so both she and her gift can flower naturally, freely, without all these cruel pressures?"

"*Exploit?*" Olivia's voice was too soft. Another danger signal. "*Cruel?* You're accusing *me,* her mother?" Leslie heard Olivia's sharp, hissing intake of breath. Then— "Mr. Martin, will you please leave this room at once?"

Leslie took all her courage together in one great armful and ran down the corridor and around the corner to the elevator. She stood there, shivering with chilly sweat,

until Mr. Martin came. She wanted to run to him and cry,
Don't leave me, take me with you! Instead she was quiet,
hugging herself.

"Mr. Martin. Thank you for trying," she said.

"Leslie, I'm sorry," he said. "But no one is guilty of
child neglect, in the usual sense. You're well-fed and
well-dressed, taken care of by your mother." He shook his
head, and then took her clammy hands between his two
large ones, pressing them hard and rubbing them. "Hold
on, my dear. Keep telling yourself there's something in
you that won't go down, no matter what."

The elevator was coming up. She had an anguished
premonition that Pauline and Naomi would be in it;
they had an unerring sense of timing where Olivia's private interviews were concerned, and now they'd be rushing back to hear, though Naomi always managed not to
look eager. Vultures, she thought. Why don't they tear out
my eyes and be done with it? She turned those eyes on
Mr. Martin, and saw his flicker as if with pain.

"You can always reach me through the Society for
Psychical Research," he told her quickly. The top of the
elevator was showing. "God bless you, Leslie."

The door clanged open. Pauline said loudly, "Oh,
hel*lo,* Mr. Martin!" Naomi gave him a regal nod. He said,
"Goodbye, Leslie." He stepped into the elevator and Leslie turned away, unable to bear watching him carried out
of her life. She could not remember losing her father, but
she knew now what it was like.

"Well!" said Pauline. "Are we all set with him, kiddo?"
Naomi gave her a cold look. "Really, Pauline! . . . Coming, Leslie?" They escorted her back down the corridor.
At her mother's door she left them, went into her own
room, put plugs into her ears, and drew a blanket up over

her head. Her chief concern was to survive her own private tornado, so that when Olivia came for her later she would not be the drowned, drained, abject creature which always roused her mother's contempt.

She came slowly back to the beach in the sun. The sea was nearer now, amiable and glittering. It was like a miracle, as if the young girl shutting herself into the black silent world under the blanket had awakened into the great sunlit universe she had tried to create for herself.

The years between that day and this didn't exist until her bemused eyes read Amy's initials scratched on the side of the thermos bottle. She was alarmed by her complete and profound immersion in the past, and began to walk around barefoot in the warm sand, then let icy water break in gentle bubbles around her toes. She climbed over the rocks and down onto a shingle beach where the water made a hushing sound as it withdrew over the rattling pebbles. She walked for a long way along the deserted shore, a small figure solitary in the great globe of sea and sky, yet not feeling lonely. She had the gulls, the song sparrows that sang out from the bay bushes, and here and there a cloud of migrating warblers that had stopped to rest and eat. All the time she was keeping herself very much aware of everything, textures and temperatures under her feet, the blue and violet qualities of shadows, the changes in the water from brilliant azure to purple over the rockweed and jade green over sand; and the abrupt shifts between the salt-edged wind and the pockets of heat in the sheltered places.

Firmly in touch with reality, as much as if she were holding it with both hands, she allowed herself to think of David.

He had come later. Olivia brought him back from the

restaurant where she'd gotten into conversation with him, and he had stood shyly inside the door, his fair head glistening with raindrops, his thin face strained and earnest as if he were trying very hard in spite of his shyness. Then he had seen Leslie and he had smiled with pleasure at finding someone young like himself. *They're not my friends,* she had said to Mr. Martin. *They're my mother's friends.* But here, she thought with a joyous lunge of her heart, here is a friend for me.

CHAPTER 6

SUSAN WENT BACK along the backbone of red rock that the children called a dinosaur. She would see David. It couldn't hurt her now.

A talk with him would be decent and honorable. It had been unfair, even cruel, to snub him as she had done, for she owed him so much.

When she reached home it wasn't time for Barry and Amy yet. She called the store and told Richard that she was back. "Oh, so you changed your mind about eloping," he said: She could hear Ella Anson's titter in the background.

"I had to," she said. "He never showed up."

"Better a present husband than an absent lover, I always say," said Richard.

"I'm going to abduct you the next good day and take you with me." Richard's laugh managed to sound wholeheartedly lustful, and she laughed too, and hung up.

Then she called Marshall Jury at the museum. After

the usual exchange of compliments she said, "Do you know if Randall Emery is still in Somerset?"

"You're beginning to sound appallingly like every other woman who's called me up in the past week. They never want to talk to me as myself; they want to know about Randall Emery."

"I'm sorry, Marshall. But my reasons are impeccable, shall we say?"

"We can say it if it makes you feel happier. He happens to be right here in the museum this afternoon. I hate to tell you this, but I'm disgustingly honest. Do you want to speak to him?"

"Please, Marshall. And thank you."

After a little while David's voice came, charmingly formal. "How do you do, Mrs. Linden? How may I help you?"

"It's all right, David," she said. "Just don't call me Leslie when you answer. How would you like to meet me somewhere for a cup of coffee?"

"I'd like it very much. Where?"

"The coffee shop at the Somerset House is nice. It overlooks the park. In—let's see—three quarters of an hour from now."

"Four o'clock," said David. "I'll be there."

She went to shower and dress. The coffee shop was not only a pleasant spot, with good coffee and fresh pastries, but a sufficiently public spot in which to meet. Anyone who happened to recognize Mrs. Richard Linden and Mr. Randall Emery would think nothing of their casual conversation at a table by the window. Somerset was not a gossipy town.

She put on the tweed outfit, remembering with a wry

little twist her euphoria the last time she had stood before her mirror in these clothes. Then she had been sure of what she had become. Now she must convince David; she only hoped that in the argument her own certainty would not be shaken.

Amy and a friend came in just as she was leaving. Their casual greeting convinced Susan that she looked the same as usual. Of course one's children never really *saw* one; they saw only something called Mother. "Stay around until Barry comes in, Amy," she said.

"Oh sure, we're going to do some work together anyway. We're going to make tea and toast first, okay?"

"Okay." They'd lately discovered the delights of tea after school, accompanied by innumerable slices of toast dripping with butter and honey. They went to the kitchen, talking all the while. Susan caught Tracy Jones Jr.'s name.

"Did you know he plays the guitar?"

"Oh, groovy!"

When she crossed the square to the Somerset House, she saw David standing by one of the big windows that looked across at the park. It was golden-leaved now, and the playing children and their mothers wore bright autumn colors. He must have seen her also, for he came across the comfortable old-fashioned lobby to greet her. She felt suddenly secure on her home ground, wearing her Somerset tweeds; she was Mrs. Richard Linden. She smiled and held out her hand. "Hello, Mr. Emery."

"Mrs. Linden." There was a quiver around his eyes that had nothing to do with his smile. "What a wonderful setting this town is for autumn. I could stay here the rest of my life."

"Unfortunately autumn doesn't last here any longer than it does elsewhere." They went into the nearly empty coffee shop and found a table by the window, as she had planned. They gave their orders to the elderly waitress, who had been there for almost as long as Susan had been in Somerset. There was no one else near them; four o'clock was past the hour when most of Somerset stopped for afternoon coffee.

"Well, David," she said, glad she had decided to meet him.

"Well, Leslie. May I say it now?"

"You may, but it doesn't seem natural. Leslie's dead, and David must be, or you wouldn't be using another name."

"I find it expedient. I'm afraid some day Pauline might light on me out of the blue with her earrings flashing and her crystal ball poised for hurling." They both laughed, and Susan's sense of freedom and relaxation increased.

"Whatever happened to Pauline?" she asked.

"She went soon after you did. She went all to pieces when the accident happened and said we'd murdered you, but I didn't have to have her tell me. I *knew*."

"Tell me about the accident," she demanded. "Where and when?"

"It was a bus going to Bangor from Boston, and it would have stopped at Belmont Falls." The waitress came, and he sat looking down at the table and rubbing his fingers across his forehead as if his memories were physically painful. When the woman had gone he said, "Three days after you disappeared this bus skidded into an oil truck just before it reached the Falls. Five people were killed. The minute Olivia heard it, she was positive you'd been on that bus. She was sure all along that you'd headed home, and she'd called some lawyer there to watch for you, but you hadn't shown in those three days. At least, not that he could discover."

He stopped and drank some coffee. His eyes were distant, he had the strained, tightened look she'd seen before. "So she was sure you'd been hiding in Boston somewhere for a few days, getting different clothes, and that you were on that later bus. She collapsed."

Susan wondered why she'd ever thought cranberry tarts a good idea. She said, "I can't imagine her collapsing."

"She loved you," he said. "She had an iron hand, yes, and a terrific force of personality, but she loved you. You were her life, and that's apart from the paintings. You were still her baby, and she must have gone through hell those three days, but she wouldn't give in. Then when they mentioned a young girl with dark red hair, no identifications—well—" He spread out his hands. "The collapse. Complete. And Pauline was having hysterics, saying we'd murdered you. I was so numb I looked calm, and Naomi took charge of everything. She and I went to identify you."

He swallowed coffee like a bitter dose. "You know, even now, knowing it *wasn't* you, I'll never forget the horror of that whole thing. The damp dark weather, and how long it took us to get to that funeral home. And the face all bandaged, because it was almost gone. She'd been thrown head first through a window." He was shaken by a shudder, and Susan too was shivering inside her clothes.

"The State Police kept after us, wanting to know about identifying marks and so forth. But it *had* to be you," he appealed. "How could it not be? You'd talked of nothing but home ever since we first were alone together. That's where we were going if I hadn't—if I—" He bit his lower lip hard, and she reached out and touched his hand.

"Don't reproach yourself any more, David. You've been through more than enough to make up for it. Let's get this over with, shall we?" She forced herself to take a bite of cranberry tart. Surprisingly, the sharp flavor was a restorative. "What about identifying marks? Naomi couldn't have known mine, I never ran around undressed or even half-dressed. I was terribly shy."

"It's the only time I ever saw her panic. Seeing you there, or rather this slender young girl with the damn' bandages hiding her face and her throat, was too much for her. She burst into tears and pointed to a long puckered white scar on one thigh and cried, 'She got that when she was small, she fell out of her swing one day onto a piece of broken glass. She nearly bled to death!' It was the damnedest thing. I thought she was telling the truth, that she really knew. She kept on crying and saying, 'And it's glass that's killed her, and she *really* bled to death!' "

"Oh, poor Naomi!" Susan exclaimed softly. "I have no such scar. I never fell out of a swing and nearly bled to death. Why did she ever—"

"To get it over with, she told me afterwards. She knew it was you, she said. But they had to have something definite. Well, they took her word about the scar—I guess her breakdown impressed them. . . . Then we had to stay for the funeral. This lawyer friend of your mother's—"

"Theodore Adams," said Susan. "She was his secretary before we went into show business."

"He made all the arrangements. Your mother wasn't able to come. She was under a doctor's care, and Pauline had gone off on one long drunk. I joined her in it when we came back."

"It strikes me," said Susan, "that for a bunch of spiritualists none of you had the courage of your convictions. Every one should have been very serene about the whole thing; hadn't I just cast off another of those annoying lives?"

"You know, that would come to me now and then through the fog. But I'm afraid that your running away and dying like that was a lot more real to me than any of those beautiful theories."

"And of course for the others," Susan said dryly, "there were practical considerations, such as the fact that an absent princess wasn't much good to them."

"As Pauline pointed out when she left. Olivia said your spirit, or rather the princess', would take over somebody else who would then be made known to us, but Pauline said in that inimitable accent, 'Don't hold your breath, kiddo.' "

"Oh, David, I can just hear her. And imagine calling Olivia kiddo."

"She'd called her worse by then."

"Pauline was a good sort. If life was at all bearable she helped to make it so. She was so darned matter-of-fact."

"Of course she was a fake."

Susan shrugged. "So was I. The difference was that I didn't know it." He drew in a sharp breath as if to speak, but she went on, "Pauline was good to me. To you, too. Remember how she connived so that we could go to the movies, and Olivia never knew? My first soda with you was my first with a man. I was in agony, trying to make conversation. I just didn't know how. But you helped, because you were bashful, too."

"How could I not be? They'd all but convinced me I should approach you on my knees. Of course," he added offhandedly, "I'd always been interested in those things. It's like madness, you have to have a predisposition that way."

"And they're not too far apart," said Susan.

"Well, isn't madness a sort of special vision gone all out of focus? Perhaps we have to be a little mad to know what we know."

There was a change in his voice and she looked up at him quickly. He was watching her intently. She felt the first prick in her self-assurance, but decided it was nothing. "Perhaps," she murmured. The thing was to be objective, take facts at face value, stop looking for hidden meanings. "Well, David, you can see what my life has been. I married Richard sixteen years ago, and we came home to Somerset and have been here ever since."

"That leaves two years unaccounted for. Where did you go when you ran, and when did you stop running?"

"I went from Boston to New York, found a boarding-house, got a job after a while."

"What did you do for money?"

"Didn't Olivia tell you? No, perhaps she didn't want to let anyone know that the Lost Princess was also a thief. I'd never had a dollar of spending money of my own, so I felt I'd earned what I took from her pocketbook."

David whistled softly. "She always carried a big roll with her."

"Yes. It did me for quite a while." She lifted her cup and drank. Her hand was steady and she could enjoy the coffee.

David watched her. "I can't get over it. Don't you ever

feel any guilt or remorse about not getting in touch with your mother?"

"Why should I feel anything of the sort?"

"Your mother—"

"My mother," she began, and then stopped. "You came *after* we met Mr. Martin, didn't you? And I never told you anything about him."

"I never heard the name before."

"I don't propose to explain it, then," she said. "But if I never felt or feel anything you think I should, I have valid reasons."

He poured fresh coffee into his cup. "Did you ever feel anything about me?"

"I was hurt because you let her talk you down that day," she told him honestly. "Disappointed and resentful. But later I understood how it must have been with you. And I could be grateful to you for the things I've already told you about. The sodas, the walks in the rain, the talk, the movies. Youthful companionship when I'd had absolutely none." She smiled at him. "So thank you, David, and I mean it with all my heart. Now tell me what *you've* been doing for eighteen years."

CHAPTER 7

HE BEGAN WITH an engaging, boyish diffidence. "Well, I stayed with Olivia for a while. I didn't want to go home, and Olivia seemed to cling to me. She kept trying to reach you through that confounded ouija board, through mediums—she couldn't believe that you wouldn't come to her in some way. With me it was a desperate hope." He lifted his eyes and smiled briefly at her. "Words are inadequate. There aren't enough *strong* enough to even begin to convey what losing you meant. So I won't try to tell you." He took a pipe and tobacco pouch out of his pocket and began to fill the pipe. She watched his fingers and thought of Richard's. She wondered what Richard was doing now with those hands, measuring rope, weighing nails, taking down a can of paint or a box of spackle, cutting a pane of glass. She was a little homesick.

"Don't think we didn't miss Pauline. Your mother wouldn't ever let her in the galleries, but she needed the messages Pauline used to give her from her crystal. Pauline was always seeing the Big Time ahead, remember? Naomi went home to Kentucky after a while. Her father was sick. I think she was glad to go, at last. Without you, there didn't seem to be any purpose to anything. Olivia kept up a brave front but—" he shook his head and stared down at the crumbs on his plate—"it was only a pretense. She was gallant, Leslie. I don't think you know how gallant your mother was."

He could have been talking of a stranger. *Mother* was a word that meant her relationship to Amy and Barry, not Olivia's relationship to her. She was a little ashamed of her coldness, but she couldn't help it. She tried to look concerned, and only felt deceitful.

"I had an idea then of showing the pictures simply as art. But she believed too firmly to give up her belief. Except that when people heard the story behind the pictures, they couldn't believe it without you. Naomi used to tell them that you'd had to go out into the world, to lose yourself among the common people—it was part of your karma. But after she went away, your mother couldn't tell it so convincingly." He shrugged. "You know how Naomi could do it and sound so damned learned. She had the occult lore of the ages right there at her fingertips. Your mother couldn't discuss things in depth the way Naomi did. She hadn't the background to hold her own with the people who were impressed by erudition. So— with Naomi gone—well, it was pathetic. She tried for so long not to give up."

He put his pipe back in his mouth and looked thoughtfully out at the street. The shadows were long and dark under the trees now, but the treetops and the upper windows of the buildings across the park were bathed in golden light. He said, "I stayed with her until she died."

Susan felt a tightening through her body. "When was it? And what?"

"Three years after you left. Pneumonia, complicated by a broken heart. That sounds mawkish, but it was true." He gave her a long look, not hard, but penetrating. "You were married by then. Couldn't you have let her know?"

"No," said Susan. "I wanted no connection whatever between myself and the past. But I have no doubt her heart was broken, to see everything she'd gambled on come to nothing. Where was she living at the end?"

"In New York, in a small hotel in the West Seventies. I went to work in a new advertising firm, and three of us took an apartment together. But I kept an eye on your mother and the pictures. She'd come over and cook something fancy for us now and then, and mend our socks, and sew on buttons. We all thought the world of her."

"I can imagine," said Susan. Olivia was a charmer to the end, apparently. But then she'd have been only in her forties, and she was always a pretty woman, in whom the essence of feminity would have been strong when she was a hundred.

"When she had to go to the hospital, I—" David looked embarrassed—"I helped out. Oh, she had a collection of old pussies around—you know the kind who were drawn to her, the ones who knew poltergeists personally, and lived by the ouija board, and heard Voices with a capital V—but they all existed on about five dollars a week and your mother's pocketbook. ... She was sick only ten days, but she knew what I was doing, and so—" He was embarrassed again, flushing slightly, studying his pipe as if he didn't know what it was. "She left me the pictures to do what I wanted with. For taking care of things."

"Well, that's fair enough," said Susan. She felt very tired suddenly, as if she'd been on a tightwire for a long time and had only stayed aloft by pure will power. "But you haven't been looking for me ever since. Not for fifteen years."

"After I saw that she was—sent home, I couldn't stand it in New York any more. The firm was folding up anyway. I stored the pictures and went to Detroit. I worked for my father there, and got married. I was an abysmal failure in both ventures."

"I'm sorry, David." She could be sincere in this, at least. She had been so happy with Richard, it would have been nice to know that David had been as fortunate.

"How could I have been anything but a failure? The experience with you and the pictures was a traumatic one. I dreamed night after night either of you or the pictures. You were in danger and calling to me as that bus pitched off the road. Or the warehouse was on fire. Death and disaster, that's all it was, constantly. Finally I knew what I had to do."

She wanted to get up and run out before David could say anything else, but she sat on, stiffly silent.

"I had to take the pictures and go to find you," he said. "I knew, after enough of those dreams, that Olivia could have been right, that you'd come back somehow and that you'd recognize the pictures. We'd be together at last." He said it in quiet triumph.

She was just as quiet. "David, if knowing me has ruined your life, I'm sorry. But I didn't choose to do it. Maybe if you'd run with me that day both our lives would have been far different. But in all honesty I can say I'm glad I went alone. I left it all behind me for good, I'm a happily married woman now in the kind of world I want. So that's the end of the search, and the end of the story."

"But what about the pictures?" he asked incredulously. "You speak as if they were of no importance whatever. Just so much paint and canvas, that's all. As if they weren't the history of a life crying to be heard, to be avenged, to find the peace it's been denied for centuries!"

"Oh, David!" Half-laughing, half-distressed, she leaned back in her chair. "You can't take that seriously now! I'm not saying that there's not a great deal we don't know about the veil between, and so forth, and I don't know how I painted the pictures. When I try to think about it I don't like what happens to me. But didn't it ever occur to you that they could be simply the results of self-hypnosis?"

"*All right!*" he said with repressed violence, leaning across the table, his eyes fiery bright with the young, ardent blue she remembered. "Call it self-hypnosis. But who knows what self-hypnosis really is? What was in your unconscious, what memories stored over thousands of years, that came out in those paintings?"

"We don't know. Mr. Martin tried to find out what I'd read as a kid. Well, I'd read so much, and so much had happened to upset me since those days, that I couldn't remember. But it might be that my unconscious memories went back no further than that."

"It's not so!" He slammed the flat of his hand down on the table and the cups jumped. Outside, the streetlight went on, turning the dusk to the blue of grapes. The coffee shop was lit by pinpoints of rosy light here and there. "You've deliberately put everything out of your mind, as you turned your back on your mother. But I've forgotten nothing. It's been my life for eighteen years, my life to the exclusion of everything else, even my children. *I* believe, and you can't sit there in your suburban smugness and say it's nonsense."

She was shaken and angry, and picked up her bag. "You're entitled to your beliefs, and I have mine. They don't include one scrap of *anything* from the first eighteen years of my life, believe me! My family knows nothing about it, and I wish I didn't. But as long as Leslie Danton doesn't mean a thing to them, I can almost pretend that she never existed." She stood up. "It's getting late and I must go."

He reached across the table and took her wrist. His fingers were very strong and they tightened with the impersonal firmness of a vise. "Listen to me, Leslie," he said very softly. "You remember what Pauline saw in her crystal and what Naomi saw in a painting? The Fair Lover from the North? The stranger in the Pharaoh's court, perhaps a captive Norseman who had once been hopelessly in love with Nen-a-tifa, and had been searching for her for thousands of years."

She sat down quickly, hoping nobody was watching this scene. "So you were fated to sit down beside Olivia that night. You were led to her."

He released her wrist and sat back, smiling. "You see? And it was the truth. I began to remember things myself, after that. Then I lost you again. But now I've found you, and this time I don't intend to let you go."

She felt the horror one must feel on suddenly discovering the person across the coffee cups is quietly but hopelessly insane. This is the Somerset House, she told herself.

I could get up and walk out. But he would follow me. We're fairly inconspicuous here, better to finish it now if I can.

"You say you knew all this eighteen years ago," she said. "But you didn't act it. Yes, you made love to me behind Olivia's back, you promised we'd get away from her, but you backed down fast enough when she cornered us. Apparently *she* didn't believe we were meant for each other, and she convinced you, so why the switch now?"

"Because she was right," he protested eagerly. "Can't you see? Later she explained to me how we weren't meant for each other *then*. I had to lose you again, suffer, work, search the whole world over for you. She made it clear to me then, and later They told me the same thing."

"They, they!" she said scornfully. "Who were *they?* A handful of harridans ready to sell their souls for money! Every well-dressed idiot who walked into a gallery was the One who'd pay. They saw blue lights and skyrockets and I don't know what else, and This was the Time. This was It. *The Money.* Is that what you were waiting for, David, with the rest of them? Why run away with me if we couldn't take the pictures too?"

"You lie. It's all lies. The harder you fight, the more you lie, the more you prove that you know the truth. You know who *They* are. Not Olivia, not Naomi, not Pauline, not any of the others who moved in and out of the circle. *They* are the Masters who kept your soul alive so you could cry for vengeance for your murder; the Masters who kept my soul alive so I could find you and we'd be together."

"David, you're—" She bit it back.

He smiled. "No. Madness comes from denying the

truth. I've never done that, but you have, and you'll pay. I don't want that to happen to you, Leslie."

"I thought the pictures couldn't do any harm now," she said, standing up. "But I've changed my mind. I think they should be destroyed, and that would set us both free."

"You would have to kill me first," he said. It didn't sound dramatic, but icily sincere. She took her bag and her gloves, nodded to him, and left him standing there.

Waiting for the traffic lights to change, crossing the street, she seemed to move in a cloud of unreality. The scene with David stayed horribly with her while she started the car and drove home. As a girl she had believed that David had been led to her not by occult forces but by God to save her from insanity. Now he was the one on the brink, and what ghastly coincidence had brought him to Somerset didn't bear thinking about.

It was almost enough to make anyone believe in supernatural influences, even if not in David's "Masters." Not just David's Masters; the rest had talked about them too, mixing Tibet and Egypt into a potent stew.

And now what? How did you make him go away again without bringing down your whole present existence on top of your head?

CHAPTER 8

LOGIC, COMMON SENSE, pure intelligence, whatever you wanted to call it, demanded that you go to your husband with the facts. But how did you begin? She got dinner by instinct that night because her mind was so busy constructing opening sentences.

Richard, there's something I have to tell you. There never was any Aunt Selma. When you told me I ought to get in touch with her I mailed the letter off to an imaginary person.

That was a great beginning. She could just see his face. . . . She tried another. Richard, I'm not what you think I am. I mean, I wasn't what I said I was. Well, you see, my mother . . . Richard, will you promise not to turn against me, no matter what I tell you?

They were all terrible. They made her sick at her stomach. No matter how she told it, it was going to disgust him, both the truth of her past and the fact that she had lied and lied. How could he be sure the whole thing wasn't pure fantasy?

It certainly sounded like fantasy. It would convince Richard she needed a psychiatrist.

And then David might start behaving openly as if he'd known her before, he was unbalanced enough to say anything. Her whole life could be shaken off its foundations before the thing was over with. . . .

"Mother, do you care if I take some of my money and get a guitar?" Amy hovered in the doorway. "There's a real beauty in Carlson's for only thirty-four ninety-five."

Susan hid her face in the cupboards as if hunting for something. "*Only!* The way you say that. Set the table, will you, dear?"

The clatter of silver was unbearable in her ears. "That's cheap for a good guitar, Mother, honest!"

"But you don't even know if you'll be able to play it, or if you'll keep up your interest in it."

"I can always sell it," Amy argued, standing in the middle of the floor so Susan had to walk around her. "They've got a good secondhand value, the man said."

"Then get a secondhand guitar," said Susan briskly. "Amy, will you please *move?* I have no objection to a guitar that costs under twenty dollars."

Amy was the tragic muse. "Oh, Mother! If only you could see it, it's so beautiful! And I told the man I'd take it!"

"You can always tell him your mother says no. He'll understand. It probably happens all the time." She patted Amy's arm, loving her enough to hug her at that moment, but knowing Amy wanted to preserve her dignity. "Or do you want me to call him, and ask about a nice secondhand guitar?"

Amy recoiled at that. "No! I'll tell him. . . ." A long

loud sigh. "Darn it." Eyelashes, mouth, shoulders all drooping, Amy began to set the table. Tracy Jones played the guitar as well as owning a Jaguar.

Barry came in, his talk divided between baseball and dogs. Amy shifted from despair to Emily Dickinson, chanting softly to herself as she moved about the table. The kitchen felt so safe and so normal, dread slid away from Susan like snow from a steep roof in a January thaw. Surely there was a way to manage David without damaging this family.

She could take care of them. She felt strong enough to do anything.

After dinner that night, with the children in their rooms doing homework, she said to Richard, "I met Randall Emery downtown this afternoon and had a cup of coffee with him at the hotel."

"So I heard," said Richard blandly. "From at least three people."

"And I thought Somerset wasn't a gossipy town!"

"Oh, it wasn't in the way of gossip. At least I don't think it was. I sold a stainless-steel double boiler, an electric clock, and a nylon clothesline, so I'm bound to think the information was purely incidental."

"My, what lovely long words you use, Mr. Linden."

"Don't I, though," said Richard modestly. "What did you and the impresario talk about? If impresario's the proper title."

"I don't know what it is. Maybe *entrepreneur*. We should ask the experts on Beacon Heights or out at the Glen. . . . Well, I was considering him for the Women's Club—"

"As a human sacrifice?"

"By the time I got through talking with him I would have agreed to that. No, for the cultural program. An explanation of his particular field in art. But—I don't know, Richard. He *bothered* me. I've been thinking about him ever since." It was enough of the truth so there was relief in saying it. "The pictures have some deep significance for him, possibly occult—"

"Spiritualism?" Richard laid aside his paper. "You know, my grandmother didn't believe in it, but she was always having strange experiences that she'd dismiss as nonsense. She wouldn't let anyone discuss them with her, or ask questions."

"Well, I suppose this is spiritualism in a way—I couldn't quite get it—but he got so worked up trying to make me see that I didn't even mention the club to him. I don't know what he might say on the platform, trying to collect some disciples." That would account for his emotional outburst, in case anyone they knew had seen it from across the room.

"I'd like to hear what he has to say," said Richard. "But not enough to get involved if he's a little unbalanced."

She went on thoughtfully. "He is, I think. I know there are people who make a life study of these things, trying to find out the truth without letting their emotions run away with them. But he's not one of them. . . . These pictures have a message, by the way. He's searching for the one person who can read the message."

"It's a wonder he didn't tell you it was you. Do you suppose he'll find the answer out at the Glen?" He reached for the paper again. "It would be nice for him to discover the object of his search had a million dollars or so." He began looking for the editorial page. "This talk of an industrial park is going to blossom into a war before winter. Listen."

She looked attentive but she didn't hear what he read. Why hadn't she leaped in back there and said, "Well, as a matter of fact he did tell me it was me." Laughing. "I was flattered no end, but I had to tell him he'd better keep on looking."

That would make it all amusing and harmless. They'd wonder aloud if that was David's line with women, or if he were really deluded, and then, no matter what he did and said after that, it would be all right.

She blushed with anger for not being able to think fast enough. If she came in with it now she'd be self-conscious, she wouldn't be able to sound natural, she couldn't force a laugh. Oh *damn it!* she thought vigorously.

She watched Richard as he read. His face was that of a self-reliant man set securely in his own frame of reference as his father and grandfather had been secure before him. His emotional stablility was still a wonderfully rich gift to her, who had known so little of it. And yet how much would that be shaken if he found out about her? What if he should suddenly discover that she was a stranger?

Wondering about this made him a stranger too. She sat there watching him, her heart beating in heavy tolling thuds, and felt as if she were seeing him for the first time in her life.

That night after he slept she lay trying to contain the straining panic that wanted to drive her out of bed to walk around the house like a ghost forbidden to rest. It had an ugly familiarity; whenever she shut her eyes she was back in those hotel rooms, and she had to touch Ri-

chard to convince herself that the hotel rooms didn't exist
for her any more. But even that didn't work after a while.
David had brought them back, a composite of them was
nastily superimposed on this long airy room; the city
smells and sounds blotted out the scent of the autumn
night. Outside the door, the hall became an endless one
composed of all those narrow, dingy, badly lit, stale-smell-
ing hotel corridors; their atmosphere was heavy with the
weight of the human woes and squalors locked behind the
doors; the pretenses, the apathy, the lonesomeness, the desperation, the panic . . . panic like hers—

She went to sleep at last, and when she woke up it was
light enough to see and recognize her own room, to gaze
at Richard's head on the pillow, to hear Barry's stealthy
early-rising movements on the stairs. She was too de-
pressed even to cry. She wished she could lie there un-
speaking, unmoving, and just let things happen as they
chose.

*Keep telling yourself there's something in you that
won't give up and go down.* Mr. Martin. She'd tried to
reach him once, to tell him that she was safe, that she had
Richard and a baby girl, but the letter had come back
stamped *Deceased,* and she cried in secret.

It was Mr. Martin who got her up now and into the
bathroom to shock herself fully awake with icy water and
begin the day.

At breakfast Amy said eagerly, "Mother, you never did
see all the pictures, and they're only going to be there another week."

Only another week. Her smile was genuinely happy. "If
I have time I'll surely go to see them."

"I wish you would. They're just terrific."

"Hey, when can we go after school to pick out my dog?"
Barry clamored.

"*Your* dog!" cried Amy.

"You can both go," said Susan. "You can go by yourselves today if I'm busy."

"You were out yesterday afternoon," said Barry suspiciously.

"Look, one way or another you're going to see the dog,"
said Richard. "So why not leave it at that? Anyone want
to walk along with me this morning?" Though they had
the two cars, Richard almost always walked downtown to
his store.

"I do," said Amy. "Only—" She looked down at her
plate.

"Only you'd like me to act as if I'd never seen you before if the Jaguar should go by. My dear girl, are there absolutely no boys of your own age in that high school?"

"They're all creeps," Barry volunteered. "Tracy Jones
is, too."

"He is not!" Amy exploded. "Just because he's rich and
refined, you're all against him!" She dashed out of the
room.

"Barry," Susan began, and then took another sip of coffee instead. Barry left the room cheerfully, and the two
parents looked at each other. "I couldn't say anything,"
said Susan. "I think Tracy Jones is a creep too."

"Even if he is rich and refined?" asked Richard.

"Last week he was *nouveau riche* . . . I'm tired, and the
day hasn't even begun. I think I'm going to stay home for
a week."

"Good idea." He went out into the hall and whistled,
and the children joined him, Amy dignified, Barry care-

fully keeping his father between him and his sister as they went down the walk.

It would be simple to stay out of David's way till the exhibit was over. She could refuse to speak to him if he called, or to let him into the house. By then he should know that it was no use to hope.

CHAPTER 9

It was a curious week. She decided that she would have another one at home sometime when she was not driven to it. She did not even go down to the store, or walk to the corner of the street to mail a letter. She told her friends who called up that she was simply tired out, and was discovering the charms of a rest cure at home. They were all enchanted by the idea and said they must try it; there were things they longed to do but needed time to get *at*.

David called her during that week. The first time she was expecting to hear from another Scout mother about the food sale, and answered gaily. David said, "Leslie, we have to finish our conversation."

"We finished it that day," she said evenly. "There's no more to say."

"Yes, there is." His assurance was chilling. "There's everything to say. When I first knew you, you told me you were afraid that you were out of your head when you painted those pictures."

"I was an unhappy child when I painted them. That's all. Now I'm going to hang up." But she could not seem to do so.

"Oh no, Leslie, you were more than unhappy, you were on the edge of madness when I met you. But I know now it was because you were fighting your karma. The soul can't stand that conflict, Leslie. And if you were so close to it then, you'll be close to it again. Because the pictures will bring you face to face with the truth."

This time she did hang up. Her hand was sweaty and trembling. He's really gone, she told herself. Round the bend, over the edge, flipped. But slang didn't help. Against her will she remembered how she had been affected by the first sight of the pictures. And there were the memories so vivid that old smells were rank in her nostrils, and old rooms surrounded her in their drab horror. But how could David know?

The telephone rang again while she was standing there, and she stared at it with revulsion. Then she picked it up. It was the woman whose call she was expecting.

There were other calls during the next few days and none of them were from David. Just when she had decided that he had given up, he called again. He sounded clipped and businesslike, like someone calling about an overdue bill and prepared to deal with any nonsensical excuses.

"Leslie, I can tell by your voice that you're very frightened. The thought of an upheaval terrifies you. But believe me, when you're on the other side of the storm, safe with me, you'll admit I was right. You belong with me."

She hung up so hastily she dropped the telephone, picked it up and clashed it into place. "That does it!" she cried to the empty kitchen. "That does it! I'm going to tell Richard about this and let him tell the police—I'll say he's insane and he's bothering me—" Breathlessly she snatched up the telephone and dialed the store. A madman, that was it. She'd already done the groundwork, telling about that conversation in the coffee shop.

The store's line was busy. Wilting, she replaced the telephone. Still, only three more days of the show, and if he was already booked somewhere else he'd have to go, wouldn't he?

She'd wait. Maybe it would all end without any public disturbance.

She left the house on Sunday to go to church. It was cold and rainy, and she and Richard drove the few blocks, so she didn't anticipate meeting David along the way. Besides, Richard would be with her, and David wouldn't be likely to lay claim to her so openly. At least she presumed he wasn't that far gone.

The children had been to Sunday School, and met their parents outside the church to go in with them. Starting down the aisle with Amy, who was trying to look religious after a giggling fit with a chum outside, Susan looked past the carefully reverent young profile and saw David. He was sitting alone in a pew at the back of the church. As if he felt her presence—or had already seen her coming in—he turned his head and looked at her. She stared through him—blank, indifferent.

The family went into the pew near the front where they usually sat, and Amy and Barry began their usual intent reading of the church calendar, which meant whispers about the hymn selections. They were honor-bound to despise each other's favorites. Then there was a quiet but fierce grab for a grip on the hymnbook they'd have to share. Whoever got it first and put a scrap of paper in to mark the responsive reading won some sort of status. Susan was glad Amy still found it important. Any day now she would surrender the whole thing to Barry with a tolerant smile, leaving him lonely in childhood while she went farther and farther away from it.

The organ played something quiet and meditative. The pulpit flowers were a blaze of chrysanthemums. The sanctuary was softly lighted against the dark day outside. The very ordinariness of routine was protection; David retreated into infinity.

Then Richard inclined his head toward her and said close to her ear, "Did you see your friend back there?"

"Who?" she murmured, frowning.

"The Man with a Mission. The Searcher for a Message."

"Oh!" She gave him a little smile. "Oh, yes. Well, maybe he'll find a message here, who knows?"

The organ crashed into the chord for the Processional.

When they went out she was afraid he'd be waiting for them and would come up all smiles. But the rain was coming down so hard now that once people had shaken hands with Mr. Montrose in the vestibule they hurried toward their cars. No one was standing about outside except a very few under umbrellas waiting for someone to come along and pick them up. Her relief made her happy. She looked forward to the long rainy afternoon with Richard home, the children busy and contented, and tomorrow they'd be taking down the pictures in the main gallery to make way for the next exhibit.

When the car turned down their street on the way home, Barry sang out, "Look, we've got company. Hurry up, Father, he's coming out of the gate."

"Oh, who is it?" Amy's face came over the back of the seat between her mother's and father's heads. "I can't tell in those rain clothes. Who could it be?"

"Someone looking for a number," said Richard as the man closed the gate and stood looking up and down the rainswept street. Susan said nothing. She knew it was David, and the meeting appeared inevitable. She shut her eyes, and in the dark all was calm and still, like the eye of a hurricane. One way or the other, it would be over. . . . "Oh, darn it, he's gone!" cried Amy. Susan opened her eyes and saw the figure in the trench coat going off down the street through the whirling fall of leaves and rain. He had reached a corner and disappeared before the car turned into the drive by the drenched red barberries.

"Now we'll never know who it was," Amy mourned. "The mysterious stranger. The unheard knock. Ships that pass in the night."

"Hey, I've got a good name for the dog," said Barry. "Ralph. We could call him Ralphie for short."

Amy groaned. Richard looked at Susan and smiled, and she smiled back, convincingly.

They had been in the house only a little while when the telephone rang. She went rigid as Amy answered, caroling her greeting; lately Amy'd been very conscious of her telephone voice. "Cripes, you'd think she was trying out for a part on Broadway," Barry muttered to his mother. "Boy, is she stuck on herself! 'Halloo-oo!' " he squeaked in falsetto. Susan shook her head at him, and tried not too obviously to watch Amy.

"Oh, I'm afraid you have the wrong number," Amy said gently, cocking her head with solicitous regret. Some answer was made, because she burst into spontaneous laughter. "Oh, thank you! It was nice meeting you, too." Something else was said, more delighted laughter, then a cheerfully intimate farewell. She hung up and said airily, "It was a wrong number."

"It sounded as if you were getting engaged," said Barry.

"Brat," she said, flipping his Sunday tie into his face, and sauntered away. It was a deliberate saunter, of the kind that made Richard take a slap at her bottom with his newspaper. She dodged just in time, turned around, and grinned. "He had an awfully nice voice," she said. "Too bad he wasn't somebody for us."

There is no need, Susan counseled herself coldly, to be sure it was David.

It was the sort of afternoon they all enjoyed when there weren't too many rainy Sundays in a row. Everyone read; television was forbidden until a special feature was due in the early evening. After a while Barry went down to the cellar to look for boards to build a dog-bed, and Amy took all her winter clothes out and gave herself a fashion show before the long mirror on the door in her parents' room. Frequently she came downstairs when she thought she looked particularly fetching. She made out a long list of things she absolutely *needed;* Susan read it seriously, as if this weren't a kind of game they played at the beginning of each new season. Amy could expect to receive one or two of the items for Christmas. She didn't really anticipate any more.

As the day coasted toward a rainy dusk, Susan went out to the kitchen to put the teakettle on for coffee. In the liv-

ing room Richard was deep in his chair and book. Amy
had stopped before the hall mirror to experiment with
her hair. She was singing under her breath. Downstairs
Barry hammered. As Susan came into the kitchen, the telephone rang. Bemused by the peace of the day, she picked
it up in all innocence.

"Leslie, you didn't outrun it," said David. "It's at your
heels."

She hung up and stood without moving, hearing the beloved sounds of her house and family grow faint in her
ears as if she were being borne away from them.

"Ridiculous," she whispered. "He's the one who wants
to look out. It's already overtaken him."

"Who was it, Mother?" Amy was in the doorway. "What
are you talking about with your eyes shut?"

"I'm uttering maledictions on this new dial system,"
said Susan. "Wrong number again."

"Oh, was it that man with the nice voice?"

"I don't know if it was your wrong number or not."
David did have a pleasant voice, she supposed, but the
mere thought of his exchanging a few joking words with
Amy made her sick.

Monday. This had to be the last day. They'd crate the
pictures and he'd go away. After all, if he couldn't sell
them here, there was always a chance at the next place. It
was like the old days.

To be safe, she went nowhere on Monday. While she was
upstairs at one time she heard the front doorbell ring, and
started to hurry to answer; but she remembered before
she reached the head of the stairs, and stood there listening, her hand unconsciously at her throat, until the ring-

ing stopped. A little later she heard the squeaking of the gate. She went to the front windows and looked down on the street but she saw nothing, or rather no one who shouldn't have been there; the mailman going toward the O'Brian house, an oil truck delivering at the Johnsons, Mrs. Novak across the street out with her dog, two pre-school children solemnly riding their tricycles.

The telephone rang. She didn't go to answer it.

The sound of tires turning into the driveway with a reckless woosh and the following slam of a car door, then quick footsteps on the side steps, were all familiar. It was Ann Ellenburg. Susan greeted her with giddy enthusiasm.

"Just in time! I'll put the coffeepot on."

Ann shed gloves and car coat en route. "I called you earlier but you didn't answer."

"That must have been when I was in the tub," said Susan.

Ann squinted at her through cigarette smoke. "I don't know if your week's rest cure did you any good or not. You probably wore yourself out cleaning the house from cellar to attic."

"I did not," said Susan. "What makes me look haggard now is the return to reality. It was a lovely week. But if you come back up too fast to Monday, you get the bends."

Ann laughed. "Well, I've got something to depressurize you quickly, or whatever it is."

"Have a doughnut," said Susan. "That's one thing I did that I haven't done for years, fried doughnuts."

"Gorgeous," said Ann. "So is the coffee. Well, here it comes. Somerset has acquired, at least for a time, a distin-guished new citizen. Randall Emery has taken a flat in the Bartlett Block. And Mrs. Tracy Jones has already snagged him for a Friday morning art-appreciation course, to be held at her house. A salon yet. With coffee, *and* a special invitation to the peasants in the lower town. Or are we the *bourgeoisie?*"

"*Hoi polloi,* I should imagine," said Susan absently. She sat stiffly still, her fingers cramped from tightening their grip on the coffee cup until she expected to snap the handle off. Her face felt as if it didn't belong to her, and she tried frantically to arrange it into a mask of naturalness before Ann looked up from digging in her bag for a cigarette. "Are you going?"

"I think we should both go!" Apparently Ann saw nothing wrong. "For one thing I'd like to get a look at some of those places. I hear she's got a pool in the living room, and Tracy Senior walked into it one night when he was high. Besides, these people in communications strike me as coming off another planet."

"The men are as crazy about hardware stores as anybody else," said Susan. "Richard's thinking of calling the store the Saturday Club. . . . Friday, you say? Starting this Friday?"

Ann nodded eagerly. "I can hardly wait. Of course, my daughter will now make my life miserable begging me to invite the Joneses to *our* place."

"Well, I can't say anything right now," said Susan. "It sounds like fun, but I don't want to say yes and then have to back out. Let's wait till I get a chance to sort out my week."

"Oh, sure, you don't have to decide till the last minute." Ann got herself a fresh cup of coffee. "What were you talking to him about last week down in the coffee shop?"

"Were you there? Why didn't you come over?"

"I wasn't there, but our dear friend Veronica was. She said you were getting along like a house afire. I said any-one who couldn't get along like that with either you *or* Randall Emery was dead and should be buried."

"I was vaguely thinking about him for the Women's Club," Susan said, "and he loves to talk and explain, no doubt about that. But I don't know if he'd do. I think he'd be way over our heads. Anyway, if Mrs. Jones has or-ganized this course, the women who want culture can choose it. I mean his kind of culture."

"You don't sound impressed."

"Well, I was and I wasn't, if you know what I mean."

"I'm not sure," said Ann. "When are you and Richard coming over for an evening?"

"All you have to do is set a date."

"Good. I'll talk to Joe. I have to dash now." She ran gaily to the car, and Susan was appalled by her own envy; it was back in full strength, the corrosive jealousy of all the girls privileged to live out a happy and thoughtless youth and move into an unhaunted maturity.

She waved to Ann and turned back into the house. *Les-lie, you didn't outrun it. It's at your heels.*

CHAPTER 10

SHE HAD TO take Barry to the dentist after school one day, and when they came out onto the street Henry Lyons was just parking his Land Rover behind her car. The two wirehairs barked at Barry, recognizing a kindred spirit, and he forgot his numbed jaw and ruffled dignity in greeting them. Henry got out and stood watching the encounter. "Soul mates," he said to Susan. "I'm seriously thinking of getting a boy for my dogs."

They both laughed. Barry dodged ardent tongues for long enough to say, "I'm getting a new dog as soon as he's old enough!"

"Congratulations," Henry said warmly.

"He's a collie-shepherd," Barry explained while the wirehairs scoured his ears and chewed his hair. "I'm going to train him like Rin-tin-tin and Lassie. I mean—" he giggled as a dog's whiskers tickled his neck—"it's almost as good as having two dogs."

"I should say so," Henry agreed. "That combination, particularly. He'll be a big dog, too, won't he?"

"Very big," said Barry. "But I like these dogs too," he added quickly. "They're an awful lot of dog."

"For compact models, yes," said Henry. Barry grinned and turned back to the bright eyes and fluffy whiskers. "Yeah, I sure love you," he breathed close to an ear. "And you *smell* so good!"

"I know you could keep this up forever," said Susan, "but Mr. Lyons has errands to do and so have we."

"Oh, don't rush them," said Henry, offering her a cigarette. She shook her head, and just as she did so she saw David coming along the sidewalk toward them. Susan felt her face grow stiff as if she had received the anesthetic, not Barry. She said, "We must go. Come along, Barry."

Henry's expression was unreadable, and she blushed with embarrassment; she must have sounded intolerably clipped and cold, and he'd remember it forever afterwards with distaste, and she *liked* him so. . . . Oh, blast you, David, she thought and swung around blindly to open her own car door.

"Oh, hello, Randall," Henry said crisply; still annoyed with her inexplicable rudeness, no doubt. He rolled up the Land Rover windows almost to the top, and went across the sidewalk to the Somerset Bookstore.

Susan dropped her car keys and David picked them up. "I've been to the dentist," Barry told him importantly.

"Lucky you," said David. "Are you joining Mrs. Jones's group, Mrs. Linden?"

"I doubt it. Get in, Barry . . . I have no interest in art whatever." She slid in after Barry.

"I find that hard to believe," said David. "And I was looking forward to seeing you next Friday morning."

"Sorry," said Susan, starting the engine.

"Maybe you'll change your mind," he said pleasantly, his hand on the door where the window was rolled down. "You and Mr. Lyons seem quite well acquainted, by the way."

Was that a threat? But of *what?* "Oh, Henry's great-grandfather and Richard's founded the town," she said lightly. "It makes it a closed corporation in many ways, but we like it." There was a warning for him, if he chose to take it that way. She couldn't tell from his expression as he removed his hand from the door and straightened up.

"I'll be seeing you again," he said. "I'm living here now, you know. It's good to stop wandering, good to find what one has been searching for all one's life." He smiled into her eyes. She put the car into gear and turned it toward the street.

The policeman directing afternoon traffic said, "How are you, Mrs. Linden?" as she drove by him. Barry saw a friend who had to be shouted at. Everything should have been reassuring, but it wasn't.

Amy went shopping after school, and came home with a secondhand guitar, an instruction book, and a chum who knew three chords. "Four really," the girl said, "but the fourth one is so hard I cheat a lot and don't use it when I should."

"Three are quite a few compared to none," said Susan.

"Oh, sure. You can sing just about everything with three chords."

"I'll be playing for you by tonight," Amy assured her mother, as she and her teacher headed up the stairs. "I'll give you a concert after dinner."

Barry brayed like a donkey, the newest sound in his circle of friends. "He does that so well," said Amy with infinitely sweet contempt, "that I keep expecting to see his ears about a foot long." She continued up the stairs, back very straight and hand sliding lightly along the banister, the guitar under her arm.

Barry stood at the foot looking up as the two girls disappeared at the top. "Who does she think she is, anyway?" he asked his mother with honest puzzlement.

Susan said amiably, "Who do you think *you* are? Aren't you three or four or even five people in the course of a day?"

He wrinkled up his face, wriggled his shoulders, and scratched behind his ear. "Yeah ... well ... I'm going over to Beaky's now, Muth." He started by her but she dropped a straight arm before him like a railway-crossing gate.

"Not in those clothes."

He groaned and ran up the stairs, taking three at a time and trying for four. His mother went back to her sewing by the sunny bay window in the living room. She had been working there for an hour and a half with no interruptions, no telephone calls, no one at the door to break the spell of the sun and the sounds of the house; the grandfather clock ticking in the hall and striking every half hour, maddening when you were lying awake and trying feverishly to get to sleep before the next striking, but a tranquil and melodious chime in the safe hours of daylight. A grandfather clock had been a part of the house she had dreamed for herself. This one had actually belonged to Richard's grandfather.

She could hear also the little Seth Thomas mantel clock in this room. Sparrows talked and squabbled loudly in and out of the shrubs and the hedge, and bluejay calls pierced everything, especially when Nellie the next-door cat strolled leanly across the lawns. When the birds were quiet, and the preschoolers who rode up and down on their tricycles were having their naps, there were the tiny sounds of the house itself, mysterious but not alarming creaks and taps.

With the children home the house took on an entirely different set of sounds. From behind Amy's closed door came the thumping of a foot keeping time, bursts of voices in song or discussion. Barry, who could be as quiet as a cat, could also sound as if he were building furniture while he changed his clothes. This was one of those times. His room was next to Amy's, so the racket was probably for nuisance value. She'd found out for herself that she could safely ignore a lot of the sniping and then effectively deal with the more serious incidents. There weren't many serious ones.

"For an only child, orphaned young and raised by a working aunt, you do very well as a mother," Richard told her once. "You must be one of the born kind. What are you blushing about? Can't you stand praise?"

"I'm just pleased," she said meekly. I can't stand lying to you, she thought. But she'd withstood the temptation to tell him the truth then, as she'd done other times; it was Susan Hedges he'd fallen in love with, and she was afraid to tell him the rest.

That was what it boiled down to. Fear. The fear that had come to live with her as a sixteen-year-old, hardly older than Amy; the fear that Leslie Danton wasn't—*right*. Susan Hedges had been a practical, brave young girl firmly rooted in reality.

There had been less and less reason to refer to the past,

so the uncomfortable times had grown fewer and fewer. When Amy asked her questions about being young, she answered as truthfully as possible, but one day she explained that she had been unhappy and lonely as a child so she didn't like remembering all that. If she had no girlhood to share with her daughter, all right; she was lucky to have a daughter, and the kind of home for the daughter that she'd always wanted for herself.

Barry left his room, pounded on Amy's door as he passed it, and came downstairs whistling. "What can I have to eat?" He couldn't stand still, had to jump and try to reach the ceiling with his fingertips, did it, and said, "Hey, how about that!" His gray eyes were luminous, his joyous smile quite beautiful. "I'm starting to grow, after all!"

"I told you you'd have to be tall, Barry. Both your father and I are."

"Yeah, but I could take after some short ancestor, couldn't I? Boy!" he gloated. "Wait till I'm taller than Amy! Oh, hey—you know who gave me a lift to the corner today? Boy, what a neat little car! He said he just got it. Those Jags are nothing!" he declared, wiping out Jags with a slash of his hand. "This was an Austin-Healey Sprite."

"Who?" asked Susan, admiring an almost invisible darn on one of Richard's sweaters.

"That man we met the other day when we came out of the dentist's. I don't mean Mr. Lyons. The other one, who said he was going to stay here for a while."

She smoothed out the sweater hard, to occupy her hands. She said, "Barry, you know you're forbidden ever to get into a car with a stranger."

"Heck, he's not a stranger! You know him, Mr. Lyons knows him—"

"We know him by name, that's all. At least that's all *I* know of him."

"Well, for Pete's sake, do you think he's going to kidnap me or something?" Barry was incredulous, and she forced herself to look at him with a motherly smile and say, "No, I don't think Mr. Emery's a kidnaper, but he's a stranger and it's better for you to get the habit of staying out of strangers' cars entirely. Now if you want something to eat you can have one apple turnover and a glass of milk. I said *one*."

"Okay!" He was gone, whistling and noisy out in the kitchen.

Kidnap. Her hands began to shake. Was David that far gone in his paranoia to think any means justified the end? Oh, don't be ridiculous, she told herself. It was too farfetched. Anyway, Barry had been warned to stay out of his car, and she'd tell Amy too, without making it seem that she was warning against David in particular.

She thought of people trying to hide from the plague; if only she could move her family out to some absolutely secure spot. On another planet preferably, she thought grimly. She went out to the kitchen to see what she could fix for dinner that would take a lot of preparation and strict attention to the detailed directions in the recipe. She chose a hearty casserole from Spain, and sent Barry to the store for the ingredients that she didn't have on hand.

The family was pleased with the results and ate with gusto. "I kept tasting, and took the edge off my appetite," she said to explain her own small helping.

When she and Richard were having their coffee, Amy

went up and got her guitar. She showed them the three chords she had learned and sang *Mama See the Tiny Ducks,* with many stops as she changed chords. Barry kept a martyred silence. When she'd finished, and was blowing on her tender fingertips while her parents praised her, he groaned.

She shoved the guitar at him. "All right, Segovia, you try it."

"Who's Segovia?" he asked blankly.

"Well, that stopped you," said Richard. "Here, let me take it, Amy."

His long hand crooked familiarly about the neck and he began to play and sing *Sweet Betsey from Pike.* His family looked at him with astonishment and increasing delight. Barry's admiration was expressed at the end of the song in one long, reverent "My gosh!"

"Daddy, *I* didn't know you could play the guitar," Amy breathed. "Did *you,* Mother?"

"I'm speechless," said Susan.

"Oh, it's just something I picked up in my youth," said Richard modestly. "We were all doing it there for a while."

"You mean everybody was crazy about guitars way back *then?*" Amy asked.

"Sure, I played at Lincoln's inauguration," said Richard. "What do you mean, way back then?"

Amy giggled. "You know what I mean. The time before anybody's born seems like a hundred years ago."

"Sing something else, Dad," Barry commanded.

"Once more, that's all. Those strings are murder when you aren't toughened up to them." He began to sing *Roamin' in the Gloamin'* with a broad Scots accent.

When the front doorbell rang, both children behaved as if they hadn't heard it, keeping their eyes fixed on their father. After a moment Susan decided they really were too fascinated to notice the bell. Usually they raced to answer that and the telephone.

The bell rang again. She got up and left the living room. Light shone from the double doors into the hall and she didn't bother to turn on another one. Someone dropping in at this hour wasn't unusual. It could be one of the children's friends or one of their own, coming on an errand at a time when the family would be sure to be home.

I'm not going to be talked into doing one more thing, she said to herself as she crossed the hall. Then she remembered the proposed industrial park; maybe there were some petitions going around for or against.

Behind her in the lighted dining room the children had already learned the refrain of the song, and were singing at the tops of their lungs.

I'll sign one against it, she decided quickly. We're losing our woods and fields too fast. She switched on the porch light and opened the door, just as the song ended with a grand shouting climax.

There was nobody there. The light shone across the porch, down the steps, dimmed off along the walk and over the lawn. Nobody out there, either. Across the street there were lighted windows, next door someone was calling Nellie in, but on the street itself nothing moved, there was no sound of footsteps or a car, though she could hear one going by the end of the block.

Behind her in the house there was a clatter of voices and dishes as the children began to clear the table. Richard came out into the hall. "What's going on?" he said. "Did I hear the doorbell?"

"It rang twice, but they didn't wait."

He came and stood beside her, and put his arm around her waist. "Practicing up for Hallowe'en. Smells good to-night, doesn't it? Good night to go parking up on Beacon Heights."

"In the Jones driveway?"

"It was still Job Shenk's pasture back in my sparking days. If you remembered to shut the gates behind you, Job never knew the difference. Of course, in warm weather you were likely to be surrounded by cows. They'd put their heads in the windows and expect to be patted. It was sort of distracting. Probably saved many a girl's virtue for her. . . ." He gave her a hard little squeeze. "This kind of weather the cows would all be in the barn at night. No difficulty at all."

"And how many girls did you relieve of their virtue on nights like this?"

"Hey, what are you doing with the door open?" asked Barry, behind them.

"We're discussing a character of Lincoln's time known as the Casanova of Somerset," said his mother.

"Huh?" He ducked his head around his father's elbow to see for himself if he was missing something. "Hey, what's that?" He swooped down on something they hadn't seen on the fiber mat, almost hidden by the doorsill on which they stood. He straightened up with a little card-board box in his hand.

"That's the explanation of the bell," Richard said. "Somebody delivering free samples."

"It doesn't say anything on the box." Barry looked at it

from all angles. "Hey, it's fastened with sticky tape." He began eagerly to tear at it, and suddenly Susan's bemused mood cracked. She took the package from Barry's hands, at the same time moving back from him.

"Come on in and shut the door," she said. "The neighbors will think we've lost our minds. What about your homework, Barry?"

"But I want to see what's in it!"

"In what?" Amy was coming down the hall. "What's going on? What's everybody been doing?" She sounded excited. Barry made a noise of disgust.

"I found it, so it's mine," he warned her. "Whatever it is."

"If you're both this worked up over a package of soap powder or a new kind of toothpaste," said Richard, "I don't know why we bother with bicycles and record players and such."

Susan walked away from them, holding the little box in a tight grip against her breast, wishing she could crush it into a powder, wishing she could make it disappear before they caught up with her. *What now, what now?* She thought she was whispering it aloud.

The children surrounded her, rushing her toward the lighted dining room, laughing and making extravagant guesses about the box. "It's the Kohinoor diamond," said Amy. "A famous international jewel thief was running away from a rival crook down our street and he threw the box away as he ran. He plans to come back for it later. We may all be murdered in our beds tonight."

"No, it's a formula," Barry decided. "Or plans for a super-super-space project, and only one guy's been trusted with them, see, and—and—" Invention flagged.

"You're right about him running away, though," he told Amy generously. "He'll be back for the whatever-it-is later. But he won't murder us. He's a good guy. At least I'm pretty sure he is." He looked worried.

"Oh, honestly," said Amy, "all you kids think about is *spies.*"

Richard wasn't with them. He'd evidently retired for the evening news, not being fascinated by free samples. Susan was glad he wasn't there to see her white-knuckled grip on the box. "Here's my knife for the sticky tape, Mother," Barry said.

Now it isn't a deadly snake or a tarantula in this tiny box, she told herself; she seemed always to be admonishing herself these days. It's not a nerve gas or an explosive triggered to go off. It's very possible that it *is* a perfectly innocent sample.

But after she cut the tape she wouldn't let either of them open it. The tightfitting cover came off with some difficulty, revealing cotton wool. Four avid young hands reached in before Susan's did, and Amy's fingers actually lifted the top layer of padding.

It looked like a small cluster of loose beads, all dull blues and reds and gold in the nest of wool. Barry was silent with disappointment, as if he'd really expected to discover secret papers but would have settled for the Kohinoor. Amy whispered, *"Oh!"* Delicately she dipped into the little puddle and lifted out a fringe of colored beads hung from a chain of gold-colored ones.

"Oh, it's beautiful!" she breathed. "It looks so old! And kind of Egyptian!"

Barry said with renewed interest, "Hey, what's this?" A folded slip of manila paper had been fitted into the lid of the box. " 'We have selected you,' " he read aloud, " 'as one of the few discriminating people in Somerset who will understand and appreciate these ex—' "

"Exquisite," said Amy, leaning over his shoulder. He jerked away rudely and his shoulder almost hit her in the jaw. From long practice she dodged in time.

" 'Replicas of ancient treasures of the Nile,' " he read on. " 'To introduce you to these lovely—' " he made a face—" 'things, we want you to have this gift. It is a perfect copy of a necklace once worn by the daughter of a great Pharaoh.' " He knew that word well, from Sunday School. " 'The Princess Nen-a-tifa.' *Bunk,*" he finished with cheerful disdain.

Amy snatched the paper from him. "It is *not* bunk. That's beautiful. I saw one almost exactly like it when our class went to the Museum of Fine Arts on our Boston trip." She read from the paper. " 'Egyptian Imports, L-t-d.' "

"That means Limited, and don't ask me what Limited means," said Susan. "What's the address?"

It was a New York one. "They hope this gift will make us want to visit their shop and see more of these beautiful things," Amy said. "I'd love to! Let's go sometime, Mother, please. I mean to New York, anyway. We haven't been for ages."

"We'll see," said Susan. "Maybe before Christmas. Now what about homework?"

Barry had already gone. Amy was holding the fringed necklace up to her throat. "What about this? Can I have it? Or can we share it?"

"We'll see," Susan said again. "I want to show it to your

father now. He might not want us to keep it, for fear these people will be pestering us, calling us up and so forth."

"But I'm crazy about it!" Amy said, already bereaved. "It's a gift, they say so. I mean, you don't have to buy anything *more*."

"You run along and do your homework now," said Susan. She stood alone in the dining room looking at the necklace. She wanted to wrap it up and bury it in the bottom of the garbage container, so it would disappear for good tomorrow when the truck came around. She'd hardly been able to keep her poise when Amy lifted it out and then held it to her throat.

Just so had she once lifted such a necklace to her own throat, for David to see how it looked. He had just given it to her, an inexpensive trinket bought out of the small wages Olivia gave him for being useful with tickets and luggage, overseeing the pictures en route, and hanging them at her direction for each new show. Sometimes she kept him with her at the gallery because, like Naomi, he gave things an atmosphere of quality.

Susan knew David had left this necklace tonight, and that nobody else in Somerset had received a sample, and that there was no Egyptian Imports, Ltd., at the address given; or, if there was, it had nothing to do with David or the introductory gift. He might have bought the necklace from them, that was all.

She was not trembling now or sick. Instead, she knew how people felt when they made up their minds to kill to protect their own.

CHAPTER 11

RICHARD SAW NOTHING wrong with keeping the necklace. "They probably turn them out for about a cent apiece," he said. "It's the same as any other sample that's left at the door. Why the doubt, Susan?"

The way he said her name startled her attention up from the beads draped over her fingers. He was looking closely at her, as if trying to find something in her face; as if some false note were clanging away in his unconscious. But that was ridiculous.

"Oh, you know how every so often there's a warning about these things made in foreign countries, toys and so forth. The paint or the stuffing is poisonous, or they're likely to burst into flame."

He reached forward and took the necklace, holding it up to the light. "I wouldn't be surprised if these are glass and made in Hoboken," he said. "But they're not worth worrying about. Throw them away if it will make you feel better."

"It will," she said firmly. As she got up to leave he said in a low voice, "Susan."

She managed not to turn too quickly. "What is it, dear?"

"You're still feeling off-color, aren't you?"

"No!" she objected, half-laughing. "I feel fine! What makes you think otherwise?"

"Things bother you that shouldn't. Trifles like that." He pointed at the box in her hand. "I saw your face when you took the box away from Barry."

"Hallowe'en is coming. And do you remember some of the sick humor that hit our town last year? The razor blades in the apples? The LSD in candy? The minute I saw the box I thought, Now what's some little sadist cooked up?"

"There were just the three incidents and the police got the boys."

"Three incidents like that are three too many for Somerset," she said angrily. With relief she let her healthy indignation take over. "And you can't tell who's going to think up what this year. The same boys could be at it again. They got probation, remember."

"You're right, I guess," said Richard, reaching for his paper.

She went over and kissed the top of his head. "Thank you, dear," she said solemnly. "Ann says that Joe has never once in her whole life admitted that she was right about anything."

"Maybe she has never been right," said Richard. He tilted his head back and grinned at her, and she said, "Oh, you men," and left him, feeling rather proud of the whole scene.

She had to take Amy to the library the next day to look up some references, and they went right from the dinner table. This was always a quiet time at the library, and while Amy sat at a table copying material from one of the very old books that could not be taken from the building, Susan wandered among the stacks. When she and Richard were first married they'd used the library a great deal. All their recreations had to be inexpensive then. But they hadn't needed to mix with crowds and spend money to be happy. With nostalgia she remembered their going home from here with armfuls of books, getting ready for a stormy weekend; reading in bed and eating apples, and laughing at each other's jokes, and making love.

A couple of kids, she thought with a smile. Happy kids. Sometimes in those days she could hardly believe her happiness. It was a perpetual Christmas morning. One outgrew the giddiness after a while, but something deeper came as one grew up.

There was a new Creasey. Richard would like that. "Hello, Mrs. Linden," someone said behind her. "Isn't this a pleasant surprise!"

"What are you doing here?" she demanded in a whisper.

"It's a public library, is it not?" There was nobody else in sight; just the two of them in a corridor of books. The lighting fixtures overhead shed a cool white light down on them, making his eyes look dark and deep-set.

"I suppose you just happened to be passing by," she said sarcastically.

"I could say that a psychic message reached me through these granite walls, but the fact is I heard your daughter downtown telling another girl that her mother was driving her to the library right after dinner." He smiled. "You see? No tricks, no illusions, no hands."

"How did you know she was my daughter?"

"She's enough like Leslie to make my heart stand still. So I asked someone who the beautiful child was."

"If Amy's beautiful it's because Richard Linden is her father," she said. She seemed to be out of breath; crowded, cramped, physically oppressed. She turned her back on him and began blindly running her fingers along the bindings.

"It's not there," said David close to her ear. "You'll never find it there. You'll find it only with me. Face it, Leslie, or face madness."

She swung around in a fury. "Will you stop this, David? You stop speaking to me. You stop making telephone calls to my house and joking with my daughter. You stop offering my son rides in your car. And the beads didn't fool me, David. They went into the trash where they belonged."

"*Leslie!*" he exclaimed softly. "Control yourself! You *are* badly upset, aren't you? I don't know what you are talking about. I did give your nice youngster a ride home one day, but what's all this other business? Telephone calls—beads—what beads, Leslie?"

He looked so solicitous she could have slapped him. She got her breath back, conquered her frustration. "If you're trying to convince me that I'm losing my mind, David," she said curtly, "watch out. You're the one who's courting madness."

He shook his head at her, smiling. "No one is as sane as I am, Leslie. I know exactly where I'm going and what I want. I fought Them for years and I nearly cracked up.

But when I knew what They were trying to tell me, and I left everything behind to dedicate myself to the pictures —*then* I found you. And as soon as you face the inevitable, you will be a serene and a whole woman."

It was a ghastly echo of the fake inspirational talks that used to bore her when they didn't turn her stomach. Eventually they'd made her feel like screaming.

"Where do my husband and children come in on this?" she asked scornfully.

"They don't come in on it, any more than my wife and children do. The facts are simple, Leslie. We belong together. As for the others, it was decided long ago that they were simply instruments to be used in helping us move from one life to another. Now their usefulness is ended. They are nothing."

The mixture as before. The same old nauseous stuff. But just words, that's all.

"How do you expect to claim me?" She gave him smile for smile. "You saw me buried, remember? There's a stone to prove I'm dead. You can't convince anybody I painted those pictures."

"I don't have to, my darling. You know it, and that's enough."

"Get out of my way," she whispered. She brushed by him and went out into the open part of the library. A few people were coming in now, and there were other teenagers besides Amy looking up references. Two were classmates of hers and the three heads were clustered together over an open book. Susan went to the rack of just-returned books at the end of the desk and fixed her entire attention on them. When she was young she could do this and blot out any unpleasantness; that was how she had been able to paint, and afterwards feel blank, exhausted, and indifferent. It had been an escape for her. After she had become Susan she had never felt any urge to paint, and for a while she'd even experienced nausea from the smell of oil paints.

David came along in a little while with a couple of books. Without glancing at her he put them on the desk, watching amiably while the young librarian checked them out. "I hope you enjoy your card, Mr. Emery," the girl said.

"I promise you I'll be a steady customer."

"Who can ask for anything more?" the girl said, looking astonished at her own daring. Pink-cheeked and dreamy-eyed, she watched him walk toward the doors, her chin on her hand. There was no doubt that David had great charm. He'd had it back then, too, though now it was much more sophisticated. Part of the charm had been de-lightful manners and a way of speaking that gave the cir-cle the impression of wealth and background.

No wonder Olivia picked him up, Susan thought wryly. All that talk about the Fair Lover from the North ... Naomi could find anything to order in the pictures. I wonder how she was able to stand it when she discovered how she'd fooled herself for so long.

David had gone out and disappeared. The girl sighed and returned to her work. Susan went back and got the new Creasey book for Richard. She thought, Is there really someone who loves David and waits for him to come back? And if he has a wife, does she know how badly he's disturbed and does she wonder what has become of him, and worry?

If there were only some way to let her know where he

was. The trouble was, Susan didn't know his real name. It could be neither David Emerson nor Randall Emery.

When they got back to the house she did not want to leave it ever again. Yet she must, or give Richard the reason why, and from that she felt a shrinking as if from something positively unclean. When they were going to bed that night Richard said, "What's the matter?"

"Matter?" She spun around from turning down the bed. "What do you mean?"

"Just that," he said. "The way you jumped. The way you looked before I spoke, when you didn't know I was watching you." He came to her and took her by the shoulders, and she stared helplessly up at him. What shall I say, what shall I say, the panicky words danced through her head till she thought he would see them in her eyes. "There's been something for a long time," he said. "What's worrying you, Susan? Are you afraid of anything? Look, if there's something that isn't quite right, and you're afraid to ask the doctor about it, just tell me, darling, and we'll go together and get this off your mind."

In her relief she could have sagged between his hands like a rag doll. "To tell you the truth I *have* been thinking about a checkup," she said. "No particular thing seems wrong, but I've been cranky and out of patience, and—oh, tired of the things I always liked to do."

"Do something different," said Richard. He was relieved too, his face softened. He let go of her and began taking off his necktie. "I was just reading an article about this. People get bored with too much activity, though how any woman married to me could get bored I don't know."

"Oh, darling!" She could laugh at that. "It's not you! I'd like to be alone with you, and the children, and the new puppy, and just wipe everybody else painlessly out of Somerset. Not destroy them, you understand. Just put them somewhere else. Or *we* could go somewhere instead. The four of us."

"Five, including the dog," said Richard. "I can see the charm of it, except that who'd buy hardware? As a substitute, why don't you join this art seminar and see if you can make any sense of it?"

"Who told you about that?" She turned away. It was coming into their bedroom. *It's at your heels, Leslie.*

"Ann was in the store running on about it. You hadn't called her yet about it, but she was expecting you to. It starts tomorrow, doesn't it? And you owe it to your daughter to get inside the Jones walls," he said drily.

"The Joneses and that Jaguar are some of the objects I'd like to see swept painlessly up by a cyclone and deposited elsewhere. I don't want to go to this thing, but if I tell Ann I don't want to go, she'll want to know why."

"You don't have to tell her why."

"The trouble with friends is that you have to take care of friendship," said Susan wearily. "I don't want to hurt Ann's feelings, and if I'm abrupt and say I just don't want to, not even once to see what it's like, not even to do her a favor and keep her company so we can talk about it afterwards—I will hurt her feelings."

She sat down on the edge of the bed and looked at her hands in her lap. Richard sat down beside her, putting his arm around her. "You don't act right, and you haven't been acting right. This shouldn't throw you. I've never known you to fuss at trifles. You call Jed in the morning and make an appointment. I'll take time off from the store and go with you."

There was no way of avoiding this, and she agreed.

Richard fell asleep while he was reading. She took his book away and turned off his lamp. Some people slept sternly, as if on guard even while unconscious. But Richard, sleeping deeply against his pillows, was relaxed and unwary. She could see now the young Richard whom she had married. The lines added by the years and the gray above his ears were superficial touches, and yet they were as dear to her as the sweep of lashes which Barry deplored because he also had them, and the tenderness of his upper lip and the deep indentations at the corners.

This was the man whom David had called *nothing*. It was simply the statement of a disturbed man, a psychopath. Yet even to think of it tightened the hair on her head, and she felt again the impulse to strike. Sitting there in bed with her knees drawn up, watching Richard's sleeping face, she began to see even more clearly how murders happened. At this moment she knew that if she could kill David without anyone's knowing she would feel absolutely justified.

CHAPTER 12

In the morning Ann called before Richard and the children were out of the house. "Shall I pick you up or will you pick me up?" she bubbled gaily. "Millicent's going too, and Nora, and—"

"I'm not." Susan didn't intend to sound so curt. Ann said in astonishment, "But *why?*"

"I don't feel like it, that's all. I don't think I could endure listening to that man for an hour. I'd rather read a book, or even clean the attic."

Ann was silent for a moment. Then she said, "Well, if you feel that strongly about it. . . . Do you want me to tell you about it afterwards?"

Susan wanted to say, No, and I don't want to hear about the Jones house and the rest of them up on Beacon Heights, either. She didn't. "Why don't Richard and I come over this evening?" she asked. That way they could leave when they were ready. "Oh, I forgot, it's the poker club. Tomorrow night?"

"I think so." Ann sounded relieved. "I'll call you anyway. Goodbye, dear."

When she turned away from the telephone Amy stood on the stairs watching her. She looked horrified. "Mother, aren't you going? I was sure you would. I told Margie you were going and that you already knew Mr. Emery—you know how he wanted to talk to you all the time over at the Ellenburgs'—and *her* mother's going, just because Margie begged her to."

"Amy," Susan said coldly, "my setting foot in the Jones house isn't going to get you a ride in that car. It's not going to get Margie a ride either, or Linda Ellenburg. I've heard all I want to hear about the Joneses, Senior *or* Junior, and the Jaguar."

Amy opened her mouth but no sound came. She looked stricken. Color flowed up through her throat and into her face. Susan walked back to the dining room and met Richard's eyes, unreproving but watchful over the morning paper. Barry looked at her with something like admiration.

"Boy, you really told her. You should've heard her on the phone yesterday. She was positive you and that creep's mother would be buddy-buddy next week—"

"Barry," said Susan. "Keep quiet."

There was a crash as Amy slammed the front door behind her.

"Finish your milk," Susan commanded. "Go up and brush your teeth. Then go to school."

"Hey, I wanted to read you my list of names for the dog," he protested. "I was just going to when the telephone rang."

"I don't know if we're going to have a dog," she said.

"Now go." Stunned, silent, he got up and went past her. She stood with her hands clenched at her sides until he had reached the door and gave her one quick backward look, in which she saw the watery glitter of tears.

"I'm sorry, Barry," she said hastily. "Of course we're going to have the dog."

"Okay," he said slowly, and left the room. But he didn't look relieved, and she knew that his world, until now to be taken happily for granted, had been shaken.

"I've hurt their feelings," she blurted out to Richard, her own eyes watering.

"They'll live through it," he said. "The Jones boy and his fancy car are wearing a bit thin around here as far as I'm concerned. And Amy had no right to try to blackmail you into doing what you don't want to do."

"It wasn't blackmail. She honestly feels I've let her down. And I shouldn't have snapped at Barry."

"You apologized." Richard pushed back his chair and came around to where she sat. "Sit here and read the paper, have a fresh cup of coffee, and then call Jed." His hand pressed her shoulder lightly, and she laid her cheek against it.

"Sometimes I think I don't deserve you. In fact I know I don't." Her voice cracked. She wanted him and Barry to get out so she could cry, and yet the pressure of his hand and the feel of his knuckles against her cheek seemed the only contact with light and warmth and sanity remaining to her.

"Don't undersell yourself," said Richard. "They always said in this town that only a saint could live with a Linden." He kissed her and went out, to walk downtown as usual.

She sat there for a few minutes, listening to the sounds of her house. But they did nothing for her this morning. She would be glad when they got the pup, something young, needing to be comforted and fed and laughed at. She could hardly wait for him to be seven weeks old.

Then she called the doctor's office. She knew she was organically sound, and all he could do for her was to prescribe a tonic, but she was beyond resenting the useless errand.

"He's out of town until next Tuesday," the nurse said. "A meeting in New York. If it's an emergency you're to call Dr. Levine."

"It's not an emergency, thanks. Just a checkup. I'll call when he's back."

"You can make your appointment now, if you want."

"Thanks, Miss Lane, but I haven't got next week sorted out yet." *I may be having a nervous breakdown next week. Or committing a murder.* Her mouth twitched with mournful humor as she said goodbye and hung up, but murder was on her mind as she went upstairs to make the beds. Purely as an intellectual exercise, how would one get rid of David? Certainly not by walking into the Bartlett Block to shoot or poison him, even provided you could get your hands on a gun or poison.

Destroying the pictures might be a form of psychic murder. He said that when the pictures came into his hands he won possession of her. Would he also believe that if he lost the pictures he had lost his rights? Would he accept that? But even if she knew where the pictures were, she wouldn't have the slightest idea of how to get rid of them.

As a criminal you're a complete failure, she told her reflection in Barry's mirror. It's too bad you couldn't have spent your youth in some useful apprenticeship. To Fagin, for instance. Or Dr. Fu Manchu.

The telephone rang. She stood by Barry's bed, his pajamas in her hands being creased by passionate and unconscious strength into fine pleats while she listened. Outside the open window the bluejays were noisy among the last of the scarlet maple leaves; as she watched, some of the leaves broke loose and spun earthward in the gray, gusty wind. One blew at the window and rustled against the screen like something scratching for refuge. The telephone kept on ringing. It could be Ann wanting her to change her mind, but there was a menacing demand in its persistence. Most callers realized that if you didn't answer soon you were in the yard or the cellar or the bathroom, and waited to try again. This pealed on and on, shrieking through the house. She was sure it was David on the line. He must have seen Richard going into the store and knew she was alone.

After a while it stopped. The fabric was wet from her hands. She dropped the pajamas on the bed, shut and locked the window, and went out of the room. She shut and locked all the windows in the house. Then she got her tweed topcoat from the hall closet, and her car keys from the desk in the living room. She hurried to the garage with the wind pushing at her, got into her car and backed out of the driveway, and drove the shortest possible way out of town and onto the road for the shore.

She had no coffee with her, and wore a cotton dress under her topcoat. When she got out of the car at the cottage, the northeast wind swept around the house and wrapped her in cold. The turf looked brown and dead, the last flowers had been blackened by frost. She went into the house and it was even colder than out of doors, with the peculiar penetrating chill of dead air. She took slacks and wool socks out of the sea chest, and found a pair of her old sneakers in the heap in the front hall closet. Out in the kitchen she shut the doors to the rest of the house and built up a wood fire. She pumped some water and put it on to heat, then changed into the warmer clothes before the open oven door. There were cocoa, sugar, and powdered cream in the cupboards, and crackers in a tin box. She made a hot drink and sat before the stove sipping it, her feet on the oven hearth. She had got so completely chilled that for a few minutes the warmth coming from the stove and the cocoa reaching her stomach was the most important thing in the world.

She felt safer out on this deserted section of coast than in her own home, where she was afraid to answer the telephone. She refused to think further than now.

When she had finished drinking she went through the other rooms to the sitting room. The wide, windswept verandah might never have held a hammock full of children, or been cluttered with swim fins, masks, and croquet mallets. The lawn, too, was empty except for the horseshoes and stakes. I ought to take them up, she thought, and then forgot about them.

Beyond the lawn the sea was a gray and white prairie. She watched it until she began to feel the cold draft that whistled around the windows. She went back to the kitchen and shivered almost voluptuously as the warmth hit her.

She stayed at the house all morning, leaving the fire to go to the other rooms on occasional errands. She planned new curtains and slip covers for the long living room. She went upstairs and considered Barry's request to move to the attic. She sorted over the jigsaw puzzles and burned the incomplete ones. She classified magazines until her hands were too cold to hold onto them. Back in the kitchen she rearranged cupboards. She lunched on more cocoa and toasted crackers.

She timed her leaving so that she would arrive home a few minutes before Barry did. Then everything would be all right until tomorrow, she assured herself. When they were all home together he wouldn't come near, and she needn't answer the telephone. Wouldn't the thing die out for lack of nourishment, if they never met?

The road wound leisurely past woods and pastures, going by farmhouses with twin elms or maples in their dooryards and great barns at their backs. Susan had always loved the meandering way and feared the time when some great widening and straightening and grading project might take place and destroy the country charm. Today it seemed impossibly long and twisting, and she was constantly speeding up and then braking, consciously loosening her grip on the wheel, trying to ease the stiffening of her body. It was as if she were holding herself in place only by hanging onto the wheel and clamping her feet to the accelerator and floor. She didn't know why she had to hurry, but the compulsion was there.

To ease it and her arms, she stopped for gas about halfway. There were two pumps in front of a general store at a picturesque crossroad, and the Lindens stopped there often. The elderly proprietor greeted her with pleased surprise. "Didn't expect to see you in this weather! You been to the shore?"

"I certainly have, and I'm frozen through," she said.

"Sure feels like the snowflakes are on the way." He put the gas in and then came around to check the oil. "Nope, she's fine." As Susan paid him, he said, "Say, did you see anybody else around your place today?" He seemed worried.

"Not a soul except some crows. Why?"

His frown disappeared. "I'm glad of that. I wouldn't have given this feller directions if I'd known you were down there all by yourself, where I never saw him before. He was real pleasant-spoken, but just the same, you can't tell what bee he might have in his bonnet. Take Jack the Ripper now; probably was a real fancy talker."

Susan smiled. It seemed to her she was always smiling now to cover something. "What did he want to know, exactly?"

"Well, he said he was new in Somerset, and out exploring the countryside, and he'd heard that Heron Cliff was a sightly bit of shore, and how did you get there. I told him the places were all shut up, but he said he was more interested in rocks and water than places."

"What kind of car did he have?" But she knew.

"Sports car. Little low dark green job. Foreign."

He went into the store to get her change. She sat there trembling. David must have driven into one end of the street as she drove out the other. But since she knew the town and he didn't, she'd lost him on the winding way out through back streets and lanes. By another fluke the Heron Cliff sign was always taken down by whatever cottagers were there for the last weekend in September. If he'd been looking for a sign, he'd found none, and had probably thought the turn-off was just another of the dead-end woods roads along there. It was possible that he'd driven down several of them and then had had to back all the way out. Maybe, she thought hopefully, he got stuck somewhere and had to walk miles to find a telephone, and missed his eleven-o'clock lecture at the Joneses'. It was wrong to be so malicious about someone who couldn't help himself, but David was so damnably smug in his delusions.

The man came back with her change. She said, "I've seen that car around town, I think. He's probably all right, but he *is* a stranger, and I'm just as well satisfied we didn't meet."

"Me too. Stop in again before the snow flies, Mrs. Linden."

"Oh, we'll be back and forth. We haven't turned off the water yet, so that's always a good excuse for a day out there."

They smiled, waved, and she swung out onto the road. Her clothes were wet with sweat on her back. She had felt safe on the cliff, and all the time he was nearby. It was only pure luck that he hadn't found her. His karma, she thought, her mouth twisting. And mine.

When she drove into her own street there was no small green car in sight and she turned thankfully into the driveway, thinking of a hot bath, a shampoo, fresh clothing and lipstick before the children got home. She wondered if she could have an injunction served on David, forbidding him to speak to her; she'd already told Richard that David had some exotic ideas, so what if she told him now that David had been calling her, trying to meet her, and had finally informed her in the library that he had been searching the world for her and that she was his?

He would sound insane. Anything he said about knowing her as Leslie Danton would be automatically dis-
counted, especially with the grave back in Belmont Falls.
Yet the thought of David trying to tell his story, David
raving and possibly in restraint, was nauseating. What if
she merely warned him about an injunction? Would that
arouse the instinctive, animal fear of a trap?

It was worth trying. Thoughtfully, if not quite hopefully, she unlocked the side door and went into the house.

As she shut the door she heard a sound which did not
belong there when all the family was out. Something was
dropped, or somebody stepped.

She froze, her hand still on the doorknob. How had he
got in? She would turn and escape as soon as she could
move her feet. There were other sounds overhead, louder.
She wondered if he were searching the rooms. If she could
only get someone to come now and catch him in the act, it
would take care of everything.

There was a crash in the kitchen that shocked her like
pain, and Richard said, "*Damn* it, anyway!"

She sagged against the door and shut her eyes for a moment. Then she walked along the short passage from the
side door to the kitchen and found him scowling at a new
dent in the top part of the double boiler.

"What are you doing home?" she asked, astonished. His
head jerked up. He looked harassed and angry.

"What are *you* doing, not being home?" he demanded.
"Where have you been?"

Ordinarily she would have answered with a simple explanation. Today, still shaken by the last few moments,
she said, "Why?"

"Barry was sick at school and they couldn't raise you
here, so they called me at the store. I had to take a taxi to

get him and bring him home. Ella's running things sin-
gle-handed over there." He slammed the cover on the
double boiler with unusual savagery. "Where *have* you
been? I thought first you'd changed your mind and gone
to this thing with Ann, so I waited till you should be
home and then I called her. She hadn't seen you. So I've
been here, and God knows how Ella's making out over at
the store."

"Ella's very capable. I always thought you underesti-
mated her." Guilt made her angry and defensive. "I'll see
to Barry."

"Oh, he's fine now. Working on his models, happy as a
clam," said Richard sardonically. "He thought he'd like a
little cereal. If it had been acute appendicitis how could I
find you before they operated?"

"Well, it wasn't," said Susan. She took off her topcoat.
"I'll make the cereal and you can go back to the store."

"You didn't tell me where you've been. What with
worrying about him and worrying about you and the way
you've been lately, I think I deserve some consideration."

"I think you do too, Richard," said Susan quite honestly. "I'm sorry. I took the car and drove to the shore,
and did a few things in the cottage."

"You could have caught pneumonia in that cold barn.
What about your appointment this afternoon?" he added
accusingly. She knew that he had really been shaken by
her unexplained absence, but she could explain it no
more than she had done already.

"Jed's out of town till Tuesday. I'll call then." She
turned the gas on under the teakettle and measured oatmeal into the pan. "You'd better get back and help Ella,
though she's probably been having the time of her life."

"Well—" He lingered. "You sure you're all right?

You didn't run off because you were afraid of what the doctor might tell you?"

"Afraid of housework," she said, trying to make a joke. It was feeble. "Wouldn't you know that the one time I played hookey I'd get caught at it?" She gave him a smile. "And now everybody knows I played hookey."

"I only called Ann."

"That's quite enough. Already she thinks I'm being definitely *odd*." She emphasized the last word.

"All right, all right!" Richard's voice was brittle. "Has it occurred to you to blame yourself for this mess? I don't know what's happened to you, Susan, but I don't like it. Something has to be done, and quickly, before matters get worse. You're like a stranger in the house." He went out into the hall. She heard him call angrily, "What are you doing on the stairs? Get back to bed."

So Barry was listening. The door closed behind Richard, not quite a slam. She stood gazing at the wall behind the stove, spoon poised over the oatmeal. After a moment she began stirring again.

CHAPTER 13

BARRY WAS UNUSUALLY meek when she brought him his
cereal. He sat in bed with his hands folded, a pious por-
trait of young Dombey. She asked him a few questions
about his stomach upset, and he answered tersely, giving
her quick, furtive glances sidewise and then looking away.
She knew it was because he had heard their angry talk.
She wanted to reassure him but, disturbed herself, she felt
as if all the right words and phrases had been shocked out
of her head. When she had decided that his upset was due
to his bolting his lunch and ice-cold milk in about five
minutes and then playing touch football, she said, "I've
told you about that before, Barry. If you can't eat properly without being watched over, we'll just have to think
of something."

Lashes downcast, he dipped decorously into his oatmeal.

"And another thing," she said, "now you know why
your father and I insist on knowing where you and Amy

are in your free time. Look at all the trouble today simply because I decided to go out and forgot to leave a note. Your father was annoyed with me, and I don't blame him."

He straightened his shoulders, as if the lifted load had been a physical one. "He sure was mad, wasn't he? Hey, Muth, when *you* play hookey, who do you take a note to, and who from?"

"That's a good question," she said pompously, and he giggled. She went downstairs, ruefully pleased with one small victory. In the kitchen she called Ann; might as well get that over with while she was ahead. She composed her face in the right expression for the manner she wanted to use.

"Hel*lo,*" she said, drawing it out. "I understand my husband had the Mounties out looking for me today."

"Where were you, for heaven's sake? I don't know whether Richard was afraid Barry was dying of strychnine or you'd been kidnaped by a sex fiend, or both. It's not like you to be so—so *unexpected!*"

Susan laughed. "Then it's time I should be unexpected, instead of the same old story that everybody knows. I simply took a run out to the shore to measure the place for new curtains—because I'd decided all at once to make some—and if Barry hadn't given himself galloping indigestion, I'd have gotten home before he did, and it would all have been very simple."

"I've got news for you, Sue," said Ann. "The minute anybody like you, or like me either, does anything on the spur of the moment, no matter how pure and innocent it is, we get hooked."

"By the spur," said Susan. "Well, I don't know whether

to go back to being good old stable me, or to start being a
reckless and unpredictable me. The trouble with that is,
you have to learn how not to feel guilty."

"Susan," said Ann, "are you bitter?" She sounded so apprehensive that Susan's laughter this time was a genuine
peal.

"No. Tell me about the seminar. How did it go?"

"It didn't. He never showed up."

"Oh, Ann!" She had to sit down. She felt as if she'd
been running, and her legs were all but elastic. "What
happened? What did you all do?"

"Well, we sat around politely ignoring his tardiness for
a while, and we then finally got to talking about it. We all
got pretty sociable after a while, and Mrs. Tracy Jones is
very nice, by the way, with a real homey midwestern accent and no side at all. . . . Well, she tried his number a
couple of times, and somebody thought she should call the
police in case he'd had an accident in that stretch of
woods that's been left unspoiled. Are you still there?"

"Yes," said Susan. "Breathless with suspense." That was
no lie. What if he'd had an accident out near the shore
somewhere, in a deserted part? Could she leave him there,
possibly to die, or would steady old Sue notify the police
that she'd seen his car out that way? . . . Ann was going on
and on, and at first it was just a clacking in Susan's ears
but it made sense after a while.

". . . called *her,* and he was very apologetic, and so
upset, but a very serious emergency had called him out of
town. It was so bad that he'd clean forgotten the seminar
until he was well past Hartford, and he'd stopped at once
to telephone. She said he sounded terrible. Well, of course
she assured him that we all understood, and we hoped

things would go all right, and would we see him next week?"

She paused, and Susan said, "Well, would we? You, I mean?"

"He didn't know. At the moment he was extremely doubtful." Ann sighed. "A man like that could have a great personal tragedy and no one else would know about it. I mean, they're perfectly charming and you feel as if you'd known them for ages, but there's the wall between. Crystal-clear but steel-hard." She repeated it, rather pleased with herself. "Crystal-clear but steel-hard."

Susan agreed with her, this being a part of friendship. She was light-headed with relief, no—with a glorious euphoria that promised to go on forever. "Maybe," she suggested, "the prospect of facing twenty women at once was too much for him and he fled."

"I don't think it was anything to be funny about," Ann protested, and Susan said, "I'm sorry." But she couldn't keep from smiling. She wanted to dance and sing. "I've got to start dinner. We'll be seeing you tomorrow night, and—" another gesture of friendship—"I want to hear all about the Jones house and that pool and so forth."

"It's out of this world, to use my dated language that my daughter says came out of the ark."

"Oh, that's not so dated," said Susan dryly. "Sometimes that's the only phrase that fits." She said goodbye and hung up, and sat for a moment with her hands clasped tightly and pressed against her breast. The Christmas morning feeling was back. She couldn't stop smiling, her face felt foolishly unsteady. She knew what had happened. When he couldn't find her out at the cliff he had taken it as a directive from the Masters to give up. So he had gone away at once. He must have been genuinely upset when he called Mrs. Tracy Jones; she had seen the way the others used to work themselves up into real distress about signs and omens. Excluding Naomi, whose belief seemed to be too deep for display, they were half-charlatan, half-savage, living in a welter of superstition and magic, scaring themselves with their own creations. Even Olivia had her jittery moments.

So if David sounded disturbed on the telephone, he probably was. Anyway, he was gone.

"You've been very chipper tonight," Richard remarked when they were going to bed. "High, in fact. If this is what happens when we let our angry passions rise, should we do it more often or consult a psychiatrist?"

"I'll tell you tomorrow," she said, "after I know what happens tonight."

He was already in bed, holding the blankets back invitingly for her. "There shouldn't be any doubt about what's going to happen."

"La, sir, how you do go on," she said, sliding in beside him. He gathered her into a bear hug.

"I've missed you," he said. "Talk to me."

"Oh, it's talk you want, is it? You've got me here under false pretenses." She pretended to struggle and he wrapped his arms even more tightly around her.

"There's all kinds of talk," he said. "Remember the time we stayed in bed all weekend?"

She laughed against his neck. "When we were very young."

"You think we couldn't do it again? Just find a place to

park the kids for a weekend and I'll prove something to you."

"It had better be out of town somewhere then. If we didn't answer the door or the telephone for a whole weekend, the street would be scandalized, half the town would know about it, and on Monday morning you'd have more women customers at the store than you'd know what to do with."

"I was thinking that," said Richard, "but if I'd said it you'd have accused me of being conceited. And what about you? Who'd guess that Susan Linden was really Helen of Troy?"

She giggled, feeling deliriously happy. "I never thought she was such a much. Walking around on the battlements to see how the war was coming along, with all the Trojan women hating her. Let me be somebody else."

"Who?"

"Susan Linden," she whispered. "First, last, and always. I love you, Richard."

"Was I your first love?" he teased her. "I mean, the first one after the man in the restaurant?"

"There was a boy once," she said honestly. "When I was seventeen. I was crazy about him for a little while but it didn't amount to much. No, you were the real one, Richard. I think I knew it the minute you smiled at me, when I bumped into you that day in the Museum of Natural History."

"So I never had a chance," he said.

"Neither did I."

Afterwards, as they lay drowsily talking, he said, "I'm glad you're back."

"Meaning?"

"You've been turning away from me even in your sleep. If I reached for you, you rolled away. It's a long time since I've waked up to find you curled up against my back. No, you'd be lying stiff as an effigy on your own side of the bed, practically out over the edge. That's worried me as much as anything."

"Next time, wake me up and bully me," she said.

"You mean, assert my rights? Have my way with you?"

"Well, I don't know if I mean that *exactly*, but—" She burrowed against his chest. "Forgive me for being difficult, Richard, and I'll forgive you any time you feel like being difficult."

"All right. But I just may take you by surprise when we have that weekend."

"Then I've got that to look forward to."

The cooked food sale for the Scouts was the next afternoon. The day was gray and bleak, as the previous day had been, but this one was irradiated for her by a pure and private sun. Baking brownies and cookies in the morning gave her exquisite pleasure; driving around town later to pick up contributions at other houses, she felt the shaky joy of the first outing after a long and near-fatal illness.

One of the women who worked with her at the sale in the basement of the public library spoke about the art seminar. "It's a shame that it might not go on," she said. "I wonder whatever happened."

"Nobody's heard anything since?" Susan asked politely.

"No. It must have been something terrible. Look, Mrs. Lyons is coming in for some hot rolls, and if I'm waiting on somebody else when she comes, will you ask her if they know anything about it? He's quite a friend of hers, isn't he?"

Susan managed to look both amused and ignorant. "*I* don't know, Marcia. But I'll ask her."

She was saved from having to do it because Marcia got a chance to wait on Pris Lyons after all. But as Susan wrapped an angel-food cake for her dentist's wife she heard the question and Pris's answer, good-natured enough not to be a snub.

"Heavens, I don't know anything about it. If he did have to go suddenly, he had no reason to let us know. We hadn't made any dates." She looked over at Susan and smiled. "Hello, Susan. You know that we haven't closed up the cottage *yet?* Henry keeps putting it off."

"So do we," said Susan. "I can just see Richard rushing out there to shut off the water in the first snowstorm."

It was wonderful not to have to keep expecting David to come in the door. The sale was a success in every way.

That evening they went to the Ellenburgs'. She would have refused to leave the children if David had still been in town. He might not have left anything outside the door again, but he could have called up and engaged one of them in conversation; he might even have come to the house, pretending he wanted to see Richard about something. She couldn't endure to think of his setting foot inside the door, and it was not only revulsion she felt but actual fear.

So the evening with the Ellenburgs was like old times.

CHAPTER 14

THAT NIGHT she fell joyously headlong into sleep, no longer afraid. A skydiver, she thought. The raptures of free flight. On the edge of sleep it seemed a wildly possible idea. She wouldn't be afraid of anything now, never afraid again. *Somerset Housewife Takes to Skydiving.* She laughed to herself, carefully so as not to wake herself up, but she must remember to tell Richard tomorrow. And remember not to forget to pull the rip cord. . . .

She slept.

She woke. She was snug against Richard's back, no reservations now, none of that instinctive turning away in sleep he'd mentioned. There was a delicate glow in the room and she thought it was morning coming. Then by the illumined clock on her stand she saw it was only a little after two. It must be moonlight in the room. The skies had begun to clear when they came home from the Ellenburgs'. She felt wide awake with happiness and wanted to savor it, to make up for the being wide awake that had

been so awful. She got up and put on her robe and slip-
pers and went out into the hall. Both the children slept
soundly, with the defenseless, heart-wrenching beauty of
all young animals asleep. The new dog-bed was beside
Barry's, where he could put a hand out to touch the
puppy when it was there. He and Amy had already had
words about that. Having given up the poodle idea for
lack of encouragement, Amy was now strong for Our New
Dog, and Barry wasn't to go around telling everybody it
was *his* new dog.

Susan had a notion that the puppy would start out in
life with the Lindens by sleeping down in the kitchen
with a hot water bottle and an alarm clock for company,
but no need to bring that up yet.

The grandfather clock chimed once for half-past two as
she went down the stairs. She walked slowly and content-
edly through her house.

The kitchen always had such a unique atmosphere
when you came into it suddenly in the middle of the
night; a place that had hummed with life all day and into
the evening, now silent except for the tiny sounds from
the refrigerator and the very soft whirr of the electric
clock on the wall, which you never heard in the daytime.
A room that was the center of the house by day was full of
temporary ghosts by night—even to the spirit of the
popcorn the children had made this evening. She could
still smell it.

She went through the hall to the front door, opened it,
and went out onto the porch to look at the street and listen to the silence. The moon was nearly full, and it
washed the street with a white light that made the street-

lights look tiny, orange, and ineffectual. The shadows of the bare trees lay black and intricate across sidewalks and lawns.

How beautiful it was, this short street of hers, now that the taint was removed. In a way, they had been like a family penned up with a murderer, cut off from all other communications but they hadn't known it. Only she had known. David wasn't literally a murderer, but what *couldn't* he have done to this family?

But he was gone, true to his Masters, and she could stand here on the porch and look at her street in the moonlight and feel a sweetness in the very chill. Presently, when it had struck all the way through her flannel robe, she'd go back up to her warm bed and Richard. In the morning she would say to him, "Richard, when you were coming back from parking in Job Shenk's pasture at two in the morning, did you ever realize how pure and sweet the world smells then? When the frost is just beginning to glisten in the moonlight?"

Someone was walking, several houses away. She wondered who else was out enjoying the moonlight. Old Mr. Barrett? One of the O'Brian boys who'd been studying late? Somebody who'd been waked by a restless dog? She remembered quite a number of those involuntary strolls herself, and Richard had said the next day, "Why didn't you get me up to do it?" She always answered, "You need your rest, and besides, I like our street in the middle of the night. I stopped by the Barretts' gate and smelled their syringa." Or she'd enjoyed the apple blossoms by moonlight. Once in early spring she'd heard wild geese flying over and had listened with tears in her eyes, not knowing why. She hadn't told Richard about the tears.

Sometimes she saw a skunk, immaculately intent on its own affairs. The dog was knowledgeable about skunks and cats, and behaved himself, but he'd danced on tiptoe at the end of his leash at sight of a raccoon. Stormy weather was something else; if he claimed he couldn't stand it to wait till morning, she hitched him to his run in the yard and stayed in the kitchen, sometimes drinking cocoa and reading, or writing out a Christmas list, until he scratched to come back in. She'd rub the wet off his heavy coat with his own towel and go back to bed, with no foolishness about lying awake.

She wondered how long it would be before she could stop thinking about David when she woke up, the pictures, her mother, the whole contents of Pandora's box.

Meanwhile someone kept walking, a slow strolling. It came nearer. She withdrew into the house, mischievously keeping the door open a crack to watch whoever went by. There was an etiquette to be preserved about middle-of-the-night walks. Unless you should come face to face, you didn't speak. In daytime you might hail in neighborly fashion the person who passed your gate, but at two in the morning you recognized their desire for solitude, for nothing to spoil the unique opportunity to be alone.

Deliberate footsteps, very close now. She had only a small opening through which to observe, but he must be passing by the barberry hedge and would soon reach the gate.

There.

David.

He stood by the gate gazing up at the house. Though she knew the porch and the door were in inky shadow, she felt against all reason that he was staring at her and trying to draw her out to him. It took an enormous amount of physical concentration to move the door those few inches and shut it without a sound. Then she leaned against it; heroines in suspense dramas were always collapsing against a door they'd just bolted, it was practically a cliché, and she thought of it now, the *non sequitur* of a woman who remembers, as she sees her husband killed by a car, that she hasn't paid the telephone bill this month.

She leaned now because she had no strength. She might never have had any. She was like a creature from whom the spinal column had been painlessly and instantly removed, so that the stairs were an impossibility, not to mention the expanse of the hall. She had the illusion that her bedroom, containing the warm bed and Richard, was now miniature with distance at the far end of a long whirling tunnel of darkness, and that Richard had slept on, oblivious, through it all. Even if he woke up and realized she wasn't there, it wouldn't much matter; he had taken on the peculiar indifference of people in dreams, when the most loved of all don't hear you when you call. Not even conscious of your entreaties and tears, they continue to walk away, forever.

She tried to say his name but her throat clogged back the sound as her chest ached to expel it. What got her away from the door finally and across the hall was the fear she might be going insane all at once, and that David was standing outside willing it to be so.

At the foot of the stairs she sat down and listened, but she couldn't hear anything else but her own breathing and heartbeats.

When the clock struck three she was still sitting there; she was like somebody waking from sleepwalking, cold and not sure how she had got there. She realized a name had been repeated over and over to her, not from outside but from inside. *Mr. Martin, Mr. Martin, Mr. Martin.*

She got up stiffly, went upstairs and back to bed. Richard stirred, and muttered, "What's the matter?"

"Nothing, dear. I just had to get up."

"You're cold."

"It's turned chilly. There's a frost. Go back to sleep." With a luxurious sigh he gathered her into his arms and she tried to relax without his knowing it was an effort. He went back to sleep, his cheek against her hair, and she was free to think. At least she felt saner than she had downstairs. Mr. Martin had done it again.

So David was back. And maybe the midnight walk was all his return would amount to; he couldn't quite give up, couldn't quite accept Their word. He might have driven back tonight late, parked nearby, and walked down here to stare at the house. And perhaps at this very moment he was driving out of town again.

She had no certainty, one way or the other. She was certain yesterday, but not now. Perhaps never again, unless it was a certainty she could see and touch. If I saw him dead, for instance, she thought wryly. Her mind touched on the hypothetical problem she'd set herself, how to kill David, and her theory of psychic murder.

The simplest, most logical, most intelligent method would be Richard.

Therefore, she thought, gazing at the ceiling, if David approaches me once more, I approach Richard. If I have to lie, I will lie and lie and lie. Besides, it will be no lie that David is insane, and that will take care of everything else he has to say.

She had decided this once, or almost decided it, some time ago. If only she'd had the courage to carry it out then, it would have been all over by now. She'd been too squeamish; she'd been at once sorry for David and horrified by him. There was the old gratitude too. Well, she wasn't going back to hiding in the house and avoiding the telephone and the doorbell. The first move he made would be the last one, at least toward her.

She went to sleep. She dreamed of seeing a girl lying asleep, with long dark red hair spread over the pillow and her face hidden. Someone said, "There's Leslie asleep, wake her up. It's time for her to wake up." Olivia's voice. "Wake up, Leslie." Susan went close to the silent figure, saying "Leslie, Leslie!" Then she saw the face was hidden under a cloth and she could not make herself move the cloth, because it would be Susan there but with no face.

Young David was talking, behind her somewhere. "Do you know what the Egyptian embalmer said to a beautiful fellaheen girl when he was trying to make time with her?"

"No, what did he say?" She was Leslie now, with a straw in a chocolate soda. Thank goodness they'd left behind the girl with no face.

"You'd make a lovely mummy."

She exploded and blew frantic bubbles in her soda.

Susan Linden woke. It was time to get up and she did. But the joke stayed with her because it had been one of David's. They used to make these silly jokes all the time; she hadn't dared to at first, it seemed vaguely sacrilegious, but then she'd got onto it, and it had relieved a good deal of pressure. The only trouble was sometimes keeping a straight face when the circle was being so portentous about new messages and interpretations. What delicious

agony, holding it back, keeping the eyes strained wide, answering in a shaky voice, not daring to look anywhere
near David. Pressing your fingers over your mouth to hold
it steady.

Then a moment together, schemed for. "I'm going
downstairs to the drugstore and see if *Seventeen*'s in,
Mother. Can I get a soda?"

"Be back in fifteen minutes. Well, twenty."

David waiting, and the nearly falling together in an ec-
stasy of mirth. All the puppy foolishness she'd never
known until then. You had to watch the clock because
Olivia would, and if it got to be thirty minutes she'd be
there, or one of the others. If Pauline came it would be all
right for them to be together. But they didn't trust Naomi
because she was so serious about the Fair Lover from the
North having to wait out his centuries. And Olivia didn't
want fraternization for a number of convincing reasons.

Now, eighteen years later, Susan realized that her
mother had wanted David at her elbow, not her daughter's. Men of her own age, though there were always
plenty to be interested in Olivia, were hard to handle.
With an attractive and well-mannered boy, she had a male
in attendance, but one she could manage. It was strange
that she hadn't fallen in love again after Bill Danton, but
perhaps she hadn't even been in love with him; for all her
delicate prettiness and feminine charm she must have
been cold to the bone.

"Was I dreaming, or did a cold woman get into my bed
last night?" Richard asked across the breakfast table.

"*What?*" she said so sharply that he looked surprised.
Then she remembered, and laughed, hoping the laugh
came quick enough after the sharpness.

"I'd gone in to check on the kids, and the moonlight was so beautiful I walked around looking out at it."

"Oh, Mother, why didn't you wake me?" Amy wailed. "Promise me you will the next time."

"I promise."

Barry snorted. "She just wants to lean out the window and moan, Tracio, Tracio, where art thou, Tracio?"

Amy sat very tall and haughty. "You might at least quote correctly. "It's *wherefore* art thou?' She wants to know why he has to belong to the family hers is feuding with. 'Deny thy father and refuse thy name,' " she recited, with a sweetly spiritual expression. " 'Or, if thou wilt not, be but sworn my love, and I'll no longer be a Capulet.' "

"What did I tell you?" demanded Barry. "There she goes again! Yuck!" He made sounds of nausea.

"And there *you* go," said Richard, "right up to your room, if we have any more of that from you." Barry heaved a put-upon sigh and stared at his plate.

Looking vindicated, Amy said, "I can try out for the Shakespeare club next year when I'm a sophomore. I probably wouldn't get an important part the first year, but I'll be learning them all. I've already started learning Juliet by heart."

"How about Lady Macbeth sleepwalking?" Richard suggested. "There's a lot of good meat in that. '*Out, out, damned spot,*' " he intoned, and Barry was illuminated.

"Hey, can you say that *right out,* on the stage?"

"That, and plenty more," said his father. "Now Barry can hardly wait to join the Shakespeare club."

"I didn't know there was anything like that in it. I thought it was just gucky old poetry."

"Oh, *honestly,* Barry!" Amy, looking ill, excused herself

and went upstairs to practice a little on her guitar before getting ready for Sunday School. Presently they heard her singing loudly *The Tavern in the Town*.

While Richard looked at the paper, Susan returned again to the jokes with David. They had discovered such sparkling springs of wit in themselves and each other, and they had appreciated their own humor so much, it was all the more incredible now to find David a True Believer.

Oh, he'd believed in the pictures then, a belief all confused with the romantic notion that he and Leslie were "meant" to meet. An equally romantic theory of reincarnation was to be enjoyed like poetry or music; it was all part of the lover's language. To see him so devout a convert, solemnly bombarding her with all the phrases she'd learned to hate, would have turned her against him even without this weird courtship of his.

He wasn't in church that morning, as far as she could see by a guarded survey of male heads when she went down the aisle. Still, there was the chance that he might come in after she did. But he did not.

In the afternoon they all drove out to Heron Cliff. She ran off a bucket of water for drinking and for washing hands, and then Richard set about shutting off the water for the winter. The children went down the cliff to the beach. They had it to themselves today, as they hardly ever had it when the little children were in the other cottages. Their cries rose in the mild, still air like bird voices as they raced along the edge of the water. After a while the shouts ceased, and when Susan looked down they were going over the rocky spine at the northern end of the beach, and soon had disappeared on the other side. There was no difference in their ages this afternoon.

Nobody else was at the cottages. The only other people visible were some shore walkers coming from the south, where the harbor lay.

Susan had done most of her closing-up chores the last time she was here, but she found a few things to do, and then went out and sat on the front steps to wait for Richard to be finished. Experimentally she remembered last night; considered from here it couldn't have happened, she felt so different. She wondered if she could have passed some crisis and would never again be so frightened. Certainly she felt able to deal with David, and she wished she could do it right now, tonight, and have it over with.

But it might be over with, anyway. She couldn't very well call him and ask him. She had to wait.

Richard came out through the cellar bulkhead and she jumped up and said, "Ready for coffee?"

He looked pained. "The last place I worked, the lady always gave me the hard stuff."

"The last place you worked she was no lady."

He considered. "Mebbe not, but I put glass in her window for nothing."

"I'll bet you did. The employment office told me to watch out for you."

"Did they?" He gave her a smile of gratified vanity.

"Good heavens," said Susan, "I hope you don't leer at your customers like that."

"Not at the men, no." They went through the cottage to the kitchen, where Richard washed his hands while Susan heated water for coffee. Then they took the tray, with the cake they'd brought along, back out to the front porch again. The shade was cool, but there was still sunshine on the steps. The children came soon, having remembered the cake. There was none left to take back.

When they stopped at the crossroads store to get some apples from the owner's orchard, Susan remembered that once more she'd forgotten to do anything about the horseshoe game.

CHAPTER 15

ANN MADE ONE of her lightning swoops the next morning. She'd been downtown. "Guess what?" she challenged dramatically.

Susan knew what, but looked ignorant. "What?"

"He's back! Randall Emery! I saw him come out of MacAllister's Drugstore." She flicked her gloves back and forth under her chin, dreamily. "Do you suppose we'll ever know him well enough to call him Randy? On second thought, no, not after the way Joe uses that word sometimes."

"Well, did he say where he'd been?" asked Susan from halfway into the cupboard under the counter.

"No, but I asked him if the trouble had been cleared up and he said he thought so, and hoped so, and if we were willing to trust him the seminar was still on. Susan, won't you think it over and come in with us?" Ann asked wistfully. "It would be so much more fun if you were there."

"I still feel the same way about it, Ann. If I take on anything more it should be something I'm crazy about doing, and to be honest I just don't have one spark of interest in that seminar."

She set a glass pie plate on the counter and gave Ann a that's-it little smile.

"I suppose you're right," Ann said. "I may not stick it to the end, if he gets very intellectual. What would you be crazy about doing, Susan?"

"Don't ask me when I'm halfway through a squash pie," said Susan briskly.

"I'll tell you what I'd be crazy about doing," said Ann. "Living like the Lyonses. Imagine deciding to go to Paris or Antigua just like *that*." She snapped her fingers. "Without even *thinking* of money. Imagine doing anything, in fact, without thinking of money. Did you ever think how it would be to live like that? It's simply there for you to use, no matter what you want."

"Oh yes, I've thought of it," said Susan. "Not enviously, because I really don't want anything else but Richard and the children and this house. But it's almost like knowing someone from Mars or Venus. Very rich people who've always had their money seem like that to me; from another planet."

Once, "very rich" had meant to her people in houses like this one; they too had occupied another planet, and they were rich because they had everything that mattered.

"They do seem like that, don't they?" Ann mused. "Pris and Henry are so darned nice, but you have the feeling that they haven't the slightest idea how the rest of us live, with dental bills and heater repairs and tax worries, all those constant irritations we have to live with down here on old earth."

"A toothache probably hurts them just as much," said Susan. "I have to tell myself that sometimes. And if they get a serious illness money alone isn't going to cure it."

"Oh, I know. And I'm like you, I wouldn't swap Joe and the kids for anything ... Ellenburgs just aren't born into money, that's all there is to it. Why, old Zieber Ellenburg would think his great-great-grandson had reached the top of the world, if he could see Joe as a lawyer."

"*And* our next county attorney!" said Susan with a politician's flourish, and surprisingly Ann blushed. "Don't even breathe it," she said. "I want it so much for him that I can't stand to think about it."

"Well, we're all going to think about it like mad, twenty-four hours a day," Susan assured her. "And after he serves a while as county attorney, there'll probably be a judgeship, and then—"

"I'm getting out while I'm ahead!" Ann hopped up, laughing. "I've got to get home and get to work, too, and I won't if I start seeing myself as a judge's wife. I'll be picking out gowns for receptions at the State House. Chow!"

"What was that?" Susan called after her. "Something about food?"

Ann struck a model's pose, spraddle-legged and angular; difficult, because she was small and rounding. "Oh, my dear, you're not *in!* That's a little Italian word we all use, you know. It's spelled c-i-a-o." She flipped her car keys at Susan. "Chow, darling! See you soonest—God bless—and all that sort of thing!"

Susan stood in the doorway and watched her back out. Then, smiling, she went back to her baking.

With the pie in the oven she went out into the yard to work around the flower borders, getting them ready for winter. There were still chrysanthemums, and the hardy stocks were sending out their spicy fragrance. A few petunias had survived the frost and they had a sad sweetness like a ghost of summer. A thicket of lilacs separated the Linden yard from the Johnsons' on the left, and on the right there was the garage and then the extra lot. Through its trees one could just glimpse the O'Brians' white clapboards. This end of the street was quiet in the sunny autumn morning. The preschoolers were elsewhere right now, and there were no sounds from the Johnson house beyond the lilac hedge. Mrs. Johnson always sang when she put out the wash, but today she must have gone shopping.

Nellie came out from under the hedge, starting up the blue jays. A tall, silvery-striped cat with grass-green eyes, she came to where Susan knelt and leaned against her hip, uttering interrogative sounds.

"Yes," said Susan. "It *is* a nice day. And you're a nice cat."

Nellie fell over on her back, her paws kneading air. "I'm not going to rub your belly," said Susan. "I know all about you. You'll grab my hand with those four feet and bite at the same time. Don't you think you're too old for such foolishness?"

Nellie shut her eyes and purred loudly. Suddenly a shadow fell across them. The cat lifted her head, staring, and turned wild all at once; she threw herself over onto her feet and was gone under the hedge. Susan looked over her shoulder. At first she thought the man standing between her and the sun was Richard, and in the next instant she knew it wasn't, though she couldn't see his face.

Her first reaction was indignation that David should

come into the yard. This was better than terror, which, after all, was unreasonable. At the worst he could be no more than a nuisance. She didn't jump at once, but went on loosening earth with her trowel.

"I heard that you'd left town," she said coolly.

"News travels," he said, sounding amused.

"Didn't you leave?" she asked. She got up and moved toward the arbor, as if preoccupied with her next task.

"I had to give them some excuse for not showing up at the first session." Smiling, he picked a grape from a cluster hanging near him, and ate it. "They were all so understanding and sympathetic, dying to comfort me."

"You're not a very admirable character," she remarked. "I wonder how long it will take them to find out."

"I suppose that when you and I have gone they'll be astonished at us both." He took another grape. "Sour, aren't they? Do you make wine of them?"

"David, let's end this idiocy here and now," she said sharply. "Do you seriously believe you can persuade me to leave my husband and children and go away with you? Do you seriously believe I'd ever *consider* it? You can't! It has to be just a long drawn-out practical joke on your part." She searched his face for answering reflexes, a movement around the mouth like held-back laughter, something about the eyes. There was no difference. He showed merely a lively interest, as if she were the curiosity, not him.

"Or else," she went on, determined not to let him rattle her, "you're getting even with me for running away that day and never getting in touch with you. But you must know by now that I couldn't take a chance on Olivia knowing where I was, and you seemed to be in her camp."

[165]

Now he was ready to laugh, as if at a child's quaint fancies. "My little love, it's nothing to do with anything else but the pictures. They tell the whole story, they hold all the answers. You and I are simply obeying the pictures. At least I am, and you'll come to it when you stop fighting them."

"Oh, those damned pictures!" she exclaimed. "Are you in love with me, or with them? I don't know what you're talking about, David, and I don't think you do either!"

"I'm in love with you," he said with infinite patience. "I've been in love for thousands of years. The pictures told me of our past together; they told me that you were the one I'd been looking for through life after life. Now, isn't that simple?"

"Very simple. It's also—" She stopped short of *insane*. You didn't throw that word at someone you suspected of being it. She sighed and was very patient herself. "The point is, you may think you're in love, but I *know* that I'm in love—with my husband. And that's final, David, no matter what the pictures tell you. Now will you please not try to talk to me again?"

He didn't move but stood smiling, his eyes dancing as if in mischief.

"Will you please get out of my yard?" she said, very softly, because otherwise she would have shouted it. "Or I'll go in and call the police."

"You say that, Leslie, because you're trying to withstand the life forces, but you wouldn't really do it. You couldn't. First, you couldn't set the police on me. Second, you feel those currents swirling about you, sweeping you along in spite of yourself, and you want to give in to them; you want to be swept into the vortex, and be tossed out safe and shining on the other shore."

She watched and listened, incredulous, fascinated by the sheer unreality of it. Being from another planet? Oh, she knew all about them, and not the Lyons variety. He smiled into her widened eyes.

"You're almost ready, aren't you, darling? You're wavering. You'll come to me because you can't stand much more of this."

"No, I can't," said Susan, "but not for the reasons you think. You're right, I don't want to set the police on you, because you were a friend to me for a little while once. And I don't want to make a messy situation for my family if I don't have to. Now will you go?"

"I'll go, because you're ready to fall down with weakness. Remember what I told you. This is something you can't fight, you can't outrun." He touched her cheek gently with his forefinger, and then left her.

She did feel limp after he had gone, but not from trying to withstand the forces he'd talked about.

She went into the house and lay down on the living room sofa, her hands gripping each other until they hurt. Tears ran out of the corners of her eyes. She found herself rehearsing again those futile beginnings. "Richard, if you'll promise not to turn away from me . . . If you can forgive me for being a liar . . . If you can stand to keep on living with a liar . . . Please don't show in your face what you must feel when you find out what sort of life I lived. . . ." How could she?

Her stomach rebelled at the sheer nastiness of it. The tears ran faster and faster from the outer corners of her eyes down toward her ears.

CHAPTER 16

SHE DECIDED in the course of the day that perhaps this was to be a new way of life for her until he got tired of it. A kind of private cold war. Encounters when you least expected them, skirmishes, hit-and-run raids. Already she knew the pattern. He'd wait at least a few days before he attacked again. How long could she keep answering him back before her nerves showed it more than they did now?

She had to be careful not to snap, not to jump when anyone made a sudden sound, not to get up and see for herself that Richard had locked everything before coming to bed. Lying there trying to relax while she became increasingly positive nobody had checked the cellar door, she asked herself, What do you expect, that he'll sneak in here and murder the rest of them and drag you off by force?

She couldn't really believe that, and yet she was afraid that his mania was feeding on her opposition. When she was sure Richard was asleep she'd make the rounds of windows and doors again. Going down cellar was a terrifying experience, reminiscent of all the suspense movies she'd used to love. Talk about your idiot heroine, she thought with grim humor as she descended the stairs. He could be over beyond the furnace, waiting to gag me and haul me away, doubled up in the trunk of that Austin-Healey Sprite.

At times it was all ridiculously unreal, the curse of her own imagination; and at other times it was all horrifyingly possible. One had only to read the papers to know that almost anything was possible. She began not reading them. Sometimes she let the telephone ring, and then afterwards someone would speak about trying to reach her, and she would lie about where she must have been when they called. She knew she couldn't keep this up.

Richard called up one morning to say they'd just changed the billing on the Strand marquee, which was almost across the street from him. It was a return of *Becket;* they'd wanted to see it before, but the kids had had flu. "How about tonight?"

"I'd love it!" she said with the extra heartiness she put into everything these days. "What about Ann and Joe?"

"Just us," said Richard firmly. "Do you know how long it's been since we've had a date?"

She laughed. "All right."

Then she began worrying about the children. They hadn't had a sitter since Amy was twelve, but then they'd still had their big dog, the best guardian possible. Amy was almost fifteen now, and both children knew better than to open the door to strangers. They had the telephone, there were neighbors close by, and they would also know where to reach their parents. On top of that Somerset was a quiet town except for the usual ratio of petty crime, and the small outbreak of sick humor that had upset everyone last Hallowe'en.

But David wasn't a stranger. If they saw him under the porch light they were likely to let him in, Amy happy to display her best manners as a hostess. "My father and mother aren't home, but is there anything we can do?"

"Oh no, I was just walking by. It's such a fine evening."

"Isn't it?" Amy would agree. "Did you notice how bright and clear Orion looks?"

Yes, she could just hear it. But if that's all it was, a little conversation and then the man leaving and the children returning to their television program—if that's all it was, even if the man were David, and she could be sure that's all it would be—but she kept imagining her and Richard's return to an empty house, still scented with the popcorn they'd made and the apples they'd been eating, and the children gone.

Yet she couldn't tell Richard that she was afraid Randall Emery might come and take the children away. He would be as stunned as if she'd gone mad before his eyes, which he could very well think had happened.

Then she thought of Hallowe'en only a week away.

She called him back in the afternoon. "Have you got a minute, or is the place loaded?" she began, businesslike.

"I've always got a minute for you," he said gallantly.

"I've been thinking about leaving the kids, Richard." Did she sound like an ordinary, preoccupied mother? "You know we were talking a while back about those rotten practical jokes last Hallowe'en. Well, it makes me a little nervous about leaving them tonight. What if somebody knew they were alone and tried to frighten them? It was different when we had Jason. Nobody'd come near the house when he was sounding off."

"Look, they won't know themselves about being alone until tonight, so they can't mention it at school. And those rotten practical jokers are about one in a couple of thousand. They can call the Johnsons or the Novaks at the slightest suspicious sound, if they're nervous. So don't worry."

"All right," she said meekly. Everything he said was right, but he didn't know what the real danger was, so he was of no help to her. And the thought of lying any more, even by pretending a headache, was abhorrent. She would have to do the best she could. This was the way the war was to be fought.

She told the children after school that they weren't to open the door to anyone that they hadn't always known. Barry said, "You always tell us that. Gosh, we know enough by now."

"There are a lot of things I have to keep telling you." She ignored Amy's obvious patience. "When you're a parent you'll get just as tired of repeating things as you are now of hearing them. We're stuck with each other, so you might as well give up gracefully."

Amy did. "All right, Mother, we won't open the door to anyone but the Ellenburgs, the O'Brians, Johnsons, or Novaks. *Or* Ted Hanson." He was the policeman who patrolled this end of town. "How about Dr. Gould, Mr. Montrose, any teachers from school, and Mr. Harrison?" He was the principal of the high school. Barry, delighted with the game, took up the list. How about *his* headmaster? And hey, what if Mr. Rogers just happened to come by tonight on Scout business?

"I might miss out on something real important if I didn't let *him* in. Then there's—"

"Just keep it up," said Susan, "and you're likely to find yourselves tucked away in bed at seven o'clock, with Mrs. Ellis ensconced in the living room."

"Mother, you *wouldn't!*" cried Amy; then she saw the way Susan tucked in one corner of her mouth, and burst into relieved laughter. She became very reasonable, explaining facts indulgently to her parent.

"But you know there's any number of people who could come here who aren't going to steal us or be sex fiends or anything like that."

"I know," said Susan, just as reasonably. "But we have to draw a line somewhere, and I don't think a lot of people are going to be offended and your lives ruined because of one evening, once in a great while. So, it's only these." She ticked them off again on her fingers. "No others. Absolutely. Is that clear?"

If only she could say, *And especially not Mr. Emery.* Children could always think up reasons for doing the one thing you hadn't spelled out in particular. What if he said, *I've got a message for your parents?*

"You all right, Muth?" Amy said suddenly. She was frowning, her head cocked. "You were talking to yourself. At least your lips were moving. And you had a kind of distraught look."

"I *am* distraught," she said with a smile. "How do people manage to argue with six or ten children?"

"Oh, that's easy." Barry returned from changing his clothes. "The kids argue with each other. Gosh, do they have fun over at Beaky's," he said wistfully. "There's always a crowd. Sometimes they have real feuds going on,

and boy, do they have fun when their mother isn't home,"
he added.

"They sure do," said Amy. "The people next door
called the police one day. They thought there was a mass
murder going on."

Susan looked speculatively at Barry, and he left quickly
before she could forbid him to play at Beaky's when his
mother wasn't home. Amy went up to change her clothes,
and left with her guitar to practice at her friend's house.
How owning a guitar was to bring her magically into communication with Tracy Jones, Jr., was not yet clear to
Susan. He was two years ahead of her, and lived at the opposite end of town. But Susan remembered how at fourteen she had gone to the library and asked for Spinoza,
after reading in a movie magazine that her favorite actor
was really an intellectual and spent long hours at his Mal-
ibu Beach hideaway reading Spinoza. She could truthfully
say afterwards—not that she ever had, except once—
that she had read Spinoza for one hour, which was more
than most people she knew had.

David had been the one she'd told. They'd laughed
about it, and he told her about falling madly in love with
his sister's music teacher, and reading up on the lives of
the composers so he could impress her with casually
learned conversation about anyone from Bach to Hinde-
mith. But the only time he'd ever had a chance to talk with
her, this exquisite woman was having trouble with tree
roots getting into her drains, and that was all she could
think about.

David, always David these days, after years of repressing
the memory of him. But it was a different David. She always saw him in these recollections as he had been, not as

he was now. Even his defection in the gallery that day was a part of the young man, and forgivable.

What had happened to him in the years between to turn him insane?

Suddenly she remembered that Henry Lyons had sponsored him here, by suggesting the show to Marshall Jury. David went out to the Glen often; perhaps he'd talked about himself to them, so they knew where his home was. He had once said it was Detroit, but it didn't have to be that now. But how did you explain asking for such information, when the man was living right here in town?

Or they might know at the museum, but on the other hand why should they have his home address, unless he was shipping the pictures directly there from Somerset, and one of the museum custodians had crated the pictures for him?

She'd been so sure of so many other things she was wary of being optimistic about this idea, but she called the museum anyway. Marshall himself answered, as usual making her feel like a lady out of another century.

"Ah, Susan. We've missed you! When are you coming to see us again? Our annual open show is on now, and I've pulled rank around here and set up a geological exhibit in the small gallery."

"I'm coming tomorrow," she said, determined to do so. "Amy's been there with her art class. Barry's already seen the geological show with the Scouts and he's gone back again by himself. Now he wants a rock collector's kit for Christmas."

"Great, great!" Marshall was enraptured.

"But will you tell me where the Leslie Danton show went from here? I'm writing to a friend about it—" It seemed as if one couldn't move without lying these days —"and if there's a chance it's anywhere near her I know she'd love to see it."

"Well, it hasn't gone anywhere, Susan. They're crated, but stored here for the time being. I don't know what his plans are. We've had inquiries about the show from several museums, but apparently he doesn't want them to go anywhere without him, and he's not ready to leave Somerset yet." He dropped his voice and became ponderously secretive. "There may be something going on."

"A chance of selling the collection, you mean?" Susan asked. "Well, I'll tell my friend she's out of luck for the time being. Thank you, Marshall. And I'll be in tomorrow."

She hadn't really expected any luck, but she couldn't fight an enervating wave of disappointment. If I had the right contacts, she thought with cynical humor, I'd know someone in the bank or the realtor's office who could find out for me what his home address is. Unfortunately, those contacts only exist in suspense novels and the CIA. And if I survive this, I'll never read or watch another suspense story as long as I live. I may go back to Gene Stratton Porter and Zane Grey.

She expected to sit tensely through the movie, unable to concentrate except on going home. But the picture absorbed her in spite of herself. When it was over she felt both frantic and culpable. By forgetting herself for a few hours she might have brought catastrophe into their lives. Richard wanted to stop and eat, but she convinced him she was dying for scrambled eggs and wanted to go home and fix them. "You know how we used to get ready for bed and then have something to eat and talk about the movie or whatever we went to," she said. "I always loved doing that. Maybe it's because I was never allowed to eat in my bathrobe when I was a kid, unless I was sick."

"You poor deprived child," said Richard. "All right, we'll go home."

The house looked and smelled the same as usual when they let themselves in at the side door. The children weren't up—they each had strenuous plans for Saturday and wanted to get an early start on their chores. Susan went straight upstairs and saw them sleeping before she took her coat off. The relief from tension was like instant intoxication. She was as happy as if nothing had ever been wrong. This must be how people managed between air raids, she thought as she undressed. When one was over you were so relieved at being alive that if you hadn't lost anyone in the raid you bounced straight up again, until the next time.

Scrambled eggs, bacon, toast, and a trial of the new grape jelly. "Isn't this better than eating in your clothes at the Wigwam?" she demanded.

"My dear wife, you are right, as always."

"And when you're finished, you can go straight down to the store and open up for Saturday, because you'll have had breakfast, and you can't sleep after all that coffee."

"Coffee," he said smugly, "never keeps me awake. What's that stuff on the floor by the cellar door where I could have walked right through it?"

Nothing was clear in the shadowy corner. Susan put on the overhead light. They saw a rusty old tray that was usually kept down cellar and used to transport bulbs and tubers in and out of the yard. Now it held ten little plastic flowerpots, of the type that hold seedlings. There were dozens of these downstairs on the shelves with the gardening materials.

Each of the ten on the tray held damp earth.

"Now what?" she said. "You guess and I'll guess and neither of us will come anywhere near the truth."

"Maybe they're trying to grow their own popcorn for the winter." The bag of popping corn had been left on the counter by the sink.

"Or they've planted dried peas or beans," said Susan. "Or orange or apple seeds. How about that? Grow your own orchard; turn your cellar into a farm."

"Were you saving that potting soil for something special?"

"Well, I had an idea of growing some flowers in the house." It had been completely obliterated from her mind ever since the Day of the Pictures. "I thought how nice a little conservatory would be in the bay window this winter. But they might as well have it for their gardening. I can get some more." She put off the light and went back to the table. "Aren't kids marvelous? *Our* kids?"

"Being ours, they'd have to be."

They held hands across the table, smiling at each other. She didn't know how she looked to him, but Richard's smile had been the same across the table in the cafeteria of the Museum of Natural History eighteen years ago.

CHAPTER 17

IN THE MORNING the children were very busy getting their work done. Barry wanted to play baseball that afternoon, and Amy and some other girls were going bicycling out into the countryside, their destination the farm of somebody's great-aunt. The two could be very energetic with their chores when it was a question of freeing themselves to go somewhere, so what with their whizzing back and forth, upstairs and down, out into the yard or to the garage and back, Susan didn't find out what they had planted until they all met in the kitchen for a sequel to breakfast.

Susan had more coffee, and Amy began making toast for herself and Barry to have with the grape jelly.

"What are you growing?" Susan asked, nodding toward the tray of planters.

"Oh, gosh, I forgot to take those downstairs," said Amy. "Well, I will in a minute. Here, *mon petit frère*, butter these while they're hot."

"What did you call me?" Barry asked suspiciously.

"Her little brother," said Susan. "What is it, apple seeds, grape seeds? Popcorn?"

"Oh, some dopey free sample again," Barry said, richly slathering the hot toast.

Amy put more bread in the toaster, took a bottle of milk from the refrigerator, and then reached into the hip pocket of her jeans. "It's really kind of mysterious and romantic and sad, too. Remember the beads? Well, you wouldn't let me keep them because the paint might be poisonous or something, but these seeds can't be. It says right here—" She brought out a small brown envelope, creased from being in her pocket, and read aloud.

" 'These tear-shaped seeds of the beautiful tear-drop plant were actually taken from the tomb of the beautiful young Princess Nen-a-tifa, when it was opened for the first time since the slender, young body was interred over three thousand years ago. Experiments have proved that these seeds will grow after being dormant for centuries, and you can have in your garden this rare and delicate flower which grows wild along the banks of the Nile. Its exquisite blossoms are said to represent the tears that flowed for the death of the Princess Nen-a-tifa.' And it's the same name and address, Mother, see?" Trustingly she held the envelope toward Susan. "Egyptian Imports, Limited. I'm sure they can't be poison, or it would have to say so . . . wouldn't it?" Her ardor died away before Susan's silence, as her mother stared at the envelope in her hand.

"How did you get this?" she asked without raising her voice or her eyes.

Amy said defensively, "We didn't open the door to anybody."

"The toast is done," said Barry. When nobody moved he went and got it himself. "Nobody rang the bell this time, either," he remarked. "I was coming down from the bathroom, and there it was on the rug. They'd pushed it through the mail slot."

"So you opened it up and planted the seeds."

This was the unexpected thing that you couldn't warn them about. They would be sure to do it and say, "Well, you never told us *not* to."

"Muth," said Amy's voice, a little smaller than usual. "I washed my hands after I touched them. But goodness, they're just like any old seeds!"

"Oh, relax and eat your toast," said Susan. She could even smile at the girl, she was so intent on not letting panic show through. "But we're going to take this envelope and a couple of pots to the police. You may have planted marijuana."

"*Honest?*" Amy looked more thrilled than dismayed. "Oh, wait till I tell this at school!"

At least Susan had a legitimate excuse to question the seeds. "They may have to send this somewhere to find out," she warned. "So don't go telling anything till you're sure."

"She shouldn't tell anything anyway," said Barry, the expert. "Because you can't tell who the pusher is, and you don't want to tip 'em off before the police catch 'em."

"Barry Linden, if you're insinuating that one of my friends is a dope pusher—"

"Stranger things have happened," said Barry, as if he were at least eighty and had long ceased to be astonished by anything.

Amy was red-faced and beyond words. "Both of you have your snack," Susan commanded. "And I'll heat up my coffee again." As Amy got her breath Susan shook her head at her. "Of course none of your friends are criminals, and these may be perfectly harmless old seeds. But I don't like the idea of these things showing up every so often. So we'll find out if the firm really exists and if it's respectable and so forth."

The conversation went on to drugs, glue, pills, LSD. Even Barry knew more about these than she wished he did, but he thought that smoking, sniffing, swallowing, and injecting were acts of a "bunch of kooks" who didn't know what real fun was. Amy felt obliged to take a more adult view. "Those people are very sick," she said.

"You mean stupid," Barry scoffed.

Amy gave her mother a resigned woman-to-woman look.

Susan sat there drinking her coffee, feeling as if at the same time she were balancing on the high wire, and if she turned her head or someone spoke suddenly, she'd fall. She wondered dispassionately if this was the beginning of schizophrenia. She could even remember feeling something like this as Leslie, being split into two persons, one here and one there.

"When are you going to take the seeds to the police, Muth?" Barry asked at lunch.

"Your father will be the one to do that. Tonight, probably."

"Hey, can we go?" Barry cried.

"Oh, yes, can we?" For once Amy was with him.

"We'll see," Susan promised.

"Anyway, they'll want to question us," Barry said importantly, and he and Amy looked solemnly at each other. The romantic legend of the Princess Nen-a-tifa was forgotten.

With Barry off to his ball game and Amy gone with her bicycle, Susan locked the doors and took a long bath. Hydrotherapy was supposed to calm the disturbed mind. In the bathtub she might be able to think constructively, which she hadn't been able to do so far.

Marijuana was a legitimate threat these days, therefore she was justified in taking the seeds to the police. This was a surface act, because she knew that David had sent the seeds; the name of the Lost Princess proved it. And she doubted that the seeds were harmful. The actual harm was in the act itself, a sly attack on Susan through her children.

So when the police found out that the seeds weren't dangerous, and then perhaps asked the New York police to look up Egyptian Imports, Ltd., and then found out that it didn't exist—or, if it did, it certainly wasn't sneaking necklaces and seed packets through mail slots in Somerset—

Then what? She couldn't tell them that Randall Emery was persecuting her under the delusion that she was his faded love.

All she would have gained would be Amy's probable loss of interest in the beautiful tear-drop plant by the time the inquiries were over. In what other way would David then try to reach her through the children?

She was cold now, and she dried herself vigorously but couldn't warm up; she bundled into bed with the electric blanket turned up and still had chills. Oh, good, she thought hopefully, I'm coming down with something.

Pneumonia right now sounded as enchanting as Paris. An oxygen tent would be a cozy place in which to spend a week. David wouldn't go near the children while she was in the hospital because his maneuvers had to be known instantly by her in order to be effective.

But she warmed up in spite of herself and, worn out by the day so far, she fell asleep.

CHAPTER 18

SHE WOKE IN late afternoon with the now-familiar sensation of having slept on guard duty and thus allowed the Viet Cong in. A fragrance of baked beans wreathed up the stairs and hurried her out of bed. She'd forgotten them. She ran down in her robe and put water into the sizzling pot, then went back upstairs and dressed. Outside an October Saturday afternoon in a small town drifted tawny and slow as a drowsy lion toward dusk.

Richard and Barry came home together, Barry talking baseball when they came in the door and not stopping until suddenly he got a powerful whiff of baked beans. "Hey, I forgot all about beans!"

"Quick, Susan, start talking while he's speechless," said Richard. Barry opened his mouth indignantly and Richard, smiling, held up his hand. "Run up and take your shower, and when you come down you'll be all rested up to tell your mother how you won the game."

Barry rushed off. "Sometimes I'd like to keep him

twelve years old, forever," Richard said. "Isn't it a wonderful age?"

"Yes, he's still too young for girls and cars," said Susan.
"I cherish every minute of it. . . . Did he tell you about
the seeds?"

"No, he's been talking the game ever since he came to
the store." Richard sat down in the tall-backed rocker that
had been his grandmother's. "Now what's this about
seeds?"

She told him. He picked up one of the planters and felt
around in it. "If they're fine seeds how can we find them
in here? Did she plant them all?"

"All. You know Amy. Thorough."

"Here's something." He brought it up between thumb
and forefinger. "Looks like a morning glory seed to me.
Could you call that tear-shaped? It's round."

"Do you know what marijuana seeds look like?"

"No. I suppose these days any well-rounded parent
should recognize all those things, so he'll know just what
his kids are growing in their little garden behind the garage."

"As far as our kids are concerned, Barry thinks smokers
and sniffers and that ilk are stupid, and Amy thinks
they're sick. They want to go with you to the police station in case there's a big international dope ring operat-
ing in Somerset. Barry insisted on sealing the seed packet
in another envelope to preserve any prints that are on it.
Of course, he and Amy have handled it, and I have, but I
didn't discourage him."

Richard laughed. "We'll take a ride down to the station
right after supper. Oh, Joe came into the store today and
mentioned coming over tonight."

"Yes. Ann and I have fixed it up." A safe evening. David wouldn't try anything again tonight, with the house full of people. . . . Yellow batter in a blue bowl. She'd always made the best johnnycake of anyone she knew. The recipe was her one authentic heirloom, passed down from Olivia's great-grandmother. Olivia used to have spells of cooking, and she was a good cook when she wanted to bother; she'd been raised on a New England farm even though she hated to admit it.

Susan was faintly surprised to find herself thinking of Olivia these days without the physical and mental reactions the name had always brought on. Maybe by being forced to remember so much she'd at last stopped being afraid of her mother, or hating her, or both.

Barry was back, refreshed in wind and voice, giving her a detailed account of the ball game, mostly in a code consisting of words like Wowee! Zap! Whoosh! Zoom! She nodded and made short comments as if she understood perfectly, while Richard read the evening paper.

She took out the bubbling pot of beans and put the johnnycake in. As she shut the oven Amy came in at the back door.

"Hi, everybody!" she sang out. She was in slacks and a Norwegian sweater, which she was pulling off over her head as she crossed the floor. Her cheekbones were flushed with the sun and wind, her eyes so brilliant that even Barry, as well as her parents, stared at her. They had always known she was pretty, but at the moment she was beautiful, an exciting and disturbing vision of the woman she might turn out to be.

"What's the matter?" she demanded. "Why is everyone staring? Am I so late? Is it really tomorrow morning?" She began to laugh. She was as exhilarated with herself and the day as Barry had been with himself and baseball.

"Simmer down, honeybunch," said her father. "No, you're not late."

"I hope you remembered to put your bike away," Barry said coldly.

"Of *course* I did, *petit frère!*"

"Hey, knock off that petty frair stuff. I'm sick of it."

"All right, *chéri!*" She ruffled his head. "Oh, you're a doll!"

"You must have had a good afternoon," said Susan, wondering if somehow or other she'd encountered Tracy Jones, Jr., and had actually exchanged a few words with him.

"Oh, it was wonderful! We went way out to Bartlett's Corner. Jenny's got this great-aunt—well, she's really a *great*-great-aunt. She's very old, but spry, and she was so pleased to see us, and kept telling us how nice we were to bother with her, and she made us cocoa. And *then*— what do you think?" She was talking fast, bouncing around the kitchen to keep her mother's eye while Susan moved from dresser to stove to sink. "She brought out a Ouija board. Did you ever hear of one? The name is made up of *Yes* in French and German. Well, we took turns, two of us at a time, and you put your fingers on this little thing, and it *moves!*" Her voice soared on the wings of fresh wonder. "Really, without you pushing it! It moves to these different letters and spells out words, and you can ask it questions, and—"

"Hey, what kind of goofy stuff is that?" demanded Barry. "If you don't push it, who does?"

"The spirits, of course. You ask, 'Is anybody there?' and

the little thing shoots down to Yes. Then you say, 'Who is it?' and they tell you. Mine and Jenny's was named Willy Hopkins, and he died in the war of 1812, only you don't say *die,* you say passed over. And the things he said to *us!*" She giggled. "He really had a line."

Susan was washing her hands. She kept on washing very thoroughly, and then rinsed for quite a while. After that she turned around, carefully drying her fingers, making a long process out of it. "That's enough," she said. She spoke to Amy, but she had a peculiar sensation that she was saying it to something else. *That's enough. I can endure no more.*

Amy stared at her. "What's the matter, Mother? Aren't you interested? Don't you think it's just tremendous?"

"Amy, slow down," Richard said. Susan felt him watching her while he spoke to the girl.

"What do you mean, he *died?*" Barry demanded. "How could he talk to you if he was dead?"

"His spirit could," said Amy in the lofty tone of one who belongs to the elite inner group. For Susan it was a horrid echo of tones heard long ago. "Mrs. Brackett told us about some of the people she's talked to. A man who used to be with Robin Hood, and a woman who was really murdered by her husband but nobody knew it. And oh, a princess who had her head cut off in the French Revolution!"

Susan moved her mouth. "Amy, will you—"

But Amy swept on. "Aunt Alice, that's what everybody calls her, says she has nice long talks every night with the man who used to live on that very same spot where her house is. He had a cabin there, and the Indians massacred him and all his family. He told her all about it when she first got him. He said he'd been so lonely all these years, because he couldn't communicate with anyone till she got that Ouija board and he could come in on that. He gives her advice, and everything."

"*Amy!*"

Had that sound come from her? It must have. Richard was standing up, Barry was watching her from eyes twice as big as usual. Amy was an extinguished candle. The voice that ripped on was Susan's, all right, but she could hardly recognize it and she couldn't stop it.

"I don't want to hear another word of this evil foolishness! I don't know what that crazy old woman was thinking of, but I do know you're never to go there again, do you understand? And if I can't trust you, you're not to go out on any more long bike rides. Do you understand *that?* Now please set the table. Barry, help her."

Amy's fine color was gone. With a strangled gulp she rushed past her mother. Barry moved as if entranced, with a furtive look back at Susan. As the door swung shut behind them, Susan glared defiantly at Richard, and turned to open the refrigerator with a trembling hand.

"What was the meaning of that explosion?" Richard asked mildly. "It didn't seem to me that Amy came to any great harm today."

"I think I'm the best judge of that."

"I don't think you are." He came and took the jar of pickles out of her shaking hand and set it on the table. "I don't think you're the judge of anything right now. Didn't you ever have fun with a Ouija board? If you didn't, you missed something."

"Those old people way back in the country really believe in those things? Seances and tea leaves and knockings on the walls—it's rotten, it's unhealthy, and I won't have Amy exposed!"

"Amy's too full of other interests to take it seriously, especially if we don't. Now you've gone and made a big issue out of it, instead of talking about it with her. Good Lord, Susan, what's come over you? You worry about trifles, or you invent worries. You're still brooding about *something*. I've seen your face when you don't know it." He stood over her, relentless; there was nowhere to run and hide from him. "When you're unhappy you're in despair or a panic; when you're happy you're like somebody delirious with a high fever. Talk about something being unhealthy! I thought you were over whatever it was, and I'd made up my mind not to pry, but good God, the way you're acting anybody would think—"

He stopped short, his face drawn in new deep lines.

"They'd think what?" she hammered at him. "Tell me what you were going to say, or don't you dare? They'd think I was crazy, is that it? Well, maybe I am. Maybe I always have been, only I hid it well. Maybe when you met me I was a fugitive from a mental hospital!"

Richard grabbed her by the shoulders and shook her. "Stop it, stop it!" he commanded. "Do you want to scare the kids to death on top of what you've done already?" His eyes glittered under the lids. It was like seeing a hostile and furious stranger looking out at her.

"You're hurting me," she said in feeble protest, not at the hurt but at the stranger.

"I want you to go to bed," he said in that hushed and warning voice, each word carefully emphasized. "And I'm going to call Dr. Levine to come over here and give you something to calm you down."

Her heart seemed to give a great bound so that it was beating and fluttering in her throat. A quieting injection, and then questions. *What is bothering you?* And, degraded by her lack of will, she would tell them, and that would be the end.

"No," she said. "Please don't call him. I beg of you, Richard, please don't." She tried to keep her voice down so he would see she was quieting herself. "I don't want him, I don't know him well enough. I'm all right now. Let's have supper."

"I don't think anyone's got much appetite." Under the ceiling light he looked ten years older, his coloring grayed. Oh my poor Richard, she mourned, what have I done to you? . . . Barry came from the dining room, shying out around her, awed.

"Amy's upstairs locked in her room and bawling," he reported to his father. "I had to set the table alone. Where's the butter and ketchup and stuff?"

"Where it always is," said Richard savagely.

"I'll call Ann right now," Susan said. "I can't face her tonight."

"You'd better let me speak to her."

"No." She couldn't bear to have him and her best friend talk about her as if she were a case demanding care and solicitude. In this way she still felt in control.

She dialed Ann's number, and then didn't know what to say. She could no longer invent decent excuses out of chaos. "Ann," she began bluntly. "Would you just as soon not come over tonight?"

"Oh, why?" Ann wailed. "I've been thinking about it all day."

"We can't have anyone in, that's all."

"One of the kids sick?"

She said stiffly, "I'm sorry not to let you know sooner."

"Well, if you can't give me any good reason." Ann was withdrawn and chilly with hurt. "Of course it's none of my business anyway." She waited, but Susan couldn't fill up the painful pause; she wanted to, she ached to, and she resented Ann for making her feel this way. Hadn't she enough to contend with?

"Goodbye," said Ann.

So there goes a friend, thought Susan. It was enough to weep for, but she couldn't weep. She went back to the kitchen. "I guess now we can eat," she said in a high clear voice. "The johnnycake should be done."

Barry said meekly, "Are we still going to the police station tonight?"

"No," said Richard.

"But shouldn't they know about the marijuana right off?"

"I said *No,*" Richard repeated.

Somehow the evening was got through. *Got through.* That was the only way to describe the wretched minute-by-minute progress of time. Amy didn't come downstairs; Richard carried a tray of milk and sandwiches to her door during the evening but she didn't answer his knock. As if someone had died in the house, Barry tiptoed around with nerve-racking caution, never mentioned his favorite television program, and of his own accord went up early to bed. Susan and Richard were left alone with whatever it was that had come to stay with them, all the more monstrous for being unseen. It was simply "This." There was no other way to describe it. They didn't even try.

Susan went to bed early. When Richard came up she pretended to be asleep. After he put his light out she knew they were both pretending. If sobs had overwhelmed her so that she couldn't hold them back, Richard would have turned to her. But what she felt was a barren soreness too dry and deep for the easy relief of tears to reach. She had become a desert, she thought, looking into the dark with burning eyes. A desert, where the ruins of pyramids stood.

CHAPTER 19

SUNDAY MORNING. She had slept after a while and waked with reluctance, knowing before she was conscious that everything was ruined. Richard was already up, and came in with a tray. He was not smiling. In the morning light he looked no better than he had last night.

"I thought you had better stay in bed this morning."

"I suppose it would be easier for you and the children," she agreed in a dead tone. "Is Amy up? I don't want her to miss Sunday School."

"They're both up, and they're both going to Sunday School."

Then we will be alone, she thought, and he will demand—what? As he moved things on her bed table for the tray, she said, "I'll go and wash my face." Crossing the hall, she heard the children's muted voices from downstairs. She felt for them the parched grief she felt for Richard, and saw again the desert that separated her from them, burning in the pitiless sun. . . . Like the desert in my paintings! she thought suddenly, with a brief attack of dizziness. Cold water restored her and she went back to her room and found the tray waiting, but Richard gone. She was glad of that.

The dryness was physical as well as mental. Coffee and fruit juice helped her mouth and throat, but nothing helped the desert in which she found herself. Time passed but she didn't know how, she remembered no thoughts, useful or otherwise. Then she heard the children cautiously passing her bedroom door and she knew they'd been getting ready for Sunday School. She imagined how they looked, all dressed up, scrubbed and combed, but without their usual sparkle. She felt a painful upheaval in the desert.

They were just beyond her door, arguing at the head of the stairs in piercing whispers. At least Barry's was piercing. Its hisses were all but visible in steaming spirals.

"I said we ought to take that thing to the police station ourselves, this afternoon! So they can get the *finger-prints!*"

"Oh, who cares now!" Amy flung back at him, and they started down the stairs, Barry still hissing at her in frustration.

If she opened the door and called to them now, would they run gladly to her, or would they look at her with those big eyes and that terrible awe? She couldn't stand that.

She got out of bed and walked around the room. When a sudden quiet in the house meant they had all gone out, Richard, too, to drive the children to Sunday School, she had a sensation of new freedom for her breathing. She went out into the hall and stood where they must have been standing when they argued; Barry frightened by what was going on, but still clinging to the exciting thing that had been promised. He couldn't imagine why it wasn't important any more. Crime was crime, wasn't it? There was no telling whose prints were on that envelope he'd so carefully sealed away—

Prints. Fingerprints. A pain shot through the crown of her head, and the desert blossomed. She'd told David he couldn't prove she was Leslie Danton. But what if *she* wanted to prove that she was? All along his chief weapon had been her fear of letting Richard know her past; she'd given it to him with her own hands in their first two meetings.

What she had given she could take away, because it didn't matter now. Everything was broken, anyway.

Once you faced that, you had faced every disaster that there was.

She dressed in one of her prettiest cottons, with special attention to her hair and lipstick, and added a light spray of her Mother's Day white violet cologne. She went downstairs and put on a ruffled dimity apron she'd bought at a summer fair at the Episcopal church, and began to get dinner. When Richard came back she was rubbing salt over the pot roast. He stopped short in the doorway, his expression guarded and wary as if he were braced for whatever wild thing she might do next.

"I'm sorry about last night," she said, matter-of-fact and busy. "*Sorry*'s a poor word for a fracas that disrupted the household, but it's all I can think of. But there is something bothering me, you're right about that." She stopped what she was doing. "I should have told you about it weeks ago. I was a fool not to. But I was trying to buy time."

He came to her and put his hands on her shoulders. "Buy time for what? Tell me one thing. Are you afraid you've got some incurable disease? Leukemia? Cancer?"

"No," she said.

There was a twitch around one of his eyes. "Then tell me what it is." He held her hard. "Tell me *now*."

"I can't. I have to get it all straight in my mind first. There's a beginning, a middle, and an end, as all proper stories should have, and I have to figure out which is which."

"Curiouser and curiouser," said Richard, attempting to crack the tension. He shook his head. "Susan, I just can't imagine what it is, and it's driving me up the wall."

"Don't try to imagine," she said quickly. "You'd better get ready for church. The children will be even more upset if neither of us shows up this morning." She smiled, and did so well she could see he was slightly reassured, at least about her sanity for the time being. "Oh, go ahead and stop worrying," she said. "After I've told you it probably won't seem much at all." *Just the end of the world, that's all.*

When he was ready to go he hesitated, squinting at her as if sun or smoke were in his eyes, then leaned forward and kissed her hard. When he'd gone she seared the meat and started it cooking on low heat, fixed a salad, and set the table. She wrote on the blackboard, "Sorry, no potatoes and gravy today, but ice cream for dessert. Eat your dinner and *don't worry*." She underlined the last two words with red and blue chalk.

Her business shouldn't take too long; she might be back before they had finished eating.

The operator gave her David's number. It wasn't answered at once, and as the ringing went on, she realized with dismay that he must have other ways of spending a fine October morning than staying indoors.

"Randall Emery speaking."

So sure he was gone, she was taken by surprise and couldn't speak at once, until he said, "Who is calling, please?"

"David, can we talk?" she said.

There was an instant change in his voice; there was always a change between Randall Emery and David Emerson, as distinct as that between youth and middle age, heat and cold, sun and rain. "We can talk," he said jubilantly. "But I'd like it to be face to face."

"Of course. Are you free now?"

"I'm going out to the Lyons' place at the Glen late this afternoon for drinks. Otherwise I'm at your disposal."

"*Good.*" That sounded businesslike. Firmly in control of events. "You know where our summer place is, you tried to find me there one day."

"Yes." There was no need for subterfuge. "But I missed your road."

She gave him instructions. "I'm leaving for there now. Can you follow?"

"Directly." His excitement leaped at her like lightning along the wire.

Driving along the shore road in the Sunday morning emptiness, she was careful not to think too far ahead. If you planned in too much detail you were often undone by one small obstruction. She was a little surprised at her poise. It was a rather pleasant, airy feeling after weeks of dragging leaden weights around.

The day grew steadily warmer and brighter. That

seemed a good omen; as if nothing bad could happen, nothing could go wrong in such marvelous sunlight. Never mind what happened later. The next hour had to be lived through first.

A horn sounded briefly behind her and she pulled over and let a long dark blue car go by. A dog bounced around in the back seat to watch her out the rear window. It was a wirehair terrier, so that could be one of Henry Lyons' cars. She hadn't seen whether there were one or two persons in the front seat. It would be just her luck if all the other cottagers decided to spend this wonderful Sunday on the cliff. David's Sprite certainly wouldn't be inconspicuous. But it was too late now to worry about gossip.

There were no other signs of life at the cottages except for the dark blue car by the Lyons garage, and the dogs running across their yard. She drove on to the end of the lane, and parked on the turnaround under the big spruce.

When she stopped the engine there was no sound at first but the birds, the cries of gulls that cruised in wide circles very far up, the chickadees and nuthatches in the woods, the drumming of a woodpecker. Then there was a joyous barking from the Lyons place, and a whistle.

She walked around the cottage and out onto the front lawn. There was still a spatter of fall dandelions twinkling in the light wind, and goldfinches twinkled among them as they ate the seeded ones. There were those horseshoe stakes she kept forgetting. She pulled up one and then the other and laid them on the top step, the horseshoes beside them, and then went to look at the ocean.

It was dark blue this morning with emerald gleaming through, white crests sparkling out to the horizon, a light surf swirling and foaming about the rocks below. On the

beach a young man was walking the tide line, stopping
now and then to examine something that interested him
in the glistening bronze-green windrows of fresh rockweed. She watched him, thinking how free and peaceful
he looked.

She herself maintained the airy poise she'd achieved on
the road. She didn't know how long it would last, if it
would stand up through the disasters that were going to
happen, but she hoped it would hold on at least through
the scene with David. Right now it felt indestructible. An
interesting phenomenon, if you were in the mood to consider interesting phenomena.

The wirehairs broke into barking, and shortly she
heard a car coming along the lane. It didn't stop at the
Newcome cottage next door but drove on to hers, and she
knew, with barely a tremor, that it was David's car. She
didn't move from where she was, watching the young
walker below as he knelt in the damp sand apparently
looking at bird tracks. A car door slammed.

In a few minutes David said in a low voice, "Leslie,"
and stood beside her.

"Hello," she said without looking away from the scene
below.

"Is that the path down to the beach, there beyond the
gate?"

"Yes. It looks steep, but it isn't once you get on it."

"Did that young man just go down it?"

"I don't know who he is. He's been walking around the
shore."

"Now we've got that over with," said David, "let's go inside."

She glanced around at him. He looked as sparkling as

the day. He took her hand in his. "Leslie, darling, when you called me this morning it was like a glimpse of paradise, if you'll let me be sickening. The gates are opening and they aren't going to close. Let's go inside, I don't want even the birds around right now."

"I'll go inside to talk if you want to," she said. "But I'm afraid you've misled yourself, David." The walker was now approaching the tide pool in the rocks. She turned away and he pulled her arm through his as they crossed the lawn.

"How have I misled myself, Leslie?" Nothing dimmed him. He was so obviously happy that she felt a maddening twinge of pity. "I feel like a boy this morning. No, I feel younger than I ever did when I was a boy. I'm becoming a youth in some blessed process of reversal."

He was so damned vulnerable! She hated the wound she was about to inflict, and now that it was time she found it hard to begin. She unlocked the kitchen door and they went in. He swung her around to face him, putting his hands on her shoulders. "Oh, my God, how I love you, Leslie," he muttered.

"David." She stood straight and stiff under his hands. "I didn't come out here to tell you that you're right and we belong together and I'm going away with you. I never had any intentions of that, and I never will." She looked earnestly into his eyes. "You simply must stop deluding yourself, and look at the truth."

He was as effervescent as if he really were a youth in his first love. "The truth is—"

"The truth is that this has to end here and now." She was very gentle. "You must leave town and never write me or call me. Do you understand?"

The change in him was appalling. He seemed to go gaunt and gray, aged all at once; the very color was leached out of his eyes. "I can't accept it. I won't let you go." His hands slid down her arms and gripped them just above the elbows like manacles. "The pictures tell the story and we can't oppose—"

"Oh yes, we can," she said. "Those pictures mean nothing. They were my romantic daydreams, wishful thinking. I was hypnotizing myself somehow. And everybody else was doing it, too. You did it and you're still doing it." She hadn't intended to be so brutal, but he left her no choice. "David, if you'd let me, I'd like to consider you my old friend. You are, you know." She smiled at him. "My *only* old friend, because Debra Jane Smalley who was my inseparable chum from the first grade to the seventh doesn't even know I'm alive any more."

"Not old friends," he said harshly. "Old lovers. That's what we are, and you know it. Through life after life we've come together again, only to be thrust apart. But no more, Leslie. *No more.* You can deny it till your last breath, but you still know the truth."

She sighed, wishing he'd let go of her before he stopped the circulation entirely. "Take the pictures and go away, David. Or sell them to Henry Lyons, if you can, and then go."

"*Sell* them?" He let go of her then, with the effect of casting her away from him. "Sell the pictures? They're my very life! Yours too, Leslie. As long as I hold those pictures I hold your life."

She felt the beginning of an enervating cold sweat, like the onslaught of illness. "All right, it's just a rumor that I've heard. Pure nonsense. So take them away with you. Maybe you'll find Nen-a-tifa in someone else, David." His expression grew outraged. She tried to humor his beliefs. "The night after I ran away from the gallery I went through hell, and I believe that if she ever did possess me she left me then, for good. Because the next day I was a different person, and I've been one ever since. Oh, believe me, David!" she implored. "She's gone to someone else, I'm positive! She's never come back, not even in a dream!"

"Because you wouldn't admit her existence. But she's been there. Why did you almost faint when you saw the pictures?"

"Because they reminded me of something hateful," she said desperately, then tried to pull back the despair before it got out of hand and made her shout at him. "David, if you don't take the pictures and go, I'll put in a legal claim for them."

"You can't." He began to smile and the impression of returning life was rather dreadful. "You're dead, remember? You told me I could never prove you're Leslie Danton."

"But I've remembered how it *can* be proved. My finger-prints are on file in Washington. When I was in the fifth grade a state trooper came and took all our fingerprints. They did it with every fifth grade."

"Your mother gave the pictures to me." His lips hardly moved.

"Did she deed or will them to you or did you simply take charge of them when she died?"

He didn't answer that but said, almost conversationally, "I thought you didn't want your husband, and inciden-tally the town, to know about your past."

"If they have to know, they have to." She shrugged. "You don't leave me any choice, except to offer *you* a

choice. Take the pictures and go, or stay here and give
them up. Even if my husband turns against me, he'll take
steps to protect me. He'll support my claim, and he will
have you arrested for harassing me." She went on, "Then
they will probably put you in the state hospital for obser-
vation, while they try to locate your people."

She paused, and he didn't move, there was not even a
twitch in his face. He might not have heard her. Perhaps
he had shut her out. She forced herself on, hating the cru-
elty of it.

"You could be locked up there tonight, David. Maybe
in restraints. Wrapped in cold sheets, or drugged. Or you
could be on your way, free. It's up to you."

Still he made no sign or motion. She said, "I don't give
a damn for the pictures. Whether you sell them or clear
out with them, I don't care. I'll even have them deeded to
you, or whatever one does, so you'll never have to worry
about losing them. But if you persist in bothering me, I'll
call my lawyer this afternoon."

Her threats seemed to bounce back at her like echoes
from a stone wall. She felt a monstrous fatigue, as if she
couldn't stand up much longer. Then David turned those
colorless eyes on her.

"You deserved your murder, after all. You must have
committed some terrible sin. You'll go on being murdered
in life after life."

"Perhaps," she said wearily.

"It was the same with Naomi, and Pauline. They had
no idea of what their true karma was, of course, until I
told them."

She was so tired she wanted to yawn. Then it got
through. *"When* did you tell Naomi and Pauline?"

He became easy and charming, giving news of old

friends. "Naomi—let's see. About three years ago. I was showing the pictures in Dallas—they're culture-mad down there these days—and Naomi came to my hotel. A handsome woman. Headmistress of a girls' school. She wanted to know what I was doing, how I'd gotten possession of the pictures, and so forth. She'd heard talk of my selling the collection."

Susan felt behind her for a chair and hoped she looked natural and relaxed when she sat down. "Did she want a cut?"

"No, she was upset at the thought. She still believed, you see. She'd thought for years that the pictures had disappeared for good. I was able to assure her I had no idea of selling, that I too was looking for a being I couldn't believe was really dead. But—" he shrugged, sighed, shook his head at grim memories. "The whole thing was tragic. I took her home and went in for a drink with her. We talked about the past, and the paintings. She wanted to read them again, she was sure they had messages to the world for today and the future. I thought I left her in a hopeful mood. But she died that night from an overdose of some barbiturate."

Susan couldn't help a gasp. "It wasn't *suicide?*"

"Who knows? The kindest thing would be to say she was keyed up, and took something for sleep that wasn't compatible with alcohol."

But that wasn't the way the conversation about Naomi had begun; there'd been no reference to a tragic accident, but to murder. She began to feel a tightness in her throat, cutting off her breath She was well acquainted with the symptoms.

Fear.

She wished she smoked. Lighting a cigarette would give

her something to do except that her hands would probably shake too much. "What about Pauline?" she asked, picking up a large blue mussel shell from the kitchen table and studying the pearly lining.

"Oh, Naomi gave me her address during our talk. She and Pauline exchanged Christmas cards each year. So later I looked Pauline up. She was living in one room in a Newark slum. A hopeless drunk."

"*Oh!*" Grief for Pauline forced out that cry of inarticulate regret. "I wish I'd known! Maybe I could have helped her through somebody else, somehow."

"She didn't need your pity," he said bitterly. "She was in a world of her own. She didn't even know when she left it."

"*You—*" She tried to stand up but he pushed her back and stood over her.

"Yes. As long as they lived they were a threat, just as they were three thousand years ago."

Her head was tilted back at an excruciating angle but she didn't dare take her eyes off him.

"But they'll live again, according to your beliefs. They'll always be a threat to you."

"And I will always have to kill them," he said tranquilly. "My karma to kill, theirs to be killed. Like yours. . . . This is something Naomi didn't discover," he went on. "It was the Fair Lover from the North who poisoned your food, because they'd given you to that idiotic young prince and I couldn't endure to think of another man touching you. You took the food, some Norse dainty, I presume, trustingly from my hand because *you* loved *me*. Afterwards I pretended to be grief-stricken." With the pleasant reasonableness of a teacher explaining a problem,

he said, "Now do you see? I have to go on killing you forever, or until the Masters set us free."

He took an elegant little leather flask from inside his
jacket, and unscrewed the silver cap, which was fastened
to the neck by a short chain.

She said faintly, "Tell me this. If I'd agreed to go away
with you, then what?"

"It would still have to be done, but not here. . . . It will
be too bad for your husband, won't it? Suicide is so much
worse than murder, I think. The survivors feel cast off,
somehow. Repudiated completely by the lost one."

"You are *crazy*," she said with a shaking mouth. "The
Lyonses are at their place. If they saw your car go by they
know you're here."

"Oh, I'm going to call on them. Very agitated. I came
out simply to walk the shore, you know, and I noticed
your car was here, but your house is locked up and there
was no sign of you along the shore, and could you have
had an accident? We'll search together. Henry and I will
then look in the window here and see you, and have to
break down the door. This drink—" he held up the
flask—"is so effective you'll be long past help when we
find you."

"Nobody who knows me will ever believe I killed myself."

"No? Haven't you been jumpy and nervous lately? If I
can see and hear the signs of strain, what about your husband? He must have noticed something. I've seen him on
the street a few times. He looks preoccupied. He knows
you've been keeping something from him, doesn't he?"
Eyes dancing, he took hold of her chin so she couldn't
turn her face from him.

"I don't take any kind of drugs," she stammered out.
"He knows that."

"But you could have gotten something from some doctor, not your own. If they can't find him, they'll think he
was too scared to admit it when the autopsy report comes
out. And nobody's going to wonder where you got this little flask. You must have bought it out of town somewhere,
a long time ago." Laughing as if they were concocting
some wonderful, hilarious, practical joke, he said, "You
know, the one thing that the family always says of a suicide is that he was the last person to do such a thing, that
there was nothing out of kilter in his life, no secrets, et
cetera, et cetera. So this will be very ordinary, just like the
others."

He put the flask on the table and, still holding her
chin, stroked her head tenderly. "Don't be afraid, my darling. It's only death. And who was it said that death is a
bridge along the road of life?"

"Tell me one more thing." It came out quite clearly,
the trembling had magically stopped. "Did you murder
my mother?"

"*No!*" The fingers clamped cruelly together on her
chin. "I did not! She was a mother to me, and I was the
child she'd longed for, the one who would never betray
her. You were born to her but you weren't hers. I was."

He pulled her head roughly against his chest and
reached for the flask. She thought, I will fight so that I'll
leave marks on the both of us. They'll know I never
drank that stuff willingly. She had her fingers crooked and
ready to go for his face.

Somebody knocked hard at the front door.

CHAPTER 20

THEY WERE BOTH startled violently out of their deadly intimacy. David swung his head irritably toward the sound, and in that instant his grip on her head shifted. She threw herself away from him, crashing against his right hand. The flask flew out of it and across the small kitchen; her surprise lunge took her after it. She swooped down on it as the only liftable thing within reach, recovered her balance like a furious cat, and as he came for her she hurled the flask hard at his face, and ran out the back door. She slammed it behind her.

She heard him cry out in pain, and kept on running blindly across the lane and plunged into the woods. There was a fluster of startled chickadees in the alders. Her feet thudded softly in the deep carpet of dead spills as she ran down the wooded hill, deeper and deeper into the unspoiled forest until she tripped on a root and went sprawling.

[THE FACE OF INNOCENCE]

An indignant red squirrel swore overhead and was echoed from another tree farther away. The chickadees had come after her in curiosity, and fluttered over her head as she scrambled up. She was too much out of breath with a cramp in her side to keep moving.

And then she realized there was nothing to be frightened about right now. The warning squirrels had stopped their chirring. No one else was coming.

She knew her way through these woods, but David didn't. There were a dozen places where she could hide like a canny deer and let him lose himself. Or she could keep on going and come out at the black road, but not walk out on it in plain view. She could go parallel with it but staying within the shelter of the woods until she came to the farm where they bought their milk and eggs all summer. From there she could call Richard as soon as she knew he was home from church.

But for now she could rest. This all had a horrid familiarity. It was like the time she'd run away from Olivia, after she'd escaped from the hotel and got lost in the crowd. But the forest had a sweet solitude and strength about it, as if the trees themselves would protect her. She crawled into a thick clump of little spruces and sat down. The chickadees settled in the tops above her, noisily sociable, but David wasn't likely to know about their friendly habits. Crows he might have noticed, they were hard to miss when they clustered raucously over any strange element in their woods. Thank God they were busy elsewhere today.

When her heartbeat had slowed somewhat she could hear other sounds clearly. The lovely shushing of the light wind in the tallest tops, a tractor somewhere in the distance, and then a car starting up on the lane and speeding away.

She knew from the sound it was neither hers nor the big Lyons car. It had to be the Austin-Healey. She could swear to it.

She waited until the sound died away. This happened quickly; if the wind had been different, or there had been no wind at all, she would have heard it after it turned off the lane and started down the steep dirt road. As it was, in a few minutes there was no more of it.

She began the return upward through the woods, accompanied by the chickadees. When she knew that a few more steps would bring her out into the open, she went very cautiously. All she could hear was the gulls beyond the cliff, calling and calling as if they'd discovered a school of herring.

The little green car no longer gleamed like a new toy under the spruces. She ran across the yard. The back door was shut and she had to nerve herself to open it, assuring herself that David couldn't have had a confederate whom he'd left hidden away to ambush her here.

When she went in, the place was unmistakably empty. One could always tell when there was no one anywhere in a house. The little leather-covered flask lay on the floor between the table and the door into the long living room. There was a glisten of liquid about it with a narrow trickle like a snail's track where the floor slanted a little.

From years of living with children and pets, her instinctive first action was to clean up something harmful, whether it was broken glass, cleaning liquid, carpet tacks. She grabbed a handful of paper towel from the roll by the sink and wiped any moisture off the flask, which still held some of the mixture. She replaced the cap and put the flask in one of the cupboards, then wiped up the floor. But the trickle had begun to dry and she was afraid of a residue that could attract an exploring puppy. And there was no water in the house.

It seemed very important that she clean it up before she left the place. If she didn't do it now she might forget it. David wasn't likely to be back; probably he believed that she'd put the police on his trail already. He might not even stop for his clothes but be already in flight.

She still had to tell Richard the truth. But she could clean up the poison first. Even if I am not with them the next time they come out here, she thought, they will probably have the puppy. And Barry's quite apt to pick up and eat a cookie or an apple after he's dropped it on the floor.

She simply could not imagine Richard's wanting her after he knew about her past. He might forgive her an illegitimate child—in fact she knew he would. But the rest of this business with its tinge of corruption and madness—even if he was sorry for the young girl Leslie, he'd hardly want her for a wife.

No water. But there was a whole oceanful outside. She took the pail which last week she had left upside-down on the drainboard, and went through the house and out the front door. The cold sea wind, fresher now, gave her a reviving buffet in the face. Revive me for *what,* she thought sardonically.

Crossing the porch she noted without interest that there was something different about it, but before it really registered she saw the gate on the cliff's edge open and swinging in the wind. For the first time since she'd escaped David she remembered why the escape had been possible.

Someone had knocked at the front door.

They must have come up from the shore then, whoever they were. Or *he*. Perhaps the walker. Why, she couldn't imagine; maybe he was parched for a drink of fresh water, or maybe—from the way he'd pounded—he'd cut himself badly on a broken bottle in the rockweed and needed first aid. She supposed she'd never know, she could only pray that he was all right wherever he'd got to, because he'd saved her life.

Maybe there'd been blood on the porch; maybe that was what had been different about it. Still carrying the pail, she glanced back at the porch indecisively, then went on toward the open gate. No matter what, she had to clean up that residue on the kitchen floor. But the mysterious knocker and his fate obsessed her, she owed him a debt. What if it *had* been a bad cut—an artery—

There was this man or boy; there was the girl buried as Leslie Danton. Oh, the debts she owed! For a whole new life given her, even if it hadn't been given to her to keep, only for eighteen lovely years.

As she reached the gate, she realized that the gulls' noise had been going on for quite a while. She'd heard it when she first came out of the woods. She looked up at them flying round and round, crying, the way they took to the air after someone fired a gun. Or if they saw a school of herring; that was what she'd thought earlier.

Or if there were something new and alien on the shore.

She looked down. A bundle of old clothes was wallowing lazily in the surf breaking over the ledges, just about where the tide pool would be at low tide, as if the bundle were caught there among the rocks. Maybe someone had plucked a scarecrow out of a cornfield and thrown it overboard somewhere as a practical joke, and the tide had brought it here.

Then, as a fresh wave broke over the tide pool, she saw the hand lift lazily out of the foam in a heavy, flopping wave and then fall down again. As the water pulled back she saw for a moment a drenched head, a profile, then it was buried in foam again.

This is what happened to him then, whoever he was. He had saved her life but nobody had saved his.

She left the pail where it was and went to get Henry Lyons.

CHAPTER 21

HENRY WASN'T in sight, but the joyous clamor the dogs raised at sight of her brought him around the corner of the house. She saw his kindly smile and nearly burst into tears. As he reached the gate where the dogs were jumping wildly, he ordered them away and opened it for her. "Come in, come in!" Then his voice changed. "What's the matter?"

"There's a man on the rocks below our cottage," she said. "I think he's dead."

"Here, come and sit down."

He put a supporting arm around her and walked her toward a chaise longue. "You're sure he's not just sunning himself?"

"I'm sure he's dead. He's in the surf."

"I'd better go and see. Lie back there and try not to be frightened." He went out of the yard. One dog stood on hind legs at the fence to watch him go, the other jumped up beside her and began to lick her ear. She hugged the firm little body to her, grateful for its ardent, wriggling life. She began to feel not better but stronger.

It seemed as if Henry was gone for a long time. No one came from the house. Evidently his wife wasn't with him today. The terrier gave up looking for Henry and brought her a tennis ball, trying to push it into her hand. The first one snatched it and ran, and they were off.

Then she saw Henry coming back along the lane through the swaying blue shadows of the spruces and out into the sharp sunlight. Though his bony face showed nothing, she kept staring at it as if in another moment it would give her some terrible message. Which it would; she knew it already. He came in and fastened the gate behind him, spoke absently to the dogs, and came toward her. He sat down opposite her and said, "Yes, he's dead."

She saw then that his shoes were wet, his slacks and pullover splashed with water. He looked reflectively at his hands. "I hauled him up to dry ground to make sure." Almost with an air of apology he went on, "I'm afraid it's someone we know. I don't know why I say it quite like that. It's tragic, no matter who it is."

"But I didn't—" she began, meaning she hadn't known the shore walker.

"Randall Emery," he went on. "He must have made a misstep on the edge of the cliff, unless he was actually down near the surf and had some sort of seizure." He looked at her with eyebrows raised. "Didn't you know he was out here? I saw him drive in not long after you got here."

She looked back, trying to think. She knew she was pale, and her ears were ringing. He stood up hastily. "Put your head down on your knees."

She obeyed, which gave her time and also took away the faintness. She kept her head down longer than she needed. I can't lie any more, she thought. I'm so tired of it. What harm if I did see David? And besides, he's dead. *He's dead.* It's really over this time. No doubt about it.

She sat up. He was watching her a little nervously, and she said, "I'm all right. Delayed shock. I've been fighting it off ever since I started over here. It was bad enough then, but to find out it's Da—someone we know." Had he caught that? He didn't look any different. She lifted her hair from her wet forehead. "He came to the back door and asked how to get down to the shore. I showed him the gate and the path down the cliff. But I thought he'd gone!" she exclaimed, remembering the car. "I'd gone walking myself, down into the woods. I heard a car start up and go away, and when I came back his car was gone."

"That's right, the car *is* gone!" They stared at each other in amazement. "I didn't see or hear it go, but then I was down on the beach myself for a while, letting the dogs run. Now how in hell—" He gave her a one-sided grin. "I'm sorry, Susan, I was thinking out loud. I can't understand about the car, unless he drove off and parked it somewhere, maybe back at the head of the lane, and *then* went down over the cliff to the shore. There's no easy descent there, but if anyone is sure-footed and nimble he'd do it all right."

He got up quickly. "Good Lord, what are we doing? I'd better call the police. Come in and I'll give you a drink, though Pris says a cup of tea is the thing for shock, not alcohol."

"She's right. Whisky would probably knock me flat, the

way I feel right now. But I don't want anything, thanks.
I'm not going to faint."

He went toward the house and the dogs bounded after
him and crowded eagerly through the door with him. He
called back through the screen, "Shall I call Richard?"

"No, he's not home, he's in church."

Left alone, she thought, It's over, it's really over. I don't
have to tell Richard anything. It will be buried now—
literally. But still she shuddered with a kind of woe. She
hadn't wanted David dead, only out of her world.

Why had he been on the shore? Suddenly, in a small
but exquisitely brilliant color movie, she saw David driving his car away, hiding it somewhere, going down the
cliff by the difficult descent Henry had mentioned; it was
well away from the first cottage in the row. Then he'd
come back along the beach to lie in wait for her, and an
accident had befallen him.

She knew there were holes in the vivid scene but she
couldn't think what they were. David had unmistakably
left, had come back, and now was dead. The circle were
all dead, now, except herself. But, true to the vicious little
irony that you never got anything for nothing, she had
given her word to Richard to tell him the truth.

Henry Lyons was coming back across the lawn, the dogs
jumping at the tray he held. "I've brought you a cup of
tea anyway," he said. "The state police are on the way. I
don't know what they'll make of his missing car. He must
have driven it away himself, but why?"

"He probably had a perfectly logical reason, but we just
can't think of it." She was glad to see how steady her
hands were.

"Yes, these whimsical actions have fogged up many a

case, I guess," he said absently. He looked into his drink, tilting the glass back and forth so that the ice cubes moved in it with a cool music. "Maybe he wanted to park the car somewhere in the open to avoid birds' droppings. That's a good reason."

"And for that it would have to be out of the lane," she agreed. They exchanged slight smiles, as if they'd just accomplished something important.

Then they heard the cars coming.

She told the young trooper what she had told Henry, that Mr. Emery had asked to be shown the way to the shore, and she had pointed it out to him. In her mind she was standing near the gate with David, and the hiker was on the shore below, but she saw no need to mention him.

He had nothing to do with it unless he had been the one to knock on the door, and that she would tell only to Richard. There was no conflict between her story and Henry's, because he didn't mention the hiker either, so probably the young man was well out of sight by the time Henry was letting the dogs run on the beach.

He knew when David's car drove in, she knew when David had joined her at the cliff edge, and she had an approximate idea of the time when the car drove off. Henry put forth the bird-dropping idea and the trooper said solemnly, "I've done the same thing myself. She's probably in a field or a clearing right close by. Those little critters can disappear behind a clump of alders."

The ambulance went off down the lane, and the trooper shut his notebook. "Well, I guess that's all for now. I know I can reach you at the Glen, Mr. Lyons. What's your home address, Mrs. Linden?"

She told him. He thanked them both and went back to the cruiser where the other trooper, who had been down on the shore with the ambulance men, was talking on the radio.

"I'll drive you home," Henry told Susan. "You and Richard can come back for your car when you feel better."

"I feel all right now," she protested. "Not brimming over with a sense of well-being or anything like that, but all right."

"Then I'll walk to your car with you," said Henry. "I always underestimate women's resilience. My wife tells me it's because I really want them to be frail little creatures forever on the verge of collapse. How would anybody analyze that, I wonder?"

"The Sweet Alice syndrome," said Susan gravely. "I used to think her whole name was Sweet Alice Ben Bolt. I thought it was lovely."

The foolish conversation got them to her back door without her having to think entirely of the last time she had come to it. Henry stood out by the car smoking his pipe while she went through the house to the front door and pushed the bolt across. Coming back to the kitchen she remembered suddenly what had taken her out to the cliff edge in the first place. There on the linoleum was the faint glisten of the dried sediment, like a snail's track.

She stood still. Finding the body had knocked the other thing from her mind for a little while, but now the compulsion was back to wipe out with her own hands this last horrible trace of David. She could look out by the window across the room and see Henry standing out by the car, smoking his pipe, looking placid and meditative the way most men looked with a pipe. She couldn't very well go call to him, "Thanks for waiting, but you might as well go back to your place. I've got to get some water and scrub the kitchen floor before I leave."

No, that wouldn't do at all. The pail would have to stay where it was, an innocuous object left carelessly by the gate, not subject to any doubts or questions. Like the horseshoe stakes that hadn't yet been put inside.

She went out quickly into the cool, bright air and the sound of goldfinches. The gulls had quieted after the strange object had been taken away.

Tomorrow, no matter what, she'd get out here to wash up the floor and take the flask from the cupboard. Portraying an efficient, no-nonsense woman, she locked the back door and went to the car.

"Drive carefully," Henry Lyons said. "Have Richard call me and let me know you're safe home."

"Call you here or at the Glen?"

"At the Glen," he said. "Somehow this place has lost its charm for me. For today, anyway."

CHAPTER 22

THE DRIVING WAS good therapy, both mental and physical. She was composed, if not peaceful, when she reached her own street. As she stopped the car behind the other one in the driveway, Richard came out the side door and stood looking at her. His face was unreadable, but she knew he must have been watching for her.

She didn't get out but sat quietly behind the wheel.

"Well?" he said without expression. "What's the story this time?"

"I'll tell you. I don't know what it will do to us, Richard, but it's time to keep my word. I'm not thinking beyond that. Are the children eating?"

"Amy was just about to dish up." He came down to the car and peered in at her. Something broke through the bleakness, and got into his voice. "What's *happened*, Susan?"

"Does it show?" Longingly she touched his cheek. "Look, slice off some meat for the children and tell them to eat and not worry. And will you call up Henry Lyons at the Glen and tell him I'm home? And then come out and we'll drive somewhere we can talk."

He went back into the house. She moved away from the wheel and tried not to wring her fingers off. Richard was about to find out what he'd really married. . . . Stop it! Think where we can talk in privacy . . . the Lang house; moldering mansion, the last one in on a dead-end road where some very rich old people lived behind high hedges and funereal evergreens.

Richard got in behind the wheel, looking surprised now instead of wintery. "Henry told me Randall Emery is dead," he said.

"Yes. I found him. Let's go to the Lang place. There shouldn't be any couples necking there at noon on Sunday."

"You never can tell," said Richard.

When she had finished the story she was in Richard's arms and had been there for some time. He had hauled her quite savagely there soon after Leslie's flight from the gallery, and had enfolded her so tightly she'd had to make him loosen his grip so she'd have enough breath to carry on with.

Now it was over, right through the moment when she knew she'd have to leave the kitchen as it was until tomorrow, and not knowing what tomorrow would be like.

He kept kissing her temples and muttering, "You little nitwit! I thought you were grown-up. How could you be so scatterbrained? Why the *hell*," he said violently, "didn't you tell me this a long time ago?"

"How could I know how you'd take it?" she pleaded. "I

had nothing to go by, no way to judge. It was horrible to me in every respect, and the longer I was away from it, the worse it became. Maybe if I'd had to spew out the whole thing to someone right after I ran away, the very next day, or even the next week, it would have lost some of its foulness. But I didn't have to tell. Everyone took me at face value, so I just buried the rest."

At the word "bury" she had a shaking chill, and Richard hugged her hard again. "Well, you're going to talk from now on," he said. "I've got a lot to catch up on. Everything I can think of I'll ask you, until we wear the subject out. Besides, there's your father and your whole background in Belmont Falls, all the good solid stuff you've been denying yourself and the kids."

"I always wanted to go back there and look around," she admitted. "There used to be an old Hedges homestead where my father was born. I can dimly remember visiting old people there when I was small, and they fussed over me and I loved that. I drank cambric tea from a little fluted cup, and there was a swing in an orchard. They're all gone now, but—"

"We'll go back," Richard said. "I promise you that. . . . As for the other business, it's not horrible to me. It's tragic, but not completely so, because you came through. You're a strong woman, Susan, or you'd have been gibbering by now, with this lunatic persecuting you."

"I expected to begin gibbering at any time."

He said dryly, "Yes, I remember the remark about being a fugitive from a mental hospital."

"That was unforgivable."

"No. Understandable. But let's erase it. And let's look at your background this way—I mean the part with your mother. If you hadn't had it, how would you and I have ever met?"

"I never thought of that!" She felt like crying, and burrowed deeper against his chest.

After a time Richard said, "What was that about no couples necking here at noon on Sunday?"

She giggled.

"I wish now I'd gone to see the damn' pictures," he said. "Where are they, do you know?"

"All crated, but stored away in the museum." She pushed away from him in fresh dismay. "Richard, he *murdered* Naomi and Pauline!"

"You told me that."

"But it's just hit me. He simply disposed of them so he could have the pictures all to himself. Richard, don't you admit that part is horrifying? That a young girl as innocent as Amy painted pictures that could cause all this corruption and insanity and *murder*?"

"When you put it that way, it does shake me up a bit," Richard admitted. "But look here, that doesn't make you responsible. The seeds of corruption and insanity and murder were there. Your mother was greedy, and cold, too, I'd say. You feel this Naomi was sincere, but she was unbalanced or she'd never have been drawn so completely into the circle. She'd have seen your mother for what she was. But Pauline sounds pretty down to earth."

"She was," said Susan. "Sometimes she'd call the whole thing 'show biz,' and Olivia would get mad and Naomi would simply not hear."

"But Pauline's business of fooling the gullible got her into the circle. And Emery, or David as you knew him, was a drifter, a misfit. You got hold of the word *schizophrenia* and thought it applied to you, but even at sixteen or seventeen you were able to think pretty clearly about it. You knew you didn't live most of the time in that world you were getting on canvas, and you didn't want to be there at all after a while." He stopped. "Listen to me. Your friendly neighborhood analyst. I don't know a damn thing about it, I'm just telling you what I think I see. And I see David as the schizophrenic and the paranoiac."

"And I brought it all out."

"Stop that! If it hadn't been you it would have been something else. It was just his luck your mother picked him up that night, because somebody else would have, sooner or later. And you don't know what never-never land he's been wandering in for eighteen years."

"He said he was married and had children, but he could be lying," she said doubtfully.

"Well, if he has any people they'll soon be turned up," he said. "Are you ready to go home and eat now?"

"I don't know about eating, but I'm ready to go home." She took his face in her hands and kissed him.

"I can eat," said Richard, "because I've got you back again. To hell with the rest of it." He started the car and drove around the curving drive, under the ivy-grown turrets and gables of the old mansion. "Our home away from home, bats and all."

"I'll always love this place now," said Susan. "Let's come here again and really neck, dear. . . . I just thought of something else. He turned white when I asked him if he'd killed Olivia. He was very upset. That business of her being a mother to him—he could have meant that, because it was the one time his poise seemed to be shaken. But I still think he lied about her situation at the time of her death."

"How so?" He drove slowly along familiar streets quieted with Sunday.

"Well, he implied that she had nothing left, that he'd helped her with her medical bills, and she left him the pictures in gratitude. She might have given him the pictures, but I doubt that she needed money. She was a businesswoman. She supported me out of the insurance my own father had left us, but she had my stepfather's insurance invested. For her old age, she said."

"Apparently she wasn't positive that the pictures would make her fortune," said Richard. "She hedged her bets."

"I told you she was a businesswoman," Susan said. "The man whose secretary she used to be took care of investments."

"What did you live on when you took to the road? Your father's insurance wouldn't have gone far."

"An old cousin of hers died, way back in the country. It turned out that he was an authentic miser, only his money was in banks and corporations, not in pots hidden in the cellar. She was his only heir. The inheritance was a big surprise, and she said it was meant for us to go."

They were almost home. She could see the house through the trees, and it was as if they'd been traveling years to get to it. She could hardly wait to see the children.

"You might be surprised by an inheritance yourself, if you go back to Belmont Falls and let them know you're alive," Richard said as they turned into the driveway.

"I doubt it," she said. "Olivia must have changed her will when she thought I was dead. Maybe she made David her heir. Maybe she felt as strongly about him as he did about her."

She started to get out but he didn't move. "What about

the pictures?" he asked. "Do you want them, if he didn't have legal title to them?"

She said, "If nobody of David's claims them, they can molder away in the museum for all I care. I never want to see them again, I have no interest whatsoever. Is that clear?"

"Quite." He grinned.

Barry was uncomplicated in his pleasure at seeing them both back. Amy was dignified, and didn't look openly at her mother. "I think I'll go do my homework," she said distantly to nobody.

Susan said at once, "Amy, I'm sorry I flew at you yesterday. It was inexcusable, and I apologize. But when I was around your age I had a very unhappy experience with Ouija boards and so forth, and I guess I was thinking about that."

"Did you really, Mother?" Amy was intrigued. "Will you tell me sometime?"

Richard squeezed Susan's fingers behind her back, and she nodded at the girl. "Sometime. Now your father and I are starved, and we're going to eat."

"Sit down and I'll wait on you! Mother, I fixed instant mashed potatoes and I made the most gorgeous gravy. Wait till you taste it."

"But don't try to guess what's in it or you'll throw up," said Barry.

Yes, she was home all right, and the miracle was that the children hadn't changed a bit since the last time she'd seen them.

CHAPTER 23

IN MID-AFTERNOON they were all down at the arbor at the end of the yard, gathering the rest of the grapes. The scents and sounds of the day had an uncommon poignancy for Susan. Not that she let herself dwell on the morning, but now and then she and Richard looked at each other across the yard and couldn't seem to stop looking. It was, in a way, like the first falling in love. "Hey, if you eat enough grapes and then lie down in the sun till they ferment, will you get drunk?" asked Barry.

A neat, unmarked car came into the drive, and a young man in sports clothes identified himself as Lieutenant Berman of the state police. "I thought you might be able to give me some information," he said. "I know a lot of people come and go in your store, Mr. Linden, and you know just about everybody in town."

"Gosh, is there a bank robbery or something?" Barry was all agog.

"*Or something* is probably it," Richard agreed. "If

there's anything for you to know, you'll find out in time. You two keep busy out here, and that's an order." He and Susan took the detective into the living room. "I suppose this is about Randall Emery," Richard said. "Thanks for the camouflage."

"I've got kids of my own, and they've got built-in radar. I always feel pretty good when I can sneak something in by them." Taking out a notebook, he said pleasantly to Susan, "They tell me that you found Mr. Emery. I have here the questions the trooper asked you this morning, and your answers. I'm afraid we'll have to go over them again in case we missed anything. You see, we're inclined to think he was dead before he went over the cliff."

Richard said, "Do you mean he was up there when he had the stroke or heart attack or whatever it was, and fell from that height?"

"Not exactly," said the lieutenant in a neutral tone that raised the hair on Susan's nape. "The preliminary autopsy report shows that he received a blow on the left side of his head that's not consistent with the damage done by the rocks, either from his washing around in the surf or from the fall. He didn't land on his head, by the way, or we might have missed this. And if the body hadn't rolled into that crevice, we might not have had a body. Not today, anyway."

Susan seemed to have run out of all reactions except a dreamlike disbelief in what she was hearing. "Somebody hit him, is that it?" Richard asked.

"We think so. There's a definite impression of an implement like a heavy poker, a pinch bar, something of that sort. We have men out there now searching the growth on the cliffside, and through the fields, but with the ocean so handy it's likely the weapon was thrown overboard. Now, Mrs. Linden."

"Yes," said Susan.

"You talked with Mr. Emery a few minutes at the gate when he first arrived, then you went about your own affairs. From the woods you heard a car leaving, and when you got back to your house, Mr. Emery's car was gone."

"Yes," she said again.

"We've found the car," he said. "It had been driven away from the lane down the dirt road a little way, then off into an alder swamp on the right, and then into a ravine. The person who drove it there had been careful to wipe off all fingerprints."

Richard said something and the officer answered. Susan thought, *The person*. A freezing phrase. Faceless and sexless, because it could be either *he* or *she*. She saw herself striking David dead, pushing his body off the cliff, driving his car away, leaving it in the aldery ravine, going on foot back through the woods; returning to the cottage and "discovering" the body. It was really so beautifully clear, as if she'd dreamed all the rest. But what would she have struck him with? That missing part spoiled the crystal perfection of the rest. There was nothing out there but turf, no big stones, nothing.

"We think he might have been struck away from the edge, maybe close to the porch," said the detective, as if answering her. "There were drag marks on the lawn, from near the steps to the gate."

"*That*'s what was different about the porch!" Susan exclaimed. Both men looked at her, the officer politely startled, Richard unalarmed, as if he knew she would make it all clear presently. "There was only one horseshoe stake there! When I first got there I put them both on the porch, I was going to put them in the house when I locked up. But I forgot. Then when I was crossing the lawn with the—when I came back and saw the gate was open, I thought there was something different but I kept on going, and of course after I saw the—uh—" The lieutenant nodded, his dark, intelligent eyes on hers.

"I didn't go back that way, so I didn't notice. But I know now it was the horseshoe stake. One was gone."

Dispassionately he wrote this down. "Mrs. Linden," he said then. "At any time out there this morning did you see anyone else besides Mr. Lyons and Mr. Emery?"

"I saw a hiker down on the shore," she said slowly.

"Can you describe him?"

"He was on the beach and I was on the cliff. I'm positive he was just some local boy out by himself."

"He was young, then. What was his coloring and how was he dressed?"

"I couldn't tell about his coloring. He wore a cap— like a ski cap. Tan, I think. And oh, just ordinary slacks and jacket—I'm not even sure about their color, whatever it was, blue or gray, or—" She shrugged.

She wanted to act stolid if not stupid, but she couldn't behave that way and hope to fool the lieutenant, who knew already that she was neither stolid nor stupid. She wished she hadn't let the word "boy" slip out. Then she could have pretended it had been just a figure down there which she hadn't noticed enough to tell whether it was man or woman, fat or thin.

When Berman had gone, after an exchange of courtesies

at the door, she burst out, "That hiker, if he was the one who came up and knocked on the door, saved my life!"

"They may never locate him," Richard calmed her. "He could be any one of five thousand people, the way you describe him."

"Why should he kill David?" she demanded.

"Why should anyone? But somebody did. You weren't the only person to hate and fear him, apparently."

She rubbed her arms absently, trying to warm the cold that raised the gooseflesh on them. "It's strange to think that somebody else around here was that intimate with him. It *was* intimacy, you know. A deadly variety of it . . . I thought I was the only one. Now it ties someone else in with the pictures, someone I don't know. *My* pictures." She looked at him in astonishment and he put his arms around her.

"You've repudiated them, haven't you? You don't really care about them after all, do you?"

"No, but it's the queerness of the whole thing that gets me and I use that word in its old sense, not this modern one that's ruined a perfectly good descriptive term. *Queer* is the proper word for this, not *odd* or *strange* or *peculiar*."

Richard laughed. "All right, use it. I won't pick you up on it."

Someone pounded on the nearest window. Barry was looking in at them. "Hey, what are you laughing about? When can we come in?"

"In fifteen minutes," Richard called back. Barry glowered, looked at his watch, and left, yelling to an invisible Amy, "Not yet, darn it!"

"Listen," Richard said to Susan, "you can't afford to get

all emotional about this man. Let's get it over with before the kids come in so you won't be bursting with suppositions. Let's say this fellow knew Emery, and knew he was going to be out there this morning. Emery might have told him, even bragged that he was going to transact a little business out at Heron Cliff."

"But that would be a foolish thing to do."

"Not to him. From what I've read of these cases they think they're superior to everybody else, nothing can stop them or catch up with them. Anyway, we're just supposing. . . . So the chap comes from somewhere else along the shore like an ordinary hiker. Now either he saw you two up there, gave you a little time and then came up and pounded on the door, or he didn't see you but knew what time David was supposed to be there."

"This is so vague and full of *ifs*," she said.

"At this point my vague guesses are as good as anybody else's. Now I'm saying he came out there intending to murder Emery, but maybe he wanted to settle something with him, and he thought the shore was a good place for privacy."

"With me up there?" she said skeptically. "And Henry at his place?"

"He could have got Emery to go farther along the shore with him, well away from the cottages. And maybe he was happy to interrupt what he thought was a lovers' rendezvous—"

"Stop that!" she said, blushing with anger. Richard was gazing raptly into space, absorbed.

"Maybe it's nothing to do with the pictures, but a simple matter of another woman," he said, as if he'd just caught the wise old trout everyone had been after for years. "This is a boy friend or a husband. Going to beat up the cultured and cosmopolitan charmer who's turned somebody's head. How do you like *that?*"

"I don't like anything about it," she said, "because all I can think is that he saved my life."

"But, my darling, if there are extenuating circumstances, and he grabbed up that stake without premeditation, he might get away with manslaughter. If they get him, that is. And he still might have a good alibi."

"I hope so," she said gloomily, and then a new disaster hit. "But *I* won't have one. Who can prove I was in the woods all that time?"

"Who can prove you weren't? And, as far as the world goes, what's your motive?" He took her into his arms again. "There's nothing for you to be afraid of."

"As a good wife I'm supposed to believe your every word," said Susan. "So I'll try. What'll we tell the kids."

"That Emery met with an accident this morning, and you found him. They'll be hearing it later, anyway, so let's get it over with. We don't have to mention the foul-play angle now."

Barry was rather ghoulishly excited; it was more or less unreal to him, a television drama. But Amy was old enough now to be touched by sudden death. "And poor *you,* Mother, finding him!" Impulsively she hugged her mother.

"I suppose it's no sense telling you two not to discuss it at school," said Richard. "But please don't embroider it."

"I won't, but you never can tell about *mon petit frère,*" said Amy. Barry rose to it.

"Whaddya mean? You knock it off, or I'll—"

"You'll nothing," said Susan sharply. "Both of you knock it off, to use your own language."

"Mother, did you faint on Mr. Lyons' doorstep? Did he

chafe your wrists, the way they do in stories?" Before
Susan could deny it Amy was off again. "I think he's
dreamy. For a much older man, of course. He's so distin-
guished and gentlemanly. When he smiles at you he
makes you feel like a lady."

"Not me he doesn't," said Barry. Amy ignored him.
"You know who he always makes me think of?" she asked
her fascinated parents. "Richard Cory. We just had that
poem in English. It sounds exactly like Mr. Lyons. Except
for the last line, of course. He'd never do that." She
laughed merrily at the mere idea. "He's got everything to
live for and make him happy, a nice wife, horses, dogs,
cars, travel—"

"*Money*-money," said Susan. "We know. Do you have
any homework to do for tomorrow?"

They left reluctantly for their rooms. When they had
gone, Susan made coffee and she and Richard sat with it
at the kitchen table. The clock ticked loudly in the silence between them. Richard is worrying about the hiker,
she thought. She herself was too bone-tired to worry about
anything.

He said suddenly, "Henry Lyons might not put a bullet
through his head, like Richard Cory, but he might be
strongly tempted to do it to someone else. Or bash a skull
in with a horseshoe stake."

"Are you *crazy?*"

"No. At least no crazier than you are for thinking you
look guilty."

"But Henry Lyons!" she objected strenuously. "It's like
accusing—well, not exactly God, or Albert Schweitzer,
but—"

"Why not?" he asked reasonably. "The hiker's nebulous. You saw him, and Emery did, but he could have been just a hiker. Who's the other person who was indisputably there the whole time?"

As she stared at him, he said, "Who introduced Emery in Somerset? Told Marshall Jury about him and recommended the exhibit. It was Lyons. Joe told me."

"Marshall told me Henry saw the pictures in some little place in New York. But that doesn't prove anything. Henry's interested in anything far-out in art."

"Consider my theory, though," he urged her. "Look at all the angles. Anything's possible. Anything could connect Lyons and Randall Emery. Who'd ever suspect a connection between Emery and Mrs. Richard Linden? . . . What are you seeing?"

"David came along one day when I was talking with Henry. I was in such a hurry to escape before he reached us that I was pretty curt. Henry turned away so fast I thought I'd offended him, and that was why his greeting to David was so short and cold." She put her fingers across her mouth. "Maybe he wanted to avoid David too. But David told me this morning, only it feels like a year ago, that he was going to the Glen for drinks tonight."

"That's no sign of perfect amity," said Richard. "I'd like to find out the name of the place where Henry saw those pictures."

"Don't talk for a few minutes," said Susan. "I almost think Marshall told me the name of the place. If I could just get hold of it." She rested her forehead on her hands and shut her eyes. Lights and faces whirled in the darkness, words and voices. Good Lord, how would she ever sleep tonight, with all this going on in her brain?

"That's right, apply some of that old ESP," said Richard mischievously, and she felt a great wave of gratitude for his teasing her about her past instead of tiptoeing around the subject. But feeling like this made it difficult to concentrate, and so much had happened between that long-ago telephone call and now. With a great effort she recreated the conditions, spoke with the assistant, heard Marshall's testy asides, and then his fluent, rolling monologue.

"The Vine and Fig Tree, of all things," she said aloud.

CHAPTER 24

THEY HAD PLANNED to go out Monday morning and wash the kitchen floor and take the flask away from the cupboard. But with the news of the murder they decided not to go until there was no chance of running into the police on the spot.

Instead they drove to New York, leaving right after breakfast. Susan had protested.

"I don't know what you hope to achieve. The police have probably already been there, trying to find out something about David, if they aren't there this very moment. And if there was any reason at all to suspect Henry they'd be on to it, wouldn't they?"

"In Somerset," said Richard, "there is no reason to suspect a Lyons *if:* A, he isn't caught in the act, and B, there's a mysterious hiker to look for first."

"You make our police sound corrupt," she objected.

"Not at all. They simply find it impossible to see Henry Lyons as a murderer."

"But apparently *you* don't find it impossible," Susan said.

"That was just a hypothesis."

"Then why are we going to The Vine and Fig Tree?"

"I just want to see the place, that's all," he said.

"It makes me feel sneaky, Richard. Really."

"Look, we're in New York for the day, we go around to the place out of curiosity. Is anything more normal?"

"It's morbid. Ghoulish, like Barry wanting to go out to the cliff and see the exact spot where the body was." She had gooseflesh inside her warm clothes, and the frost-bright morning was dimmed.

"Listen, my dearest wife—I have three, you see; dear, dearer, and dearest—they haven't got the hiker yet, they haven't found out anything about Emery yet. Maybe by tonight there'll be a forward movement in the case, and we can decide then what we're going to do. But for now it's low water slack, and we're away from Somerset and that damned telephone for the day."

She couldn't question that. The telephone had rung constantly since the news had come out on radio and television last night. And each time that she answered and had to make conversation about the discovery, she had felt sicker and sicker. It seemed as if she were lying each time, even though her relationship with David was certainly not the business of any of those people.

The hardest thing was talking to Ann. She and Joe had come over during the evening, and all Susan's guilt at keeping Ann in the dark for so long had almost overwhelmed her into blurting out the whole thing to the Ellenburgs. But Richard seemed to know, and a glance from him was at once control and comfort. "Let's start having

some old-fashioned fun this winter, Ann," she said impul-
sively. "We used to love to go to the movies, remember?
Let's start going again. I've been hating myself lately, and
I've decided to be frivolous now and then."

"I'm with you there, chum," said Ann. "Life's too
darned real and earnest these days. We need some foolishness for leavening."

"Queer thing," Richard mused, as they drove through
the autumn landscape, "when I walked out to the car with
Berman yesterday he said that according to Emery's papers he was a complete loner. No hint of family or even of
friends—no pictures, letters, anything of that sort. His
driver's license was issued in Detroit, but that was about
the only thing to pin him down."

"That's where he came from," Susan exclaimed. "And I
know he had parents there, because he used to talk about
them. Of course they could have died in eighteen years,
but he said—this time—he had a wife and children."

"Could be, but not in Detroit. I called Berman this
morning, after the kids left for school and you were getting ready, to tell him we'd be gone for the day. He told
me the Detroit police had checked out all the Emerys in
the phone book, and the only Randall was nine years old.
Nobody was missing; at least, not that anyone would
admit."

She tried for a smile. "There's another mystery. Maybe
somebody's glad he's gone, so they're not saying a word.
. . . This is just *awful*. I wanted to be rid of him, not have
him dead!"

"Apparently somebody else wanted to be rid of him,
too, or at least to give him a good scare, if they didn't intend to kill him. . . . I wonder if The Vine and Fig Tree

is too poor to have a telephone." He pulled up at a phone booth near a filling station and went in to study the New York City directory. She saw him writing something down, and he came back smiling.

She adored everything about him, the way he walked as he crossed the pavement against the brisk breeze that whipped at his topcoat, the long creases in his cheeks from his smile, the way a cowlick flipped up from his crown, and the very set of his ears. When he got into the car she said, "Richard, I love your ears."

"That's the most passionate thing that was ever said to me. For that I would follow you across the seven seas. They've got a telephone."

"I still don't know what you expect to find there."

"Psychic emanations, maybe. Remember my grandmother's experience. I may have inherited her gift, and give you some real competition." He put his hand on her knee and squeezed it. "Hey, there's a real groovy motel. Hows about stopping there, baby?"

"Yes, let's, instead of going to The Vine and Fig Tree!"

Richard laughed.

The Vine and Fig Tree was in a basement apartment. The front windows held some arrestingly brilliant paintings, and as they went down the steps Susan tried to see what the pictures were about, but they were great clashing masses of color that seemed to be their own reason for being.

Going in, she felt self-conscious, but the new Richard escorted her as if he had been in and out of such places all his life. The front room was the gallery, and at this hour in mid-morning there was only a scattering of people there, most of them young but not obviously hippy types, though there was some long hair and exotic apparel. There were a few older people, casually dressed but no more so than some of the Somerset artistic types.

Susan, still set against the whole idea, was too embarrassed by it to look around. She walked immediately to a painting where there was nobody else, and began staring at it. The title was "Thou and I," which didn't help a bit in the interpretation. She gazed so hard her eyes felt glassy. A strong whiff of fresh coffee made her think nostalgically of her early breakfast.

Richard joined her, and she whispered, "I can't figure out if that brownish shape there, with the gold edge, is *thou* or *I*."

"The empty space is I," said another voice, not Richard's, and as piercingly clear as Amy's could be at times. The girl stood by Richard's elbow, arrow-slim in mini-jumper and striped turtle-neck, her yellow hair strained back in satin smoothness from her brow and falling down her back. "*I* is a ghost, you see."

"You *are?*" said Susan, and the girl giggled. Her ridiculously thick eyelashes made her look like a Disney baby animal.

"Susan," Richard said, "this is Victoria Holmgren. She's a kind of hostess."

"Goodness, are you old enough to be out of school?" asked Susan.

Victoria wasn't offended. "I go to ballet school, and I have this morning free." She looked at her watch. "Till eleven-thirty, anyway. Would you like a cup of coffee? Nita's just finished a fresh batch of doughnuts and they're terrific."

"I'm starved," said Susan.

"So am I," said Victoria. "Oh—do you want me to explain the pictures first?"

She was obviously more interested in the fresh doughnuts. Richard said, "I think we can understand them better on a full stomach."

She grinned and glanced around, and then whispered, "You won't be able to understand them then, either. Even the artist doesn't. I think he was on pot or acid when he did them, honest." She led the way into the back room. Susan, looking at the straight back and the fall of shining hair, wondered hopefully if the girl were as innocent as she appeared, and how she managed to walk unharmed in a jungle where pot and acid flourished.

"I've got a couple more, Uncle Ed!" Victoria sang out.

"Is he really your uncle?" Susan asked.

"Yes, and I live with him and Nita while I'm going to school. . . . Uncle Ed, they'd like coffee and doughnuts."

Uncle Ed was stout and wore glasses well down on his nose. He shook hands firmly, and said in a Vermont accent, "Take a seat, folks. Vic, you look out for 'em like a good girl. Arnie just called and he's in a bad way. I have to go."

"It *is* acid, isn't it?" Vic looked distressed.

"I'm pretty sure." He shook his head at Richard. "Real gifted boy. This show's brought some serious people. But he's escaping—or thinks he is. And from what?" He shook his head again. "Sometimes I think he never should have left home."

He went out through the gallery, looking worried. Vic said, "Imagine trying to drop out just when you're getting somewhere. I can't understand those people." She went off to the kitchen. Richard and Susan sat down at one of the long trestle tables of scrubbed wood. The place was more dimly lit than the gallery, but it smelled and felt clean. In a shadowy corner someone was playing a guitar in gentle melodious chords. The few other people at the tables talked in low voices, or read if they were near a lamp. One boy was obviously studying. At the end of the Lindens' table a woman was writing in longhand. Her hand moved on and on, giving the impression of unreeling miles of smooth, rhythmic script. Utterly absorbed, she hadn't even looked up when they sat down. From the corner of her eye Susan could tell when she turned a page in the big loose leaf notebook and started at the top again.

"It's pleasant here," she said to Richard. "I can see why Henry likes it." Then she recalled their discussion of Henry, and she fell silent again, and wished they hadn't come. Vic came back with a tray. She'd included a mug for herself, and the doughnuts were puffy, golden, and aromatic.

"Whom do we pay for this feast?" Richard asked.

"Nobody. It's Uncle Ed's idea of hospitality. If he hadn't had to go and see Arnie, he'd be sitting down here getting your life history. He's so curious about people. It must be a Vermont trait, don't you think?"

She asked it so seriously that Susan smiled, and Richard said, "It's a human trait, that's for sure." He didn't glance toward Susan but she knew what he was thinking. Had Uncle Ed gotten David's life history?

Richard said, "We must bring our daughter here. She's

becoming really interested in art. We just had the Leslie Danton show, and Amy was very much impressed."

Vic's eyes widened. "Are you from Somerset? Where Mr. Emery was—"

Susan looked into her cup. Richard nodded somberly.

"Isn't it awful?" Vic exclaimed. "A plain clothes detective was here last night asking Uncle Ed about him, trying to find out who he knew in New York, and so forth. But we didn't know anything about him except when he was here."

"What kind of man was he, Vic?" Richard asked, as adult to adult. "When something like this happens to a person, you wonder what he really was like, inside. What was there about him that made someone hate him that much?" She was watching him with fascinated eyes and he said softly, "I don't mean anything bad, necessarily. Some people can't stand goodness in other people, you know. Or charm, or talent, or good looks. So they strike at it, like a jealous child."

Vic was plainly flattered by his approach, and intended to do her best. She frowned, laced her fingers and looked at them with her head on one side, then gazed long and earnestly at Richard. Amy had the same mannerism. "Well, it's really hard to say. He saw me as a child, you know, so I never had a chance to talk with him as we're talking now. Oh, he was always very nice, very *gallant*."

She gave it the French pronunciation; Amy all over again.

"When he was in Somerset," Susan said, "he talked about an occult significance of the paintings. He said the artist had been in a trance when she painted them, and they were really messages from the past ages."

"Oh, I didn't hear anything like that!" said Vic. "Gosh, that sounds fascinating!" She was clearly disappointed at what she'd missed. "But he used to talk a lot with Mr. Lyons. You must know him, he's from Somerset, too. Maybe Mr. Emery told him about the—uh—occult significance."

"Oh, yes, we know Mr. Lyons," said Richard smoothly, as Susan took a hasty gulp of coffee. "As a matter of fact, he sponsored the show in Somerset."

"Now, Mr. Lyons is *really* terrific," Vic stated. At the rising emphasis, the woman at the end of the table looked up, studied the girl thoughtfully, caught Susan's eye, and they exchanged slight smiles. Then she lowered her head and went on writing. Susan retained an impression of ruffled dark hair, thick, dark brows like charcoal strokes above wide-set eyes that smiled more than her mouth did; a strong smooth throat.

Vic was still talking about Henry Lyons. It was Amy all over again, and Richard Cory. "Honestly, a man like him makes some of these boys look so *uncouth*. I'll bet he was sick about this. He's so nice, it must be awful to think he was kind of responsible for Mr. Emery's death."

Richard raised his eyebrows. "How responsible?"

"Well, he got him into Somerset, didn't he? Not that he'd ever dream of someone killing him. But Uncle Ed says you never can tell what will happen in a small town. Where he comes from in Vermont they have at least one murder a year."

The woman at the end of the table was looking up from her work again, her chin on her hand. She was gazing over Susan's and Richard's heads toward the door from the gallery. The smile was back in her eyes but with a difference.

It was on her mouth too, in a gentle curve; the whole effect was of quiet radiance.

Susan turned instinctively toward the door and saw the face of Henry Lyons. It would not be true to say it reflected the woman's glow. It had its own illumination.

And then he looked down and saw Susan.

His expression changed at once to the mild, kindly one of every day. He said, "Why, Susan, what a pleasant surprise." He came forward. Richard looked around and got up, and they shook hands.

Vic said, beaming, "Hello, Mr. Lyons, we were just talking about you! And it was all good, too."

"I'm glad to hear that, Victoria. Well, what brings you people to such a far-out spot as this?" He sat down beside Richard. "Vic, would you get me some coffee?" She sped off, her hair flying.

"Curiosity," said Richard. "We're in town for the day, we were passing through this street, we saw the sign, and —" He shrugged. "Susan's taking an intellectual approach to the paintings, but I'm purely materialistic about these doughnuts."

"Nita's a genius," said Henry. "I can't say the same for the current exhibitor."

"What will happen to Emery's paintings, by the way?" Richard asked.

Henry smiled at Vic and thanked her for the coffee. "No doughnuts, thanks . . . I don't know. I suppose they'll go to his next of kin, if they ever turn anyone up."

"Vic!" someone called from out of sight. She was gone again.

"How did they ever come into his hands, anyway?" Richard said. "Did he ever tell you?"

Oh, let's go, let's go, Susan pleaded silently. You didn't

see her face and his, Richard. You didn't see anything. Let's get out of here. . . . Her heart was thudding so hard it seemed to be half into her throat, and yet in her stomach too.

"He said the mother of the artist willed them to him because he took care of her in her final years." Henry did not look toward the woman, who had begun writing again almost before he sat down.

"Richard, we really should go," Susan said more abruptly than she'd intended. "I know this place is seductive, but we've got errands." She stood up.

"I'm sorry to have you go," said Henry, also standing, "when I've just arrived."

"We come to New York so seldom," she said, forcing a smile. "And we try to do so much."

Richard, getting up more slowly, said, "Was there anything more on the case before you left home?"

"They think they have the hiker. Or rather *a* hiker."

The word was a punch in Susan's stomach. She distinctly remembered, in that moment, being punched hard in the midriff in a fight with a boy when she was seven. Now she couldn't sit down hard, sick and gasping. She had to stand there, glad the light was dim, not able even to start moving toward the gallery. The men's voices were at first a meaningless buzzing in her ears, then words became clear.

". . . someone at the harbor. They saw him coming from that way, around the base of the cliff, just before noon."

"Good enough," said Richard. "What does he say?"

"The news report didn't go that far. I heard it on my car radio when I was driving in. They'd just picked him up."

"Well, it will be something if they clear this case up

within twenty-four hours, won't it?" Richard asked. He took Susan's elbow. She gave Henry Lyons a steady smile.

"I don't know what I'd have done yesterday if I'd been alone out there. If I didn't thank you properly, I'm thanking you now."

"You're welcome, Susan," he said gravely. "I'm glad I was there to help."

He still stood there as they left the room. *I will not look back,* Susan promised herself, and him too. *I will not look back.* She walked fast ahead of Richard toward the outer door, called goodbye to Vic, who was talking with two bearded young men, and was out on the street well before Richard.

"Well, what did you find out?" she asked him defiantly.

"I might have done better if Henry hadn't shown up just then."

"Pumping a child. I'm ashamed of you."

"It seems to me you threw in something yourself. The occult significance and so forth." He laughed at her. "Come on. Got your shopping list, or did you lose it in your agitation?"

"No, I've got it." She wanted to tell him at once what she had seen when Henry came in, but a busy New York sidewalk wasn't the place. She didn't know how to begin, how to describe the two faces and the effect they conveyed of almost tangible lines of communication shimmering between them. Remembering it gave her the same sensations all over again.

"Let's walk through the park," she said.

The sun was warm, and Central Park was full of people enjoying it. There was no bench where they could sit alone and talk, and the longer she put it off the less she

wanted to tell it. By accident she had witnessed something tremendously private, and she wished she could assure Henry Lyons that it would be kept secret. Besides,
maybe she was wrong. She hoped so, she prayed so. Maybe
there was nothing but a warm friendship, maybe the
woman loved *him,* but knew it had to be denied. Good
Lord, forget it! she told herself. Worry about that hiker.

Until now she'd seen him as her rescuer. But what if he
were saying at this very moment, "Sure, I was out there.
But I never touched anybody. I'll tell you what I did do,
though. I went up to the end cottage and knocked, to ask
for a drink of water, and I heard this man and woman
shouting at each other, see? She screamed, and something
crashed, and man, I beat it out of there."

What if Lieutenant Berman were waiting at the house
when they drove in? *Mrs. Linden, would you answer a few
more questions, please?*

Richard was saying something. She gave him a dazed
look and saw strain around his own eyes. That poor man,
she thought angrily, he's thinking about it too, and it's all
my fault for not telling him the truth in the first place.

"You're right, coming to New York for the day was a
good idea," she said vigorously. "Let's not worry about
what's going on in Somerset until we get back there.
That's what you suggested this morning." I got through
something once, she thought; I'll get through this, too.
She smiled at him and squeezed his arm; he squeezed
back, and said, "For auld lang syne, let's go to the Museum of Natural History and look at the elephants."

The rest of the day was a success in terms of determina-
tion and courage. If she felt quite a few years older, she

also felt infinitely stronger when they turned in to their own street at dusk. Seeing the lights streaming out of the house and no cars waiting, they both relaxed slightly, looked at each other with the tight grins of comrades in danger, and went almost happily into the house.

The kitchen smelled of baking gingerbread. Barry was doing homework at the table, and Amy was on the telephone, giving the instrument as much intense charm and attention as if it were Tracy Jones, Jr., in person or, at the other extreme, Henry Lyons.

"Oh, here they are now! Would you like to speak to my mother? All right, I'll tell her. At seven o'clock ... thank *you*, Lieutenant Berman." She hung up and turned around, shining. "He's got the nicest voice on the telephone. He's coming over at seven."

"Hey, they got the guy who did it!" Barry exclaimed.

"They don't know who did it," Amy reproved him, "and a man's innocent till he's proven guilty." The timer rang, and she rushed to take her gingerbread out of the oven.

So more courage was called for, to get through dinner with two children who wanted to talk and be listened to, and who wanted to hear all about New York. Richard vetoed any more discussion of the case. How queer it was, thought Susan, that David had been so disturbingly alive yesterday morning and now he was nothing but two words: The Case. What was that policeman going to say? What was *she* going to say?

When the meal was over and Richard went into the living room with his paper, he gestured with his head for her to come, too. She followed, her throat tight. He said, "I think we should call Joe and ask him to come over."

"Why? If I have to tell the whole story, why can't I simply tell it?"

"Because talking to the police is not simple," he said patiently. "Berman will probably want you to have your lawyer present, too."

She had the physical sensation of losing color, and Richard moved swiftly and took her by the arms, tightly. "You'll be all right, darling," he whispered. "Don't be frightened. Nothing's going to hurt you. I won't let it."

She put her forehead against his shoulder for a few moments; then, hearing Barry on his way, she straightened up and said, "Well, I'd better help Amy clean up those dishes. Yes, call Joe if you want to, dear."

"Hey, Mother," said Barry, "how the heck can you use 'asperity' in a sentence? What's it mean, anyway?"

"The dictionary's in the living room. Be my guest. But as a hint, it's what I feel when you greet me with *Hey*." She rumpled his head as he passed her, and he dodged, giggling, and said, "Hey, stop it!"

Susan was the one who let Lieutenant Berman in. She tried to see something in his face, but it was quite as usual. She'd read that when a jury found a person guilty of murder they never looked at him when they came back into the courtroom, but this might not hold with a policeman.

"What a great evening," he said. "I suppose your two are too old now to be excited about Hallowe'en, but mine can hardly wait."

"Oh, Barry still likes to dress up." Susan led the way into the living room, proud of her poise. Richard got up, looking hospitable. He and the children were watching Walter Cronkite, and he turned the set off. "Upstairs now," he said to the children. "Anything we want you to know we'll tell you."

Barry sighed loudly as he left. Amy gave the officer a ravishing smile and made an exit. Richard shut the double doors behind them, and then the door into the dining room. Coming back he said, "We were in New York all day, but we heard that you had the hiker."

"Yes." The lieutenant was taking papers from an inside pocket of his jacket. "He claims he never went up on the cliff at all." He frowned at a long envelope, and laid it on the arm of his chair. "He's got a good reputation. He's one of the Harbor boys, a medical student home for a few days rest after a virus attack."

Susan's voice wouldn't come at first. She had to clear her throat. "He doesn't sound very dangerous."

"He isn't." Berman gave her a slight smile. "He's home again." He picked up the long envelope. "Well—"

Richard said politely, "Would you mind waiting a few minutes until Joe Ellenburg gets here? He's our lawyer as well as a close friend."

The lieutenant looked surprised. "Oh, I don't think we need him. This will only take a few minutes anyway." He took a closely typewritten sheet from the long envelope. "This came to us around five o'clock this afternoon, from New York, by special messenger. It's signed Henry Lyons. His wife verified the signature, and also the facts given in the letter, because she knew them already. He'd informed her of them this morning. Quite a woman, Mrs. Lyons."

He began to read aloud. The letter was addressed to him, and formally requested that Mrs. Linden be apprised of the contents as soon as possible.

"I did not kill Randall Emery intentionally," the letter

went on. "It was done in a moment of blind, uncontrolla-
ble rage. I had made the mistake of thinking I could reason with him. I should have known long before that he
was beyond reason. I'd known him for a month, but now
it seems as if his evil has been tainting my life for years,
though I am not passing over my weaknesses which made
his influence possible.

"I met him at The Vine and Fig Tree, where he was
showing the Danton pictures. At first I liked him; I
thought we had a great deal in common. Then, by accident, he discovered something about my personal life. He
trailed me, spied upon me to make sure, and then he
began to blackmail me.

"At first, I thought he simply wanted to force me to
sponsor him in Somerset, where there was a concentration
of money. But then he suggested that I buy the Danton
collection for a half-million dollars. When I refused to be
blackmailed, he threatened to approach my wife. I had
tried for a long time to keep her from being hurt, but
now I knew that the hurt was inevitable, because I had already done her serious harm. But at least she would hear
the story from me and not from a scoundrel.

"So I didn't kill him to keep him from telling my wife,
as I was about to do that myself. I killed him, as I said, in
rage, and in disgust. He had invited himself to our home
for drinks on that Sunday night, and I knew I couldn't
endure his presence there. I had gone to the Cliff that
morning to think things through, owing a duty not only
to my wife but to my unborn child and its mother. When
I saw Emery's car drive in a little while after Mrs. Linden's, I decided to go find him and tell him not to come
out to the Glen that night, but to leave Somerset fast, before I had him arrested for attempted extortion.

"I walked down the lane and out onto the Lindens' lawn. He was standing there looking at the sea. He was not pleasantly surprised, he seemed to be in a bad mood. I asked him where Mrs. Linden was and he said he didn't know where she'd gone. I wanted to be sure there was no witness to our talk, so I asked him to come back to my place, but he laughed and refused, saying he was sure I didn't have a sociable drink in mind. He didn't believe me when I said my wife was to know everything as soon as I could tell her.

"There's no need of going into details. One word led to another. He wasn't about to give up a half-million dollars so easily, and his frustration turned him into a madman. As for me, after a lifetime of being what I was expected to be by virtue of background and training, the inevitable explosion occurred. I remember picking up the stake, and he dodged away from me. I don't remember striking him, but I saw him lying on the ground by the steps, and the stake was in my hand. I dragged him across the lawn to the gate, and tumbled him over the cliff. He was dead. Then I threw the stake as far as I could into the sea. Next I drove his car away, and returned to my own cottage.

"I didn't see the hiker that morning, so I had no intention of his being accused. I thought that the surf and tide would sweep the body away, and the mark of the blow would be camouflaged. I felt no guilt, because Emery would have gone on damaging lives wherever he went, some of them far more innocent than mine. I do take the responsibility for my own flaws, and I have been forced to face their consequences.

"My plane will be well on its way by the time you get this."

Berman folded the paper and put it back in the envelope. "It's signed, and Mrs. Lyons says he signed it."

Susan sat in an aching silence. Richard didn't move either. Then he said, "Would you like a drink, Lieutenant? Your throat must be dry."

"I'd like one, but I'll wait till I'm home with my feet up, thanks. It's been a long thirty-six hours."

"Long for Henry, too," said Richard dryly. "That was quite a document."

"Yes." The lieutenant seemed as bemused as the Lindens were.

"Of course we'll never know if Emery really was an extortionist," said Richard. "We've only Lyons' word for it."

"Oh, I'd believe Henry Lyons," said the officer with quiet, unprofessional emphasis. He stood up. Susan and Richard got up with him. Susan was seeing two faces irradiated in a dim room. She had to know something before Berman could leave. "He said 'my plane.' Is he *alone?*"

He smiled one-sidedly. "No, the woman's with him. They flew by chartered plane out of the country, headed for some place where there's no extradition. We're not sure which one yet. He must have spent a busy morning lining things up." He shrugged. "When these gentle people break, the crash is heard around the world. If it's not somebody else who gets it, they kill themselves."

Like Richard Cory. "I'm glad Henry's still alive," Susan said defiantly. "Even though I'm sorry for Pris."

The men nodded vaguely at her, then shook hands, and as the lieutenant went down the walk Joe was coming in.

Susan escaped to the kitchen, saying she'd make coffee, while Richard told Joe briefly about Henry's confession.

Joe was as shocked as they were, as shocked as the rest of Somerset was going to be when the end of the case was announced. Richard behaved as if he knew no more about the whole thing than what the police had let him know. Susan's silence was accepted as natural. She'd found the body, she'd talked with Henry perhaps only a half-hour after he'd killed the man, and she liked him. Didn't everyone in Somerset? No wonder she couldn't think of anything to say.

Joe hadn't got out to his car before Susan was in Richard's arms there in the front hall, clinging to him as if he had to save her from some fresh bit of awful knowledge.

"Henry protected me, do you realize that?" she whispered. "He was the one who came to the door, just in time. He must have heard us, he couldn't have helped hearing us. Maybe that's why he pounded so hard. *He* was the one, Richard. And we went spying on him!"

He shushed her and drew her back out to the kitchen, shutting doors behind them while still keeping one arm tight around her. "He must have known it was all up when he saw us in there," she said. "That look between him and her wasn't meant for us to see. I'll never stop regretting that."

"Listen," Richard persisted. "It was all over with him before he came in there. He knew they had the hiker. He had no way of knowing what they could dig up as evidence against the boy, and he couldn't let an innocent man be held. He's Henry Lyons, remember. No, he'd come to tell her to get ready, I could swear to it."

"But how can I live with myself, knowing what I've done by my foolishness? If only I'd told you the truth at the first!"

"You would have saved us some grief, but you couldn't have done anything for Henry. He'd already set certain forces in motion, this woman was carrying his child, and the blackmail had begun. How did he phrase that?"

She sought out the words, fumbling for them, seeing Henry's face all the time, illumined in a dim room. " 'He found out something by accident . . . trailed me to make sure . . .'—oh, something like that. David could have seen what I saw, Richard. It was as plain as if it had been written out in flaming letters. Then he probably sneaked around, asking questions and handing out five-dollar bills for the answers."

"You hate him now, don't you?" Richard said quizzically. "All the time you were telling me about his persecution of you, you didn't sound like this. Strange."

"Because I thought he was insane and I was sorry for him," she said. "Now I know it was all a cold-blooded act from the start, deliberate torture on his part, trying to destroy us all by making me look like a mental case and then a suicide."

"Oh, he had great plans for himself," Richard mused. "He made the contact with Henry, maybe by pure accident as you say, catching a glimpse of something he wasn't meant to see. That one fatal instant started the whole process. The next thing he was out here in Somerset and snuggling up to a potential fortune. Imagine his horror when he turned around in Joe's library that night and saw the one person who could stand in the way of his making that fortune. *You* could claim the pictures. And what he went through to try to get rid of you proves that he had no legal hold on them whatsoever."

He pulled her roughly into his arms and squeezed her hard; it hurt, but it was a good hurt. "He went out there yesterday to get you out of the way, but his viciousness came back at him like a boomerang. He'd made the mistake of thinking Henry was soft and that his position meant more to him than anything."

"I hope Henry has as good a life as possible, wherever he is," Susan said defiantly. "I know he's done wrong, but he saved my life, and he never mentioned knocking on the door and hearing voices, so he's probably saved my reputation, too, though that's a small thing beside my life. I'm sorry for Pris, I could cry for her if she loves him as I love you. But she's young yet, and she's not the exile."

The telephone rang. Upstairs there was the sound of a stampede toward the extension, but Richard reached out a long arm for the kitchen phone and said, "I've got it. Hang up, kids."

Susan waited, passively. There couldn't be anything else today, could there? They couldn't have discovered anything worse than what they'd already found out. She sank into the rocker, feeling absolutely boneless.

Richard's face was long and somber at the telephone. "Tomorrow, then," he was saying. "Yes, we'll be there. Any time after two ... certainly. ... Thank you very much. Goodbye."

He hung up, then looked down at her with his splendid gray eyes and said not a word.

"*What?*" she asked, hardly breathing.

"The puppy's ready to go," he said, and smiled.

Elisabeth Ogilvie has written many children's books and short stories, which have been widely serialized. This is her fourteenth adult novel. Last year she published *Bellwood*.

Miss Ogilvie spends most of the year on Gay's Island, Maine, where her activities include writing, beachcombing, exploring and lobstering. Few authors have so inspiring a retreat.